THE WEAPONS OF
WOODMYST

The Weapons of Woodmyst

THE WOODMYST CHRONICLES BOOK IX

Robert E Kreig

WHITEKEEP BOOKS

For Dorothy and Frank.

The Realm

THE FROZEN WASTE

THE CORE LANDS

BLACKROCK HAVEN

WINTERMARSH

IRONFIELDS

ERIMOOR

WHITEKEEP

BLACKSHORE

THE CANYONS OF TERKEITH

REDLOCH

LIGHTHOUSE

MALLOWHILL

STRONGHOLDT

THE SEA OF SOLACE

MELAMWED

THE PILLARS OF MOHAA

HAVENCREST

KALIBARD

CLEARFOOT

OAKBEACH

BROOKNESS

WINTERSPRING

THE FOREST OF KHUN

MEADOWMOOR

WOODMYST

NEWHOLT

OSTFORD

DELLMOOR

OLDCASTLE

GRASSBEACH

THE WESTERN SEA

PRYHOLT

GREYROSE

LUNKHUL FOREST

BELBURN

DWEAGAN

BARROWFIELD

THE SEA OF LUNKHUL

REDEDGE

LINPORT

THE EASTERN SEA

BUTTEREDGE

BYVIEW

ROSEFORD

FREYMOOR

BELMORE

W   E
S
N

Prologue

Winter's curse had arrived in full glory.

Bitter wintry winds swept across the open plains, smashing sleet and hail against sharp rocky crags that poked sporadically from the ground like strangely angled jagged teeth. Waves of speeding snow rushed from the mountains in the east, placing a thick layer of cover over everything in Wintermarsh. Anything not battened down or stored away blew asunder or carried to the sea, never to be seen again.

The hounds locked away in the kennels howled as the gale whistled through cracks and crevices that it found in the neat stonework of the castle and the surrounding buildings. The guards on the parapet, tucked in the towers or standing by the gates huddled together for warmth as they tightened their cloaks about them with one hand and tried their best to keep a grip upon their shields that so wanted to fly away in the wind.

Inside, every fireplace blazed. Logs burned and crackled as tall flames danced in the many hearths located inside the palace walls. Soldiers inside the barracks gathered as close to the fire as they could, thankful that they weren't on guard duty, cursing the fact that their time to go outside was yet to come. Kitchen servants were glad to be slaving over a hot stove, or at least delighted to be near such glorious warmth as they sliced potatoes or seasoned the meat intended for the night's supper.

The largest fire had been lit in the throne room.

To the side stood a deep inglenook, almost the size of another small room. It was alive with bright orange flames that sent an intense glow throughout the room. A large log rested on an iron grate.

Isabel stared into the flames from her seat by Takmel's right side. She watched the flames bite into the timber as it skipped along the surface of the log.

"My lord." A guard lowered himself to his knee at the foot of the marble dais. "There have been sightings of Dakoth Risha near Ironfields."

"Is General Versel aware of this?" Takmel asked.

Isabel glanced over at the man by her side. She had had strange feelings towards him. Something inside of her found him repulsive, like an uneasy stirring in the stomach that was still building. Yet, she felt love for him also and wanted nothing more than to be by his side.

The conflict was unbearable. She wanted to cry, but pressed her emotions down. Her body remained composed. Her face wore the expression of dignity.

Inside, there was turmoil.

A raging war of disposition.

"Yes, my lord," the guard replied. "She has sent word that all is ready. She asks what you wish for her to do with him."

The White Queen watched the Maji carefully. He looked over to her and gave a quick smile. She responded in kind.

"What do you think, my love?" he asked her.

She thought about how she would like to peel his skin from his face.

At the same time, she envisioned herself lying with him in their large bed upstairs.

"I wouldn't presume to advise you on such important matters, Maji," she replied.

He turned away from her.

"And what do you think, my queens?" he asked, leaning to his left.

Isabel's eyes felt hot with fire as she looked past Takmel to the twin girls seated on his other side. She thought they appeared older. It could have been the way they dressed. Each wore a gown similar to hers, only one was in scarlet and the other in lilac. They tied their hair back in a braid and draped over their shoulders like hers. It was as if the Maji's influence was infiltrating to their core, as it had done with her.

But there was something more. There was a level of maturity or the appearance of a type of wisdom that harboured behind their eyes. Something had been imparted to them; something that Takmel had shared with the girls. Something that caused an uncomfortable fear to stir inside Isabel's stomach.

Both girls turned their faces to Takmel and responded to his question in kind. Their eyes leered and their lips turned up in twisted grins. They slid their fingers over their throats, giving their new husband the answer he was seeking.

"There you have it," he said, turning back to the guard. "Take that answer to the runner."

"Yes, my lord," the guard said, returning to his feet. As he strode to the door, Isabel moved her gaze back to the roaring fire. She watched the flames dance upon the log and felt herself becoming transfixed. Her mind drifted to a state of nothingness, and she welcomed it.

"You seemed troubled, my love." His voice almost made her jump. He took her hand and pressed the back of it to his lips. "What can I do to make you feel better?"

"I'm fine," she lied with a smile. "Just tired."

"Perhaps you should take rest," he suggested.

"You need your queen by your side."

He lowered her hand back upon her armrest. "I have two more," he told her.

She felt a hot, burning sensation move along her spine. The sudden urge to tear the two little girls' heads from their slender necks was overwhelming. The desire to take Takmel's face in her hands and plunge her thumbs deep into his eye sockets was almost arousing.

She wanted blood.

"I'll stay," she said. She offered a pleasant smile and a playful tilt of the head.

"My beautiful queen," he whispered. He looked at her with adoring eyes.

"My wonderful husband," she answered.

Another guard entered the room and approached the throne.

Takmel turned from Isabel and set his attention upon the soldier.

"What news?" the Maji asked.

"My lord." The guard dropped to his knee.

Isabel returned her gaze to the fire.

As she watched the flames dance, her mind ventured to the world beyond the castle walls.

The wind howled and spread more ice and snow over the rooftops.

The increasing layers of blanketing frost were becoming burdensome upon the beams and supports of the township's structures.

Creaking, moaning timber groaned painfully as the falling snow applied more and more pressure.

Cold bitterness overcame any life, warmth, or hope. Existence itself was seemingly swept away in winter's bane.

And somehow, as she thought about this, she knew it wasn't just the season that had this effect on all things in Wintermarsh.

She too, was undergoing such a change deep inside.

Everything she once had been was slowly dying or was already dead.

She hated herself for feeling this way.

She hated what she had become.

As the warmth inside her faded, she contemplated what she should become now.

Her heart drifted away from the Maji. But she still felt love for Takmel.

She despised him for what he had done to the twins. But she understood the reasoning behind his actions.

She was torn.

Composing herself, she pushed her emotions away.

The flames spun and twirled over the log's surface.

The orange flicker and glow spilled throughout the room.

But she didn't feel the fire's warmth.

She felt empty and cold.

Winter's curse was inside her, too.

One

"I apologise for disturbing you, my lady," the guard said, as he led the small band past closed cages occupied by men loyal to the Maji. "He requested an audience with you. When I told him to go fu—" He shot a hesitant glance to the girl who looked back at him forbiddingly.

Glaun stood behind Alice, shaking his head as a warning to the guard.

The guard took a deep breath and chose his words carefully. "When I told him no, he refused to eat. He's been without food for almost three days. I wouldn't have been that bothered with this, except the boys say that you wouldn't want him to starve to death in the cell."

"The boys are correct," she replied.

"He's an old fellow, too," David put in. "He won't last long without something in his gut."

"How does he fare otherwise?" Alice asked.

A prisoner reached through the bars and grabbed a handful of her cloak. She spun on her heels, took his arm in her hands and thrust it to the side, snapping bone against the iron cage.

The man screamed in agony as he dropped to his knees. His forearm dangled awkwardly from halfway along its length.

"Keep back for your own safety," another guard following the group quipped. "I say it every time. But do you bastards listen? No. Serves you right."

"Someone best see to that," Alice said, gesturing at the prisoner.

"Paul," one guard shouted, turning to face back the way they had come. "Job for you. Broken arm."

1

They turned a corner and descended a short flight of stairs. A large cell sat at the end of a short passage. Five men dressed in dark clothing sat upon cots. A sixth was lying down, covered with thick blankets. Alice almost didn't recognise him. His features were withdrawn and his skin had turned sallow.

"He doesn't fare well, my lady," the first guard replied, answering her question from before.

Alice approached the bars slowly and peered at the old man. The torchlights posted on the walls in the corridor, and the fire burning in the hearth to the side, illuminated the area well. Yet the flickering glow caused the shadows in the corners near the ceiling and floor to grow most dark. And, although she could feel the warmth flowing from the flames, she could tell that the men in the prison cell were cold. Bitterly cold.

"Get these men more blankets," she ordered. "They're not animals. I want them treated with respect."

"Of course, my lady." The guard turned and silently signalled with his eyes for the other guard to fulfil the command. The man started away, complaining under his breath and not realising that his voice carried through the stone room, amplifying it for all to hear him grumble.

"Thank you, my queen," one prisoner said.

"Shut it," Glaun snarled.

Alice kept her attention on the old man, who stirred slightly beneath the layers of coverings.

"Master Drayton?" she called. "Are you awake?"

He lifted his eyes to her. It took him a moment to realise who was calling.

"Mistress Warde?" He lifted himself, grunting as he swung his feet over the side of the cot. His feet were bare, revealing blue lines, twisting and branching just beneath the skin's surface. She felt a lump form in her throat as she stared at his yellow toenails.

"Where are his shoes?" she asked the guard. "His socks?"

The guard shrugged. "He may have traded them for the blankets."

"Traded?" She glared at the man.

"Not our doing, my lady." He held up his hands. "The prisoners make such deals among themselves all the time."

"They wouldn't if they had all they needed," David stated.

"Begging your pardon," the guard said, "but it has always been this way. Even when you were chief of this city. We received limited supplies then, and we receive limited supplies now."

"We didn't have any prisoners then," David responded, attempting to justify the lack of supply to the prison during his time as leader.

"We need to bring more blankets and provisions for the prisoners immediately," Alice instructed the men with her. "We can't have people freezing to death during the winter."

Porf shook his head and pursed his lips.

"What is it?" she asked upon seeing him.

"People may have already taken most of the stock to cater for their needs," he replied. "Blankets are scarce at the moment."

"Having trouble keeping the balance, my queen?" Drayton chuckled.

"I'm not your queen," Alice replied to him before turning her attention back to Porf. "Do what you can. There must be something that can keep these men warm."

"I'll see what we can scrounge up."

With a slap on Glaun's arm, a signal that he wanted the other to accompany him, he retraced his steps through the corridor of the prison.

"You may not wish to be called queen," the old man said, lifting himself to his feet, draping a blanket around his shoulders. "But that is what you have become."

"I don't have time for games, Master Drayton," she said briskly. "Tell me why you have summoned me."

He approached the bars, gripping one in his withered fingers as he met her gaze.

"I don't believe I ever noticed how beautiful your eyes are," he mused. "Such blueness as I have never seen. Not even in the clearest sky. They were brown before, were they not?"

"Master Drayton!" She scowled. "I have other things that require my attention. So, if you don't mind..."

"And your hair," he continued, ignoring her warning. "Almost like the snow falling in places. But, not quite."

"I think we're done," Alice said to David. She started away with the others in tow.

"But it won't last..." Drayton smirked as he called after her. "Will it, my queen? All things must come to an end, eventually."

Alice stopped in her tracks. Her feet had almost reached the bottom step of the short stairwell. She turned on her heels to face the old man.

"What do you know, Master Drayton?"

"I know you won't be this way forever," he replied. "You have already started to change. Your time is short, and I fear you won't reach him before that time has passed you by."

"I will face him," she assured him, stepping through the small band of men that followed her. They parted to the sides to give her clear passage. "You have my word on that."

"He gave me his word too." Drayton bared his teeth. "He even called me his friend. But he lied. One thing that I believe, my queen, is that he will slaughter you and everything you love. Including that one-armed little milksop husband of yours."

David started forward, gripping the hilt of his sword and lifting it slowly from the sheath strapped to his waist. Alice quickly put her arm out and placed her hand on her father-in-law's shoulder.

"Steady," she ordered.

"Sorry," the old bookkeeper slurred. His sardonic grin spread wide across his face. "I forgot. How insensitive of me. His mother is dead. Isn't she?"

David looked at Alice with fire in his eyes. He wanted so much to kill this man.

"You can't let him get away with that," he growled.

She lowered her hand and stepped towards the cage.

"Where do you come from, Master Drayton?" she asked. "I mean, originally. Before you came to Woodmyst. Where was your home?"

"You know this," he replied. "Here you just were saying that you don't have time to play games. That you have other things that require your attention."

"Perhaps you and your fellow bookkeepers don't need the extra blankets after all. Perhaps you don't need your socks or food. Perhaps," she added as she turned to the guard, "we can forget that this section of the prison ever existed."

She turned towards the short stairwell and started away again.

"All right," he called after her, realising her threat was not a bluff. "I'm from Dweagan. I grew up there and came to Woodmyst after the war with the Mirikin."

"I don't really have much of a recollection of that time," Alice said, turning to face him again. "I was very young. When, exactly, did you come to us from Dweagan?"

"I don't remember. A year or two after the war."

"Not even one year, to be sure," David said. "I don't quite recall why you became Master Bookkeeper. I sanctioned it. This much, I recollect. But why would I do such a thing?"

"Because *he* wanted it so," Drayton answered. "He manipulated you. Twisted you and fashioned this city the way he desired it. Preparing it all for when it would be his time. He whispered in those seven bitches' ears and allowed you to think the worst of this one." Drayton gestured to Alice with his chin. "And nearly everyone, in some way, did his bidding. All except you, my queen. You and your husband. But, oh how much he wanted you."

Alice felt her mouth droop into a frown. She forced her composure to remain as she kept her eyes locked on the old man's.

"He summoned me here," Drayton continued. "He would talk with the traders from Dweagan, and he established a relationship with the city. You must understand, we were loyal to him before that. We were simply waiting for him to contact us. He saved us from the Mirikin. We owed him our lives.

"They wanted to wipe us all out. They almost did. The women of the city saved our hides. They hid us in cellars and beneath straw stacks in their stables. The Maji saved them, claiming all the women for himself before the White Mistress slaughtered them all.

"So, when he called, we came running. When he summoned me, I knew it was for a greater cause. I kept the books. I moved the numbers. I made sure the projects that he wanted to be kept secret were kept secret.

"I did it all for my lord," he said. "My Maji. My friend."

"Only, he lied to you." Alice furrowed her brow. "You said so yourself. He wasn't your friend. He used you just as he did everyone else."

Drayton stared at her blankly, as if contemplating her words.

"Listen to me, Master Drayton," she said calmly. She looked at the other men sharing the cell with the old man. "All of you should give ear to this. I won't lie to you. I'll be your friend."

"Pray tell," one bookkeeper said sarcastically. "Why should we trust you over the Maji?"

"Well," she said smoothly, "I am here, and he is not. He ran away like a coward. Also, I will tell you a truth right now. Would you like to hear?"

"Go ahead." Drayton wagged his head. "Please tell us."

"I destroyed Blackrock Haven," she replied. "I killed the Scarlet Queen."

The bookkeepers gave their full attention to her.

"So?" One of them shook his head. "That's one. The Maji still lives."

"Yes," she allowed. "He still lives. But the Black Queen, my own aunt, does not. She threw herself from the rocks by the Eastern Sea. I saw it with my own eyes. The Jade Queen is dead as well. Do you know where she was when she died, Master Drayton?"

"You lie," he spat, his eyes glaring at her like wildfire.

"I burned the docks of Dweagan," she told the prisoners. "I set the tower aflame, but I didn't destroy the city."

The men in the cell appeared fractionally relieved. Still, they leant forward with anticipation. They knew there was more to this story.

David stepped up to the bars.

"The Haigok of Mohaa did that," he taunted. "Burned it all to ash, they did. Nothing, no one left living. All gone."

The old man shook with fury.

"Curse you and your dragon-riding devils," shouted Drayton. Tears welled in his eyes.

Alice waited for the old man to settle down. Drayton plonked himself on the side of his cot and placed his head in his hands as he wept.

"So," Alice continued. "Why did you summon me, Master Drayton? Was it to gloat over how your friend will bring me and my allies to an end? Was it to tell me how wonderful his plan was and how stupid we were to fall for his devices? Because it seems that we have seen the end to four of his queens, the allegiance of another swayed in our favour and the annihilation of not just one of his strongholds, but two. Blackrock Haven and your beloved Dweagan. We took Newholt back and you know what happened here."

"You bitch," the old man spat.

Alice placed a hand on the bars.

"We will defeat him, Master Drayton," said the girl. "We will see an end to the Maji and the Mirikin once and for all. You, on the other hand, will see nothing beyond these walls for the rest of your life. You are an enemy of the people and deserve no better treatment.

"Be thankful that we don't follow the same laws as Dweagan once did. Otherwise, you might face a far harsher sentence.

"I hope my visit was everything you desired. From here on, you will continue to receive your regular meals. You will be given more blankets and provisions to keep you comfortable during the winter. I'll be sure to send the apothecary to check upon your health regularly...at least until you don't need his services, which won't be too much longer, if you continue to refuse to eat and persist in walking upon the stone floor with bare feet."

With that, she turned and started back down the corridor.

Drayton listened to the footfalls of the company growing more and more distant as he dropped his head in his hands again. The noise of boots falling upon stone became fainter and fainter, and the sound of sobbing men grew clearer.

Blackrock Haven was gone.

Newholt had been reclaimed.

Dweagan was a ruin in ash.

With four queens dead, how would his master triumph?

How would his friend survive?

Friend?

His friend had left him to rot in a prison cell.

He lowered himself to his side and pulled the blankets over his head. He wept profusely onto his pillow as he tucked his knees as close to his chest as his ageing body allowed.

All was lost.

There was no more hope.

Dweagan was gone.

He wanted to die.

Two

General Risha peered down upon the township of Ironfields. It appeared quiet and still. He had seen no sign of the bitch, Saruun Versel, and her nine followers. In fact, he hadn't seen hide nor hair of anyone for quite some time. But, with the howling wind and barrage of sleet, it did not surprise him they would all cower inside, keeping from the bite of winter.

Five hundred men on horseback formed up loosely to his sides. There wasn't any structure to their gathering, except that he positioned himself before them.

They watched him carefully, waiting for him to command them, give a signal, anything. Eventually, he snorted something back from his nose and into his throat before spitting onto the frozen ground.

He gave his steed a slight kick, urging it forward.

The others followed suit and started down the hill.

The mob fanned out as they neared the village. Some guided their horses through narrow lanes between buildings. Others kept to the wide streets.

Risha moved to a crossroads in the middle of the town. He gestured for a group of riders to stop and dismount before pointing to a cluster of huts to their right.

Fifty men slid off their steeds and pulled their swords free. They dashed to the tiny cottages and knocked down the doors with their boots or by throwing their bodies at the entrances.

Wood splintered and cracked.

Screams reverberated along the streets, only to be carried away in the gale.

It wasn't long before the men returned from the huts with blood-stained swords. Some even dragged hapless women and children into the cold after slaughtering the men inside.

The general gestured for others to start their assault. The riders complied by jumping from their steeds to ransack shops and buildings by the roadside.

A fire was lit in the stable house at the southern end of the township. It was a roaring blaze within moments.

The men continued their attack, whooping and cheering as they broke into more houses. They dragged more women and children into the street. The captives shivered and shook as the weather assaulted their underdressed bodies.

"Line them up," Risha commanded.

His men placed their victims onto their knees in a long line in the centre of the main road, in and out of Ironfields. They pressed blade edges against necks.

"Saruun Versel," the general hollered. He waited for a reply.

None came.

He called to her again. Louder. Longer.

Still no reply.

"I will kill these women," he shouted. "I will kill their children. Show yourself and I will spare them."

The wind continued to howl as Risha's men pulled the barkeep and several women from the tavern. The general looked at them, silently asking if they had seen her. They shook their heads as they dragged the barkeep and the others, kicking and screaming, into the line of townsfolk.

"Saruun Versel," he called again. "One last chance to save these people. Show yourself and I will let them go free. Hide away, and they will die."

He waited. He moved his eyes about, searching. He trained his ears to listen carefully beyond the shrieking wind.

A child cried from along the street.

"Shut that thing up," he barked to his men.

One of them flashed his blade and silenced the infant.

A woman screamed.

Another sword responded.

Silence again, except for the breeze.

A soft pitter-patter, rapid and distant, grabbed his attention. He turned on his heels and peered into the cloudy flurry. It was as if a thick, white cloud had suddenly surrounded them, blotting out any chance of seeing much farther than the end of the street, shielding their view of the hill they had descended only moments before.

"Where did this fucking storm come from?" one soldier asked.

"Quiet," Risha spat, trying to listen to the approaching sound.

He squinted into the white flurry as he noticed a blob appear in the road. It grew larger and larger.

The pitter-patter grew louder and louder.

It was something running towards them on all fours.

Too small to be a horse.

Too thin to be a bear.

Too fast to be a man.

Risha shook his head. His confusion and curiosity increased with each step that this strange creature made towards him.

Closer and closer.

Louder and louder.

Clearer and clearer.

General Risha's eyes widened.

He knew what this thing was.

"Oh shit," he spat.

The dark creature lunged into the air. It gripped the man beside Risha by the throat, using its teeth and claws.

A thick spray of blood splashed over the general, staining his cloak and armour and splashing over his face.

The creature sprinted away, disappearing into a tiny alley, leaving the soldier to writhe in agony.

"Kill them," Risha roared, pointing to the prisoners in the street.

Several arrows stuck into the chests of men nearby. They fell to the ground as a roar erupted from the western side of the village.

Three hundred men wearing the white tunics flooded into the streets on foot. They waved their swords above their heads as they charged towards Risha's men.

A hundred dark creatures accompanied them. Thin, leathery skinned beasts with large, gnashing teeth lunged at Risha's unprepared soldiers and began tearing flesh from bone.

General Versel sat atop her steed and watched the carnage unfold from the northern end of the wide street that ran through the middle of Ironfields. Her nine men grouped behind her, awaiting instructions.

Risha spotted her.

He started towards her, sword in hand and fire in his eyes.

A dark creature to his left lunged for him. He saw it and swung his blade, slicing through its forehead and opening its skull. It let out an ear-shattering scream as it fell to the frozen ground. Dark blood spat from the wound as it flipped and twisted violently in the snow.

Risha continued onwards, his face stern and focused, his complete attention fixed upon Versel.

She dismounted and handed the reins to Willis at her side. Her other companions remained on their horses, watching her as she strolled casually towards the other.

Versel pulled her sword free of its sheath and lowered her helmet's visor over her face.

The fighting around her had become intense as the dark creatures tore into Risha's men, as the soldiers in white tunics attacked fervently with sword and bow. Steel smashed against steel, ringing noisily around her. The calls of pain filled the air as men fell. The shrieks of the creatures were deafening as they were either struck down or mauled.

The women and children being held prisoner used the opportunity to flee back into their homes or hide in buildings nearby as the battle continued.

Horsemen from both sides clashed at the southern end of the township. Foot soldiers wrestled and duelled along the streets. Dark creatures skulked, gnawed and scratched as they assaulted the renegade army. Several of Risha's cavalrymen were tackled from their saddles as the beasts lunged seemingly from nowhere, through the air and pulling the unsuspecting soldiers to the ground where the men were torn asunder.

Versel gripped the hilt of her sword. She stepped over pooling blood, steaming entrails and body parts scattered across the frosted road.

Risha quickened his pace. He lifted his sword high as he drew nearer to his mark.

Versel blocked his first blow with her weapon. She spun quickly, crouching low, and hacked her blade into the false general's thigh.

He roared, dropping to his knees.

Before Versel could offer him another taste from her sword, he rolled onto his back.

She overshot her target and stepped too close to him.

Risha grabbed her ankle and tripped her onto her front.

She crashed to the ground beside him in a heap, her armour emitting a loud crunching sound upon impact. She tasted blood in her mouth.

Risha lifted himself to his knees and brought his blade over his head, directing it towards her back.

Versel rolled away from him quickly. Still lying on her back, she looked over at the false general. His sword sliced into the snow where she had just been.

She seized her opportunity and stabbed her own blade towards him.

He saw it coming, but could not get out of the way quickly enough. The wound in his thigh was sending a sharp pain along his leg and up his spine, slowing his movement.

The tip of her sword penetrated his lower abdomen, just below his chest plate. She was a good aim, he thought, as the blade passed through a thin join in his armour. It continued upwards into his chest cavity and out of his back, between his shoulder blades.

She held it there, twisting it slightly to make more damage inside of him.

He glared at her.

"Bitch," he gurgled, spilling a thick flow of blood over his chin.

Keeping the sword buried inside him, she gripped the hilt as she lifted herself to her feet. He was forced onto his back as she pulled her blade out of his body.

Risha kicked his legs out straight and coughed as body fluid filled his lungs.

"By the command of the Maji," she said, peering down upon the dying man through her visor, "I relieve you of your duties and reclaim Ironfields in his name."

He kept his angry eyes upon her as he continued to cough and spit blood over his own face. It soaked into his hair and beard, dribbled into across his cheeks and left spatter marks over his forehead.

Versel kept her gaze fixed upon him, seemingly oblivious to the slaughter unfolding around her. When Risha finally breathed his last, she strolled away, moving unconcernedly through the fighting back to her steed.

"Kill them all," she called to her soldiers as she lifted her visor to reveal her face. "Leave none alive. Larson, Coogan."

"General," two of her trusted men replied, urging their horses to move slowly towards her.

"Usher the surviving women and children from the street and into the tavern," she commanded. "Owen, Freed and Grosset. I want you to inspect the houses to the north and find any surviving men. Bring them to the tavern for treatment. Reilly, Norris and Walters. Take the houses to the south and do the same."

"Yes, General," Norris replied, before charging away with the other two.

"What about me?" Willis asked, handing the reins of Versel's horse-back to her.

"You stay by my side," she commanded. He gave her a small smile. "It's not that," she told him. "I need your eyes. Keep watch for any stealthy bastards trying to sneak up on us."

"Yes, General," he replied, a little disappointed.

After a while of silence, as blood splattered over the street and shrill screams echoed through the air, she leant towards him.

"I need your eyes now," she whispered. "I need the rest of you tonight. Understand?"

He smiled again, appearing like a giddy schoolboy. "Yes, General."

The fighting continued.

More of Risha's soldiers fell.

Finally, the last man fled into an alley in a desperate attempt to escape.

Several creatures and men in white tunics gave chase, cornering the young renegade soldier in a small rectangular yard hedged by three buildings joined together.

Versel and Willis followed on horseback, arriving in the enclosure just in time to see the soldier drop his sword to the ground in surrender. He raised his hands in the air.

The creatures lowered their heads and stalked towards their intended prey. The men in white turned to the general, awaiting orders.

"I said to kill them all," she reminded them.

It was too late for them to act.

One creature lunged and tore into the throat of the soldier.

He reacted by trying to scream as he reached for his dagger, still sitting on his belt. With two quick jabs, he stabbed the dark beast in the chest.

It let go with a yelp and fell to its side.

The soldier crumpled to his rump and held a hand to his throat. Blood streamed through his fingers and over his chest plate before spilling onto the ground.

Before long, he toppled to his side and lay still.

As if by some form of intervention, the storm suddenly ceased. Versel seemed unnerved by the spectacle, pointing to the wounded creature. It kicked and screamed, rolling in circles on the ground.

"Put that thing out of its misery," she commanded.

One of the foot soldiers in white complied, piercing the beast's ribs with his sword and giving a sharp twist. The creature hissed a long breath, sending a white cloud of warm vapour into the cold air before it closed its eyes. The foot soldier withdrew his blade and placed it in his sheath.

The other creatures started emitting strange clicking sounds as they watched their companion die. A couple ventured over to the body of the beast and sniffed, offering soft whines.

"I didn't think they mourned their dead," Willis said, watching with curiosity.

Unexpectedly, the two whining creatures sank their teeth into the fallen beast and tore chunks of flesh away. Within a blink of an eye, other dark creatures joined the frenzy. Dark blood splashed in all directions, forcing the men in white to back away in horror and disgust.

"It appears they don't," replied Versel with a wry grin.

Three

He opened his eyes slowly.

They seemed heavy and took a while to focus. The fire was the first thing he noticed, orange and bright, flaring to his left inside the deep inglenook. The flickering torches hanging on the walls were next.

The light cast shadows through the room and it took him a moment to recognise the shapes, even though he knew who was in the room with him. He noticed the tall shapes of the guards positioned at intervals along the walls. The white of their tunics splayed across his vision, gradually pulling back to form the profiles of men.

The marble walls, floor and light timber ceiling with its dark beams and large, iron, circular lighting minstrels hanging by thick chains; all became clearer and clearer.

"What have you done?" he heard her ask. She stood at the foot of the marble dais, staring up at him compassionately. "You look terrible."

He wiped his eyes before reaching his hand out to her. Lifting her white dress slightly with one hand, so as not to catch it beneath her boots as she climbed the steps, she moved to her seat by his right.

"Come," he said, grabbing her forearm as she started by him. He pulled her gently to his lap and wrapped his arms around her.

"Why do you look so tired?" she asked.

"I've been busy, my love," he replied. He stretched his neck and kissed her cheek.

"The guards told me you've been here for some time," she said, furrowing her brow. "What kind of activity could make you this way without leaving the room?"

He smiled and tightened his embrace.

"You're so curious suddenly. I've hardly heard a peep from you in the last few days. And here you are, questioning and questioning."

"I'm concerned," she answered, placing a gentle hand on his face.

"No need to be," he told her. "All is well. In fact, it is better now than it was."

"What do you mean?"

"Another question," he said, trying to look playful. He could see his pretentious act wasn't working on her. "I'll tell you. Ironfields is back in our hands. Dakoth Risha has been vanquished and General Versel is now in command of the region. There may still be a few renegades in the hinterland for her men to take care of, but the township is ours again."

"And that is why you appear so tired?" she inquired. "Because you have really been there while you have been sitting here?"

He stroked her face and moved a lock of her golden hair from her face, placing it gently behind her ear.

"I'm here now," he assured her, "with you."

"And the girls?" She frowned. "Where are they?"

He looked at her curiously.

"Are you jealous?" he asked, raising his brow. She shook her head. He saw through it. "Yes, you are. They're a necessity," he assured her. "A means to an end. I need their presence to fulfil my destiny."

"Just as you did with us?" she asked, getting to her feet. "Were we simply a means to an end? Joanne, Tricia, Gilda, even Lucy?"

"I loved them all," he answered. "I love them still. They will always be a part of me, and I wish they had never perished. I miss them all."

His eyes welled with tears, but she wondered if it was all an act.

"You need us," she told him. "You need nine to feed your power. You have six."

"Seven," he corrected her. "I have seven wives."

She stared at him for a while before realising that he was including Catherine in his total.

"She betrayed you," she reminded. "She tried to kill you and you still count her among us?"

Isabel struggled with her disposition towards Catherine. Part of her saw the girl as a wretched, putrid example of filth that needed to be dealt with harshly. Another part of her admired the girl for fighting and defeating the influence that the Maji had once held over her.

"She is still my wife," he replied calmly. "And I still love her. I loved her before I loved you. She was there for me at the beginning of it all."

"She won't be there for you at the end." The tone of her voice was biting.

"We'll see," he said, smirking. "We'll see."

***

The ocean breeze flowed through her hair, pushing it over her shoulders and away from her face. She closed her eyes and soaked in the fresh air. The salt filled her senses with each breath. She found it soothing.

Upon opening her eyes, she peered down from the citadel steps to the ruins of Oldcastle. Not one structure remained intact. Even the pillars and towering walls of the city's central hub behind her were a crumpled heap of stone.

"We go back?" Nola'ee asked eagerly. She was surveying the land to the north, keeping watch for movement upon the open plains now littered with snow.

They had posted other guards as watchmen on the upper platform. A tent had been erected, and a fire set at the northern edge. The men preoccupied themselves with keeping warm by the flames, allowing the Agrodien warrior to temporarily perform their duty.

"Just a little longer," Catherine replied, looking down at the many fires that had been lit among the toppled buildings between the citadel steps and the waterfront.

The docks had all been destroyed, set to flame long ago, leaving charred and rotting posts behind that jutted from the rolling water. Beyond that, lay the Sea of Lunkhul.

Far upon the horizon, several black dots appeared. She squinted, hoping it would make the image clearer.

It didn't.

"What's that?" she asked the reptilian, hoping her vision was better at discerning distant objects.

Nola'ee turned abruptly and peered into the south. Her tongue flicked out and recoiled; something Catherine had seen small lizards do.

"There are men," the Agrodien reported.

"Out there?" the girl asked, pointing to the horizon.

"Yes," the other answered, stepping closer to Catherine.

"How can you tell?"

"I can smell them," Nola'ee told her.

Catherine looked down to the campfires below, noticing the thin plumes of smoke wafting northward on the breeze a short distance before dispersing into the air.

"Are you sure you aren't just catching the odour of our own people?"

"Men are on ships," the reptilian said.

"Are they friend or foe?" one guard asked, stepping over from the warmth of the fire after spotting the dark blobs in the distance.

"My eyes are good," Nola'ee told him, turning to look at the man. He took a step backwards, suddenly afraid of the reptilian's glare. "But, not that good." She turned to Catherine. "We go now?"

The girl nodded.

The two started down the steps together. It was a long way to the bottom.

When they reached the ground, they made their way directly to Schoenbach, who was snuggling with Karlena by an open fire. Others had also gathered by the hearth, including Catherine's mother, Emily, and Akasati.

"Do you still have your spyglass?" Catherine queried, ignoring the conversation that was underway around the fire.

"Nice to see you, too," Emily responded. "You could begin with a simple hello."

"Hello," the girl offered with a sarcastic smile, accompanied by a curtsey to her mother. She then turned her attention to the sea captain again. "There are ships on the horizon. Do you still have your spyglass?"

"Ships?" Schoenbach spat as he jumped to his feet. "Where?"

"In the sea," Nola'ee informed him, pointing her leathery finger towards the waterfront. "That way."

"I know which way the bloody sea is," he grumbled, moving away from the fire. He pulled the spyglass from his coat pocket and started towards the steps that Catherine and the reptilian warrior had just descended.

By the time he returned, excited and in a rush, Catherine and Nola'ee had made themselves comfortable by the fire. They had just shared some bread and were handed a steaming bowl of stew that some soldiers had made over another hearth not too far away.

"Twelve ships," Schoenbach said as he passed by in a flash. "A galleon and eleven frigates from Dendadia."

"How do you know?" Brondt called after him.

"They fly their colours above the masts," the captain called over his shoulder. He was hastily making his way through the campsite and onward to the waterfront.

"The eagle?" Brondt asked, lifting himself to his feet and giving chase.

"Carrying the war axe of the pit guard," Schoenbach replied.

"Bugger me," Thornton huffed, standing up and following his commander excitedly. Within moments, Lieutenant Brook and the rest of Thornton's men were gone, leaving the women and Agrodien warriors by the fire alone.

Amicia looked over at Ursula in question, then to Catherine. The younger girl shook her head and shrugged before digging into her bowl of stew.

"Boys and their toys," Ursula said, peering after the men rushing towards the waterfront.

"I suppose this is a good thing, then?" Emily asked.

"I suppose," Akasati replied, tearing some bread from a loaf before passing it on to Yuri.

"What is *pit guard?*" he asked as he stripped a portion of the loaf away.

Karlena reached over and took the loaf from him.

"They're the meanest sons of bitches that ever wore a uniform," she explained.

"Bad men?" he questioned. "Enemy?"

"No," she replied. "Honourable men who keep to their duty. They guard the citadel and temple in Dendadia. Not the sort of men to be trifled with."

"Why *pit guard?*" Catherine asked. "It seems a bit of a putdown."

"It is said that they originally chose the guard from the survivors of the fighting pits," Akasati clarified. "I've seen no fighting pits during my times in Dendadia, and some have said that they outlawed the custom long ago. I guess the name stuck with them. A kind of tradition, perhaps."

"Fighting pits?" Ursula asked, furrowing her brow.

Catherine looked at the other, perplexed.

"Surely you must have heard of such things as fighting pits?" the girl queried.

Ursula shook her head.

"I was going to say that perhaps you lived a sheltered life," Karlena said. "But then, I just remembered what your occupation was in Whitekeep."

"I've seen and heard many tales in the tavern. But nothing about fighting pits."

"It's not that surprising," said Akasati. "As far as I know, they haven't been in operation in more years than my lifetime." The Erilian lifted her mug and took a sip of the hot liquid inside. "The fighting pits were places where men would meet together and fight to the death. Others would place wagers on who they thought would win. And that's basically it."

"Sounds horrendous," Ursula remarked. Her face wore an expression of revulsion.

"It probably was," said Emily. "Men killing one another for sport."

A longhorn trumpeted from the sea, announcing the arrival of the fleet. The women looked towards the source of the sound, but they saw nothing but the piles of rubble and soldiers sitting by their fires.

"At least we will have some more company tonight," Amicia said.

***

Alice straddled the chestnut stallion uncomfortably. She had grown used to the movement of Liana sweeping through the air. The horse didn't provide as smooth a ride, forcing her to stand in the stirrups now and then to reposition herself.

"It's been too long," she explained under her breath to David, who was clearly entertained by her wiggling about. He even laughed out loud once in a while, earning a scornful glare from the girl. "My arse hurts."

The northern men pretended not to notice her fidgeting, keeping their faces blank as they looked to the left and right to the snow-covered trees and shrubs they passed. Ruttger, who had joined them in Woodmyst along with Andris, stifled a chuckle as the girl stood up again to rub her backside.

"The saddle on Liana is much softer," she explained. "I don't know how I ever sat in this."

"Give it time, lass," the old warrior advised. "You'll be used to it before we reach the glade."

"Either that, or she'll need to sit in the cold stream for a while to make the swelling go away," David jested.

"Not funny," she grumbled.

"Yes, it is," he replied with a chuckle.

She shook her head as she looked over at Andris. He was quiet and withdrawn. He seemed to watch something distant and unseen as they rode.

"How do you fare, Andris?" she asked.

He snapped back to reality. "I'm fine," he answered with a thin grin.

"No, you're not," she told him. "You have something on your mind."

He wagged his head a little as he shrugged.

"I don't know what to say to her," he replied.

"To Sevrina?" Alice asked.

"Yes. How do I explain to her all of what happened?" he questioned. He didn't expect an answer. "How do I tell her of the things I have done for Joanne? How do I explain my actions?"

"You tell her the truth," the girl answered. "You tell her you had no choice. You tell her that the Maji threatened you with her life and the life of your unborn child. You say that my Aunt Joanne commanded you and you had to follow your orders."

"Only, I didn't follow my orders," he said. "Not all of them."

Alice watched him for a moment, sensing his thoughts.

"So, you didn't lie with her," she announced. He looked at her, surprised. "Good for you. For whatever reason, she couldn't bring herself to punish you for that. But, I assure you, the Black Queen wouldn't have been so lenient if you had disobeyed any of her other commands. At least you can go to your wife and tell her that much."

He looked away again. His eyes seemed to gaze at something distant and unseen. Eventually, he nodded, accepting Alice's words.

She felt a small sense of achievement and her face brightened.

"Good job, girl," David whispered from her side.

Alice grimaced and squirmed. Suddenly, she stood up in the stirrups again and rubbed her backside.

"Bloody saddle," she huffed.

Four

When she arrived back at the glade, it surprised her to see so many dragons.

She felt her heart skip a beat as she pulled the stallion to a stop just so she could look upon the great beasts as they lay about in the snow or spread their wings to absorb the warmth of the sun, or chirp, call and snap at each other in a friendly gesture.

Liana was moving among them. To Alice, she appeared more excited than usual, bobbing her head and chirping as she greeted each of her own kind. The magnificent beasts rubbed cheeks together, emitting a low rumbling purr.

"You're back," Arthur called from a cluster of tents. He was standing with her uncle, Lor, Gruloch and a few other Haigok that she didn't recognise.

"By the gods," David gasped as he stared at the dragons. "There must be fifteen of them."

"Five clans," Gruloch explained. "Three riders from each clan. Thirty dragons exactly."

The bald man shook his head in disbelief.

"How many dragons are there?" he asked, lowering himself from his horse. "In total, I mean."

"Uncertain," the other replied. "My clan has the most. This much I know. Most other clans can boast five or six. But, they are a dying breed. There aren't many egg layers left."

"You have an egg layer," Alice said to him, approaching her husband to embrace him.

"Correct," Gruloch said. He gestured to a young Haigok standing nearby. "This is Erugoth. Leader of the Kazrekh."

"The Spine Mountains Clan," Arthur interpreted. "They come from the lands near the ruins of Kailibard."

Erugoth placed a hand on his chest and bowed slightly. He dressed in a long robe and wore a curved sword on his hip. David couldn't help reminiscing about the time when the Night Demons attacked. Their clothing was very similar to that worn by the leader of the Spine Mountains Clan.

"Erugoth is treating with me for dragon pups," Gruloch explained. "He has none that lay eggs anymore."

"I'm sorry to hear that," David said sincerely.

"A great deal of loss was experienced during your Realm Wars," Gruloch replied.

"You're talking about what happened to your people in the marshlands," the large man said. "We weren't there for that. I wasn't even born," he added defensively.

"I know." The Haigok placed a friendly hand on David's shoulder. "There is no blame. Not anymore. My father did a great wrong to your people. I was merely telling you what happened to these beasts."

David lowered his gaze, embarrassed by his sudden flare. He felt heat swelling in his cheeks and around the back of his neck. He didn't know why he felt angry; only that he did.

It was so long ago;; he thought. *It's barely a memory.*

Still, something stirred deep inside. Old feelings of dread, fear, and hatred suddenly came sweeping back.

"Our people formed clans after the great war," Gruloch continued. "We gathered what we could and regrouped. But we lost many eggs and some of the younger, more curious dragons were killed by men. I'm sure you have heard tales of great dragon slayers during your childhood."

"Only one," David said with emotion in his voice. "Richard Dering. The lone adult survivor of Woodmyst."

"I've hit a tender spot," the Haigok acknowledged by lowering his head, "and I apologise. I didn't mean to cause any distress."

"Where are the livestock?" Alice asked her husband, hoping to change the topic and bring back a friendly feeling to the atmosphere.

"I had Corandra, Koryn and Alan help me herd them into a small field near the Rakmha Trench. We used rope and timber to fence them in. They'll be safe out there."

"As long as the rukyul and those dark devils of Takmel's keep their distance," Ruttger muttered.

"There wouldn't be many of those things left," Alice told him. "Liana made sure work of most of them at Blackrock Haven." She turned back to Arthur. "Why is she out here and not in the cave?"

"Have you ever tried to stop a dragon with one arm?" he asked her with a little attitude. "She only ever listens to you."

Alice smiled and put her arms around his neck before kissing his cheek.

"Sorry," she whispered in his ear. "Should we get something for our guests to eat?"

"I've killed three sheep," he explained, gesturing with his eyes to Alice's cottage. "Galonia and the other Agrodien women are up there now preparing a feast for everyone. She kicked Becka and your aunt out of the kitchen some time ago. The northern women didn't even dare go anywhere near the hut. I stayed down here where it's safe."

"What of Sevrina?" Andris asked. "Is she safe?"

"She's in a hut near the end of the clearing with Becka and Linet," Arthur said, pointing. "She's fine."

Andris kicked his horse and started away.

"Andris," Arthur called after him. He pulled his steed up and turned to face the other. "It's good to see you."

Andris nodded. "Thank you, Arthur. It's good to see you as well."

***

"This is Queen Amicia Elynbrigge of Newholt," Brondt announced, ushering a man dressed in naval regalia into the encampment. The other bowed politely, clicked his boot heels together and stood to attention.

"My queen," he said in a deep, husky voice.

His gaze went straight to the Agrodien sitting by the fire. He appeared to be cautious of them, wary of their appearance.

Yuri measured the man, glaring at him guardedly. He didn't seem like the man who, in his eyes, appeared to have never seen battle. His uniform was clean, without a spot or wrinkle on its nice deep blue fabric. Golden epaulets on his shoulders and aiguillette strung across his chest looked as if they had just been tailored.

He wore his bicorn a little askew, revealing hair closely cropped to the scalp and his beard was so neatly trimmed that Yuri believed the man looked better suited to parlour duties, serving tea and cakes, than to commanding a fleet of ships.

"This is Commander Willard Zakhar," Brondt informed the others. "He has offered us his assistance."

"I am yours to command, Queen Elynbrigge," Zakhar proclaimed.

Amicia rose to her feet and inclined her head politely.

"I am honoured," she replied. "But, please call me Amicia. Amicia Brondt."

Her husband furrowed his brow and looked at her for a seemingly long time. A sudden urge to ask her why she had made such a statement, regarding her name, filled him to the brink. However, he held his tongue and turned his attention to the other commander.

"You must be hungry after your journey," Brondt said. "Won't you join us?"

"I don't know if I should," Zakhar answered, glancing to Nola'ee and Nakrah sitting by her side.

"These are our friends," Amicia explained. "They are brave Agrodien warriors led by Yuri, their commander."

Yuri stood to his full height, towering over the fleet commander. He stared into the neatly dressed man's eyes and extended his leathery hand.

"Yuri," he growled.

"Zakhar," the other replied nervously, taking the reptilian hand in his. Yuri squeezed a little too tightly, causing the other to wince. Nola'ee tried to hide her smile, forcing the corners of her mouth downward.

"You eat," the Agrodien commander said, letting go of Zakhar's hand. He gestured to the pot dangling over the flames on a small tripod. "Food good."

Zakhar nodded, clenching and flexing his hand.

"Thank you," he said as Brondt escorted him closer to the fire so he could meet the others.

"Have you seen much action on the sea, Commander?" Ursula enquired.

"A little," Zakhar replied, as Brondt dished up some stew from the pot. "We generally perform escort duties and patrols near and about the Crystal Islands in the south. Oh, thank you," he said, taking a steaming bowl from the soldier. He dipped a piece of bread into the stew and shovelled it into his mouth. "Mmm. Good."

"The Crystal Islands," Catherine said. "Sounds fascinating."

"Palm trees and sand," the fleet commander replied. "Very warm for the most part of the year. There seem to be only two seasons. Sunshine and rainfall. And, both can occur in a single day."

"Sounds marvellous," Ursula put in. "Perhaps we should all go when this is over," she mused.

"I'd be happy to take you," Zakhar offered. "However, I have been reassigned to the naval base in Dendadia. Who can tell when I will see the islands again?"

"Crystal Islands?" Thornton asked. "Why the *Crystal* Islands?"

Zakhar swallowed a morsel that he had just plopped into his mouth.

"I think it's more to do with the water than actual crystal," he answered. "It sparkles a deep blue when the sun hits it just right. More of a thing to see for yourself than have someone explain to you."

"But what action did you see?" Jendryng asked, hanging on every word since Ursula first asked the question.

"Well," the commander said, still chewing on a piece of bread. "We seized control and cargo of some pirate vessels. Our ships outran theirs and we forced them to surrender. There were a couple of times we appropriated black powder kegs from smugglers who were trying to supply renegade traders near the Isles of Erilia."

"Did you ever fire your cannons and sink ships?" the young soldier pressed.

"Ah, no," the other replied. "Afraid not. Well, not unless you count training missions where we practised our aim upon vessels we confiscated from pirates and smugglers."

"But no battles?" Vawdrey asked.

"No," Zakhar admitted. "But my men are all well trained in the art of war."

"I see." Vawdrey reached his bowl over to scoop some more stew for himself.

Yuri let out a long, deep groan. Amicia sidled up to him and nudged his arm gently.

"Play nice," she instructed him with a grin.

"He no warrior," he said to her quietly, watching the sea commander with a wary eye. "He no fight before."

"Perhaps not," Amicia agreed. "But, he's all we have out there for now."

***

Isabel sat in a high-backed cushion seat by the fire in the drawing-room. A servant had brought her tea and left her to her thoughts.

She watched the flames dance over wood chocks as her mind ventured to Takmel and his new fascination for the twin girls. She knew he was with them now.

A frown formed on her face as she considered what he was doing with them. Envy, jealousy moved through her like a torrent, causing the skin around her jaw, her cheeks, her forehead to burn.

With care, as if he might hear her, she placed her cup of tea on a small table by her side and rose to her feet. Curiosity had got the better of her. She started for the stairs to the upper level.

Passing guards, who pulled themselves to attention as she drew near, she made her way through stone corridors to the girls' room. She expected to see the door closed; the lock held fast and Takmel's voice coming from within.

It was not so.

The door was wide open, and the room was empty.

She turned and retraced her steps to the lower level.

"Where is the Maji?" she asked the guard by the main door.

"I believe he went to the stable house with the young queens, my lady," he answered.

Young queens, she thought.

She started past the guard to move through the door.

"Open it," she commanded. He did so obligingly.

"Perhaps an escort, my lady?" he asked.

"To the stable house?" she inquired. Her voice relayed anger, and the appearance on the guard's face showed he had heard it. "It's only a few yards along the path. Why would I need an escort?"

"It's dark out, my lady," he explained. "An escort could carry a torch for you. I didn't mean to antagonise you, Your Majesty."

Her heart sank a little. She felt a small sense of shame as she came to realise that the guard was merely looking out for her.

"I would appreciate an escort very much," she breathed.

Within moments, another two guards were accompanying the White Queen as she walked along the wide path to the stable house. A bitter breeze blew, sending drifts of snow scurrying across the cobblestones near her feet.

A bright flickering light emitted from the crack of the stable house door. As she approached, she could hear his voice speaking calmly.

"Turn it like this," he said as she pushed the door open. A long creak ensued as the guards stepped to each side of the passage to allow her through. "Now, tighten the yarn."

She stood with mouth agape as she looked upon Takmel and the girls.

They sat on the floor, encompassed by mounds of straw, baskets of twining, and bundled twigs. Scattered across the floor were hundreds and hundreds of tiny straw men with little wooden arms and legs, not much bigger than the length of her hand.

"Another one done," he said, tossing a completed straw doll onto the floor, where it toppled over the others before coming to rest. "Close the door, my love. You're letting in the cold."

"What are you doing?" she asked, stepping inside and pushing the door shut behind her. She gestured to the crude dolls on the floor. "What is all this?"

"This," he stated, as he grabbed another handful of straw and some twining, "is something my mother did. She would spend hours and hours making these little straw men. I thought these young ladies might enjoy learning how to make them. Would you like to try?"

"For what purpose?"

He looked at her, a little perplexed. The two girls glanced to her suddenly. Tiny dots of white light shone from their pupils. Isabel's heart almost stopped and a tight knot twisted in her stomach. There was magic here. Dark magic.

"Why, for my purpose," he replied. "They serve me."

She shook her head in disbelief. "Little straw men will serve you?"

"Don't be silly," he said playfully as his hands worked. "These little straw men are representations of the ones who will serve me."

"Representations?"

He tossed another completed doll near her feet. The girls were still clumsily working on the ones they were making when Isabel had first opened the stable house door.

Takmel gestured to the floor farther inside the stable. She saw piles of little straw dolls stacked against the pen walls. There were thousands of them. More than she could count.

"How long have you been out here doing this?"

"A few days," he admitted as he gathered materials to make another doll. "On and off. The ladies just came out with me for the first time tonight. They've made three each. And they're very good, indeed," he finished with a kind smile towards the twins. They replied in kind and continued to wrap the twining tightly around their little dolls' necks.

"There are so many," she murmured, stepping past him and moving into the stable. Horses housed in the pens watched her curiously as she looked over the mounds of tiny straw men. "You made all of these?"

"Yes," he answered.

"Why?" she asked, turning to face him. He tossed another completed doll to the floor. He was fast with his hands. She surmised it was unnatural, the way he formed them and completed the task so quickly.

"I'm building an army," he answered. "One large enough to wipe out all who oppose me and drive fear into those whom I allow to survive. That's why."

Five

Alice sat cross-legged on a horse blanket by the hearth. The Agrodien women gathered empty plates from the guests and returned to the kitchen to clean. Her cabin was behind her. Several of her friends had gathered on its porch to watch the proceedings.

Arthur sat on the edge of the veranda, his boots scraping through the snow-covered ground to make small trenches. They were deep and cut down to the dirt beneath the frosty covering. The talks had been going on for some time; long enough for him to have noticed the moon rise over the pine trees to the east and move far enough across the sky to dangle high above their heads.

He kept his eyes on the gathering of Haigok leaders surrounding the campfire. Alice was talking to them, but he couldn't hear her words. Gruloch, seated on a cushion beside her, translated. Three of the others nodded, seemingly in agreement with what Alice proposed. One, however, gestured with a wave of his hand to the north and spoke angrily. Arthur could hear him, as clear as day, but didn't understand what was being said.

"What do you think that was about?" Lor asked from behind the boy, seated on the bench that ran along the front of the cabin.

"Don't know," David replied from his position near the door. "But he didn't seem too happy."

Alice was gesturing to the west as she spoke. Her hands moved to the north, then to the east.

"She's explaining the Maji's plans," Becka told them. "That one comes from the Frozen Waste."

"Ganda," Arthur said, keeping his eyes on the meeting. "Leader of the Nrarukh. His people are so far to the north, no man ever ventures there. Gruloch told me he was the only leader who had second thoughts about attending this gathering. Ganda would rather remain in the north, hidden from man. He would rather have all of his kind join him and let man fall away by their own devices."

"Sounds like a lovely fellow," Glaun remarked.

"I don't think he's wrong for having that opinion," Arthur told him. "If you consider what happened to them, what our people had done to them, he would be in his right to hide away. If it weren't for Alice, I would consider doing the same."

"What our people did to them was a very long time ago, son," said David.

"The Haigok hold onto memories the way we would with precious jewels," his son explained. "It's why Woodmyst fell when you were a boy. It's why Richard lived. Gruloch's father held onto that memory so tightly, it shaped him to act violently."

"Ganda holds onto that memory, also," Arthur continued. "The stories his father shared of what man is capable of drove his people north. Gruloch told me that the Nrarukh have a saying; *To hide is to survive.* It may sound cowardly, but I don't disagree with them. If I didn't believe that Alice could defeat Takmel, I would take the same path as Ganda and his clan."

"And go north?" Kygra enquired.

"No." Arthur shot him a curious glance. His hand moved to his left shoulder. "But I would hide."

As they were speaking, Alice rose to her feet and bowed respectfully to the five clan leaders. They responded by standing up and bowing with their hands on their chests.

Alice then raised her hand to the sky and spread her fingers. In a quick motion, she swept her arm down towards the fire.

The flames died.

Thick smoke wafted into the air as darkness fell upon the meeting area.

"Meeting adjourned," Becka announced as they watched Alice turn towards the cabin with Gruloch by her side.

"I make tea," a gruff voice said from the door. Arthur turned to see Corandra, Yuri's daughter, poking her head through the entrance. "On table," she announced.

"Thank you," Arthur replied.

"You come in, Kayl'sro," the reptilian called softly. "Too cold for mother."

Alice smiled as she drew near to the hut. She dropped her blanket on the porch.

"I'm not a mother, yet," the girl replied, reaching for Arthur with one hand while rubbing her belly with the other. "I don't even have a bump."

"You will before you know it," Sevrina said, lifting herself from the bench, struggling a little with her belly sticking far out before her. Andris offered his help by taking her elbow.

"That seemed to go well," said David jovially. They moved inside and regrouped.

"Well enough," Alice replied, sitting at the head of the table. Corandra started pouring tea for all of them.

"Four clans will give their support; in return, they want to openly lay claims to the lands that they currently occupy," Gruloch relayed. "One will not join us. Ganda has decided to keep out of the fight."

Arthur looked across the table to Gruloch.

"Will this affect us greatly?" the boy asked. "The decision made by the Nrarukh?"

Gruloch shook his head. "The Nrarukh Clan is the smallest. They have seven dragons in their keeping, and all are very small compared to those raised to the south of the Frozen Waste. Not all are capable of fighting. Ganda believes he is risking a great deal by bringing three of them here. He will leave tonight under the cover of darkness.

"All other clans have pledged their dragons," he continued. "Alice only asked that they do not risk all of them."

"I tried to persuade Ganda," Alice put in. "He argued he was too far to the north for the Maji to be concerned with. I told him how the Maji plans to extend his influence across all lands to the west, to the east and eventually to the north. But, he wouldn't have it."

"Ganda is one of a set mind," Gruloch explained. "It would be hard to change his perceptions after being away from all of us for so long. I believe my clan is the only one to have visited his people since the time of your Realm Wars. He has never ventured outside of the Frozen Waste until now. Quite strange, now that I think about it."

Arthur tilted his head and contemplated the Haigok's words.

"So..." David leant forward as he reached for his steaming mug of tea. "How many dragons does that give us?"

"I can commit nine," Gruloch answered. "Five of my females are laden with eggs."

"That's good news," Alice said earnestly.

"Not all the eggs will survive, sadly," the Haigok told her. "Fewer and fewer hatch with each brood. We don't yet know the cause of it. The Kazrekh Clan has offered eight riders. The Eranak, seven. Traruk, seven as well. This gives us thirty-one."

"And Liana makes thirty-two," Alice added.

David raised his brows. "That's a lot of dragons."

Becka sighed deeply before sipping her tea.

"What is it?" Linet asked from beside her.

"I'm concerned," she replied. "Do we really want to go down this path?"

"What do you mean?" questioned Lor.

"I saw the devastation caused by one dragon," she explained. "After Richard killed the first, the other wreaked havoc upon Woodmyst. Its breath was so hot, so intense, that it melted stone. The entire city and its walls were destroyed. Nothing stood afterwards. Not a thing. And now, you say we have thirty of them?"

"Takmel will use whatever he has at his disposal to occupy these lands," Alice told her. "After that, he will want more. He won't stop. We must stop him."

"But there are people in the cities that he already controls," Becka argued. "Families. Children. Richard wouldn't want this."

Alice nodded, absorbing the widow's words.

"This is war," the girl said. "None of us wants war. But war has come. Takmel won't sit idly by and simply allow us to walk in and take over. He will have prepared his forces.

"If we don't attack," she went on, "he most certainly will. He won't concern himself with families and children if he returns. He has already shown what he is willing to do to little boys and girls.

"As much as I don't wish to see innocent lives damaged by conflict, I need to admit that it could happen. The dragons give us an advantage, and I intend to use them."

***

Arthur walked down the embankment, towards the little bridge that crossed the stream. The snow crunched loudly beneath his boots. He thought the Haigok encampment across the way would surely hear him approaching.

A piece of parchment gripped in his hand flapped in the gentle breeze. He pulled it to his chest, protecting it as best he could with one arm.

With care, he stepped across the little wooden bridge. The timber planks creaked a little. The stream bubbled as it slid over smooth stones and continued on to the south.

He saw a silhouette move between tents. An orange flickering glow rose behind the figure.

It was a cloaked Haigok with a curved sword in his hand. He called over to the boy, using words that Arthur didn't understand.

"I wish to speak with Ganda," the boy called. "Clan leader of the Nrarukh."

The Haigok spoke in his own tongue again, stepping forward and displaying his long blade for Arthur to see. Arthur held the parchment out to his side and turned in full circle to show the other that he was unarmed.

"Ganda of the Nrarukh," he said. He heard several dragons rumbling to his left. He started to doubt his actions, thinking himself a fool for coming on his own.

The Haigok stepped over to Arthur and glared at him with his large, bulbous, yellow eyes. He seemed to measure the boy carefully, moving his gaze up and down the boy's form. His blade tip slid beneath the flap of Arthur's coat as if searching for hidden objects concealed beneath, first right, then left. The Haigok's eyes fell upon the empty left sleeve of the coat.

"Arthur," the Haigok grunted.

The boy nodded.

The figure sighed a deep breath and signalled with a nod of his head for the boy to enter the campsite.

They had placed the tents in a rough circle around a large hearth. Apart from the Haigok accompanying Arthur, a few others sat by the fire talking in low voices. Three were rolling up bedding and folding tarpaulins into small bundles to be carried away. The Haigok by the fire looked over to the boy in question.

"Ganda?" Arthur questioned. One of the Haigok gestured with his thumb over his shoulder to the three packing their equipment.

Ganda, crouching near to the ground so he could fold the tent canvas, looked over at Arthur. He stood up and peered at the parchment in the boy's hand. Slowly, the Nrarukh Clan leader moved towards Arthur, pointing at the parchment as he spoke quietly in his own tongue.

"I've come to treat with you," Arthur explained. "I've come to ask that you reconsider."

Ganda shook his head as he passed by the hearth, not understanding the words coming from the boy's mouth. He looked around at the others and spoke again. The others responded with words of their own. None of it made sense to the boy.

Arthur jutted his chin towards the dragons.

"We need them," he said. "We need you. We can help each other. All of us."

Moving closer, Ganda reached out his hand and snatched the parchment from Arthur. He waved it in front of the boy's face and growled some words menacingly. Arthur felt his heart racing as fear gripped him.

Ganda turned and approached the fire, holding the parchment out to the flames.

"Wait," Arthur called desperately.

He didn't need to.

Ganda had frozen in place. His eyes fixed on the parchment in his hand.

Orange flickering light passed through it, revealing a crude scrawl over its surface.

"Khadzh," Ganda spat. He spun on his heels and glared at Arthur. More words ensued as he held the parchment towards the boy, displaying the image drawn upon it.

Arthur didn't need to look at it. He had drawn it; a charcoal sketch of a thin, black figure with long claws and large teeth.

Ganda grabbed Arthur by the collar of his shirt. He growled words that the boy didn't know as he waved the image wildly in Arthur's face.

Another voice called out in the Haigok tongue.

It came from behind Arthur, but Ganda's grasp prevented him from turning his head to see who it was.

Ganda stopped suddenly and looked over Arthur's shoulder. He released the boy and took a step back.

"Are you all right, Arthur?" asked a familiar voice. The boy turned to see Gruloch standing behind him with Alice by his side.

"I'm fine," he replied.

"You silly fool," Alice muttered, moving to her husband and wrapping her arms around him. "What were you thinking?"

"I was thinking of you," he replied.

"They could have killed you," she scolded.

He nodded apologetically before looking back to Ganda.

"What was he saying to me?" Arthur asked Gruloch. "Before you told him to stop."

"He wants to know how you came about the image of Khadzh," the other explained. "It's a word I am unfamiliar with. But it is what he is calling that beast you have drafted."

Arthur looked to Gruloch.

"Could you translate for me, please?"

The Lord of the Haigok nodded.

The boy put his attention back upon Ganda. He moved away from his wife and approached the leader of the Nrarukh Clan cautiously.

"That," said Arthur, pointing to the image, "is a creature which is under the control of the Maji. How do you know it?"

When Gruloch had finished relaying the message, Ganda spoke. Gruloch translated for Arthur to understand.

"This is Khadzh," he replied. "They are many. They come from the mountains far in the north. An area we call the Ice Spires. They sleep during the coldest times, but when they wake, they need to feed. Khadzh raided our stores and killed our livestock. We hunted them, but they are good at hiding. We would only ever kill a few at a time. But they are many.

"A few moons back, one killed four children. Sneaked in and took them from the Haigok huts during the night and feasted upon them in the ice fields. All we found were their clothes and frozen blood.

"But they are all gone. Khadzh have left the Ice Spires. We looked for them. They have all gone."

"Not gone," Arthur told him. Gruloch translated. "They are here. Alice's dragon killed many. But there are more. And when the Maji is finished with us, he will send them back. Your livestock won't be safe. Your children are not safe. Help us. Please. We can defeat the Maji together. We can destroy all of these dark creatures." Arthur pointed to the parchment.

Ganda stared at the boy for a long time after Gruloch finished relaying the message. He looked down at the image again, then back to the boy.

Eventually, he nodded as he reached out his hand to give the parchment back to Arthur. The boy took the sketch and tossed it into the flames. He then took Ganda's hand firmly in his to seal the agreement.

***

He gave a polite wave to Gruloch, who replied in kind as he closed the door that led into the cavern behind the cottage. Alice lifted his coat from his shoulders and dropped it on a chair before taking him by the waist and leading him to their bedroom. They passed a closed door, from behind which they could hear David snoring loudly. Arthur smiled and paused to listen, but Alice took his hand and pulled him away.

She was strong, and he was too tired to resist. He complied and followed her to the edge of the bed.

With a wave of her hand, the door closed gently. The candles on the bedside table flickered a little in response.

Alice moved away as he sat on the bed to unlace his boots. It took him some time, as he was still getting used to performing such trivial acts with only one hand. Eventually, he used his right toes to push the boot off the left foot. He repeated the action, alternating his feet. He reached down and placed the boots neatly, side by side, at a space beside the door.

He turned to face Alice, to talk with her, as he felt shame regarding his behaviour. He wished he had spoken to her before he approached Ganda, before he had even drawn the creature on the parchment.

"Alice," he started. "I'm so sorr—"

He paused.

He stared with mouth open as he moved his eyes over her.

The candlelight caressed her smooth skin with a soft, orange glow. The deep shadows accentuated her curves as she stood by the bed, waiting for him.

"You're taking too long," she told him.

He got to his feet, feeling a tingling sensation move down his spine.

She slid her fingers around his neck, and over his shoulders, pressing her body against his. Her lips touched his cheek.

"I leave tomorrow," she said, unbuttoning his shirt.

"I know," he replied. He started loosening the cords of his trousers. "I am sorry about tonight."

"I'm not," she replied, almost tearing his shirt away. She kissed the newly healed skin covering his left arm socket. It felt tender to him, but not painful. A pleasurable tingle moved over his skin.

"I shouldn't have gone without you," he admitted as his trousers fell to his ankles.

"Shut up," she whispered. She pushed him onto his back. "Just shut up."

"All right."

She giggled and bent to kiss his neck.

With a wave of her hand, the tiny flickering flames of the candles snuffed out.

Six

She woke early.

Dawn was approaching; she could feel it.

She stretched and moved to get out of bed.

"Don't," Arthur groaned sleepily, reaching his hand out to her and grabbing her arm, keeping his eyes shut. "Stay a little longer."

She moved onto her side, pressing herself against him and slipping her leg over his. She kissed his neck where it met the shoulder.

"I need to go," she told him.

"I know," he replied, opening his eyes to look at her. "I don't want you to."

She rested her head against his chest.

"I don't want to either," she said. She listened to his heart drumming deeply and calmly in his chest. "You did well last night."

He smiled. "That's a compliment worth waking up to."

"Not that," she said, smacking him softly on the stomach. "I mean the negotiation with Ganda. You did well."

"Almost got myself killed," he reminded her. "I feel so stupid."

"But you didn't. You convinced him. I still don't know how you did that. How you knew to do that."

Arthur took a deep breath and gave his mind to his actions of the previous night.

"It was something that Gruloch said," he replied. "How Ganda and the Nrarukh had never left the lands they have occupied. Not until now. I suspected it was because something else took priority. I suspected it was because of those dark creatures. The Khadzh."

"You couldn't have been sure of that," she interjected.

"I took a gamble," he admitted.

She nestled against him. "You were brave to do so."

"You're the brave one, remember." He kissed her head. "I just read books."

"I'm not brave," she told him. "Most of the time I'm pretending."

He tilted his head to see her face.

"What do you mean?"

"I don't know," she answered. "I just do what I think is the right thing to do. But, I'm uncertain it always is the right thing. Remember what Becka said. About Richard. How he wouldn't want me to use dragons. About there being children and families. I can't get that out of my head."

"You are the bravest person I know." He tightened his arm around her shoulders. "You ran the Kyhur Circuit in less than an hour. You leapt over the Rakmha Trench on foot. Twice. You defeated the Agrodien and became their Kayl'sro. You tamed a rukyul. You ride a dragon that tried to kill you once, if you recall. You've defeated squadrons of men, single-handed, with barely a scratch on your skin. If that is pretending, then I've been wrong about you since we were younglings."

"That was all training," she told him.

"Training didn't make the Agrodien respect you," he told her, moving to look her in the eyes. "Training didn't bring the people who followed you from Woodmyst to the glade to live with you. Training didn't give you the incentive to strike up a treaty with the Haigok, with whom we are now friends. That was all you, Alice."

She touched her belly as tears welled in her eyes.

"I'm scared," she admitted. "I can feel the power of Gwendra leaving me. How can I be brave without that power? How can I be sure that we will return to you?" She gestured to her stomach with her eyes.

"You will," he smiled.

"How do you know?"

"Because you are Alice Gyfford," he explained. "My wife. Daughter of Tomas Warde. You are the most powerful sorceress that I have ever known. Even before you were given this new power." A lone tear streaked over her cheek. "Besides," Arthur continued. "You don't believe in the gods, remember. Even if this power leaves you, you will still be Alice Gyfford, mother of my unborn child and the bravest person who I have ever known. That's how I know you will come back to me. Both of you."

She wiped her eyes and kissed him hard.

"Thank you, Arthur," she whispered into his ear.

***

Alice steered Liana in a south-westerly direction. She wore her bearskin beneath the leather cloak, made and given to her by the Agrodien females. She pulled her cowl over her head and wrapped her scarf about her mouth and nose. The only distinguishable feature visible were her striking blue eyes.

Forming up behind her were three more dragons with riders; the representatives of Kazrekh, the clan of the Spine Mountains.

They passed low over the Lunkhul Forest, leaving the glade and Woodmyst far behind them. A white coating of snow dusted the world below. Crooked, twisted fingers stretched up to them from the forest floor, bare trees with dark limbs that seemed to ache for warmth to return.

For the best part of the journey, the dragons followed the path of the Western Road that led from Woodmyst to Oldcastle. Once they reached the edge of the forest, however, they shot skyward over the plains to get a wider view of their surroundings.

It wasn't long before Alice saw the ruins of the war-torn city by the sea. The great mound of steps that once housed the citadel still towered above it all. The citadel itself was a tumbled mound. Most of it had rolled down the stairs in large pieces to the ground where it crushed houses and smaller buildings surrounding the once impressive structure.

She carefully looked through the streets, and nooks from her high vantage point, but saw nothing. If her friends were there, they would have surely come out to welcome her.

There were signs they had been here, though. Black marks and steaming embers dotted the ruins.

She heard a sharp whistle, and looked over to Erugoth, who was flying near to her right flank. He was pointing to the west, into the Sea of Lunkhul.

Alice followed his gesture to a group of ships on the horizon. Twelve ships.

It was difficult to tell if they were friend or foe. In fact, she had no way of knowing.

In either case, she intended to let them know she was here. She urged Liana to turn towards the sea. The dragon gave a loud call that shook the sky as she turned towards the fleet.

Yuri pulled his steed to a halt. He was certain he heard something on the air. A gentle wind was blowing from the east, and he knew he heard a voice carried upon it; a voice not belonging to one of the many men behind him.

"What is it?" Nola'ee asked him, peering in the direction he was looking.

He shook his head slightly.

Emily pulled up beside them and turned in her saddle to peer back the way they had come. The region looked clear to her, save for the hundreds of soldiers in tow.

"There," Yuri eventually pointed. Emily followed his finger to the sky. She could see nothing. "Four of them."

"What is he looking at?" the auburn woman asked, perplexed and seeing nothing.

"Dragons." Nola'ee smiled. "Four dragons. Kayl'sro Alice has come."

They passed over the land's edge after spying the great multitude moving westward, and dived for the water, levelling out just above the surface. Travelling at such an intense speed, the beasts kicked up white spray, leaving four fine lines of wake in the sea behind them.

Liana chirped as she dipped her wing tips into the liquid. Alice kept her eyes on the ships coming up on her right. She saw cannons and finely dressed men carrying sabres.

A deep blue flag, with a golden eagle carrying an axe, was flying upon each vessel. She wasn't familiar with it, and therefore, couldn't tell if they had good intentions towards her friends onshore.

What she knew was that the fleet was running through the sea almost parallel to the forces onshore. They weren't that far out from the coast, which meant Commander Brondt had probably seen them.

"Commander!" one of the ship's crew called to Willard Zakhar. "Dragons!"

Zakhar turned to see four great monsters gliding over the waves at great speed towards his vessel. His eyes stayed transfixed upon the lead creature. All he saw were immense teeth and giant claws.

His jaw dropped open when he noticed the rider. The form was unmistakably a young girl. For some stupid reason that he could never be able to explain, he waved to her and smiled.

Alice couldn't believe her eyes.

The little man in his nice uniform was waving.

She didn't know how to respond, so she waved back.

Liana turned sharply to the right and swung tightly around the fleet, before turning to shore. Alice leant back in her saddle, urging Liana to head to the sky again. The girl turned her head back to see other crewmen on the vessels with their hands held high.

Friendlies, she supposed.

***

"Who is the little man on that ship out there?" Alice called as she jumped from Liana's back, lowering her cowl and scarf. Emily smiled as she watched her daughter approaching. Three cloaked Haigok were in tow, leaving their dragons to rest on the ground. "Do you know he had the gall to wave to me?"

"You waved back," Catherine replied. "I saw you."

"Yes." The girl stopped in her tracks. "Well. What was I supposed to do?"

"I think you're referring to Commander Willard Zakhar," Brondt informed her. "The fleet he commands comes to us from Dendadia. He has offered his services."

"His services?" Alice stared out at the ships as Emily dropped from her steed and started towards the girl. "To what end?"

"To defeat the Maji," Brondt told her.

"To reopen the trade routes to Newholt, more like it," Ursula put in.

Thornton smiled as he raised his brow at Lieutenant Brook by his side.

"Smart, that girl of yours," remarked the lieutenant in a whisper.

Emily wrapped her arms around Alice from the side, locking the girl's arms in place.

"Hello Mama," Alice grinned, nestling her head into her mother's chest.

"Who are these with you?" Akasati enquired, pointing to the three Haigok behind the girl.

"Oh!" Alice stepped out of Emily's embrace and gestured to the leader. "This is Erugoth, clan leader of Kazrekh. I don't know the names of these others with him, but they escorted me from home. They have agreed to assist us, but they must return to their home first."

"Assist us?" Amicia questioned. "How?"

"The Haigok met together and have committed their forces to the fight," the girl explained. "Thirty-six dragons in total."

"From these Haigok?" Schoenbach asked excitedly as he looked over to the cloaked figures and held a hand to his chest. "We thank you from the bottom of our hearts, gentlemen."

Erugoth copied the gesture, placing his own hand upon his chest, followed by a slight bow.

"He doesn't understand you," Alice explained. "And no, not just from the Kazrekh. That's what all the Haigok can spare in total."

Alice turned and bowed politely to Erugoth, who returned the motion before turning and ordering his companions back to their dragons.

"They're leaving already?" Ursula asked, watching the three retrace their steps.

"They have much to prepare," Alice answered as she turned to face them. "And, so do we. A great deal of travelling needs to be completed if we are to make Greyrose in three days."

"Greyrose?" Jendryng called from behind his captain. Thornton turned to scowl at the young soldier, but not before Jendryng blurted out again. "Three days? May as well not sleep if we're to do that."

"Will you shut your pie hole?" Thornton growled.

Alice smirked as she turned to watch the three dragons lift into the air.

Liana spread her wings, eager to follow. The girl whistled, to which the dragon instantly looked over to her rider and folded her wings, returning them to the ground where she used them as forelimbs.

"You'll see them again, girl," Alice told her as she moved closer to the beast. She stretched out her hand and rubbed Liana's snout reassuringly. "Soon. I promise."

The dragon turned her neck to watch the other three climbing higher into the sky, moving away to the north. She gave a sharp chirp, as if trying to call them back. It echoed across the open plain, sounding very lonely. The girl's heart sank a little as the dragon called out after the three again.

They didn't respond, being already too far away, almost mere spots in the sky.

Seven

Arthur ducked beneath a low branch as he followed Alan on into the woods. He had a hunting knife strapped to his waist and a water skin slung over his right shoulder so that the strap crossed his body, allowing the container to rest against his left hip. Alan carried a bow in his hand and a quiver of arrows on his back.

"I don't see why I can't carry the knife," Alan said as he started up a small rise.

"Gives me something to do," Arthur replied.

"You could carry the bow and quiver."

"And if we come upon some game?" Arthur smiled. "Which arm should I use to hold the bow and which should I use to load the arrows?"

Alan turned and gave him an incredulous glare. "I said, carry. Not go all Alice on me."

Arthur chuckled as they started forward again, picturing his wife leaping over fallen logs and flinging countless arrows into countless targets.

"You know," Arthur said after a short time, "there are times I forget."

"Forget what?" Alan asked. "Alice? Don't know how you could forget her."

"No." He gave the other a hard look after sensing a hint of what he thought to be salaciousness in his friend's words. "Not Alice. By the gods. Let alone her being my wife, she's your cousin."

"I meant nothing like that," Alan bit back, turning to give the other a questioning stare. "Where do those books that you read take your mind to?"

"Not there," Arthur replied. "I was talking about my arm. I sometimes forget it is gone."

"Oh." Alan started walking again. "What? Do you try to scratch an itch with it or something?"

"Something like that," Arthur answered, following the boy's footsteps up the embankment. The snow crunched loudly beneath their boots as they neared the top. "Take this morning. I was making tea for Alice. I was holding the pot with my right hand and reaching for the mug with my left. Only, the mug didn't move. But I could swear to you it felt as if I was reaching for it. I could feel my fingers closing and opening."

"Must be good to have a woman," Alan said suddenly as he peered across a shallow dell. The remark caught Arthur off guard. It was almost as if Alan hadn't heard a single word he had just said, responding to something totally unrelated.

Arthur looked at him and saw loneliness on the other's face.

"You'll find yours one day," he said.

"I'm thirteen," Alan said. "I've got my whole life ahead of me. Of course, I'll find mine one day. Or so my father tells me. But I can't help feeling some envy for what you and Alice have. I hope I have that with the one I find."

"I'm certain you will."

"I don't know if you saw too much in Woodmyst," Alan said with a grin. "What, with your head in your books all the time. But, not everyone is happy with their wives or husbands. Some marry out of necessity. Some marry for the sake of having children. Others marry because of strange arrangements between their parents. I don't want to marry because of those reasons. I'd like to marry someone for the same reason that you and Alice did."

"Love?" Arthur asked. "You're speaking of love? Not what my father initially thought about Alice and me, which was that I couldn't keep my trousers on?"

Alan laughed. "Yes. Love," he answered.

"Plenty of girls in Woodmyst," Arthur reminded.

Alan shook his head. "They all still play with dolls," he replied. "And those that do so less often frequently ogle the young soldiers or woodsmen's apprentices. More so in summer when shirts are discarded. They have no interest in someone like me."

"You want someone with a heightened level of maturity?"

"I don't want anyone old," Alan stated. "Someone my age would suffice."

"I meant, in the mind," Arthur pointed to his head. "Not in body."

Alan nodded. "Hard to find at our age," he admitted as he scanned the dell. There was movement from beneath the trees on the far side. He gestured with his chin for Arthur to look as he took an arrow from the quiver on his back.

Arthur peered across the small clearing to see a large boar shovelling snow with its snout, tearing up dirt with its tusks at the base of a thick tree. He guessed the pig was after truffles or grubs.

"A young woman," Arthur whispered, seemingly to himself, as Alan took aim and pulled back on the bowstring. "Mature minded. About our age, not old. Just what do you have against wrinkly ones?"

The arrow flung through the air, skimmed over the surface of the dell, sticking deep into the flesh behind the boar's ear. It squealed a little before falling to the ground.

"You bastard! You're so lucky that hit," Alan said, stifling a laugh and trying to appear angry.

"I never had a doubt," Arthur said, slapping his friend on the shoulder before setting across the clearing to retrieve the kill.

***

Sub-Commander Landon Wake stood upon the waterfront with Captain Davine Staiger by his side. She had her arm tucked beneath his long coat and wrapped around his waist. His was around her shoulders as they watched a barge, laden with a small crane and large timber beams, being guided by men with long poles to the far end of a new pier being constructed.

"That looks like hard work," he said in a low voice as he observed two men on the front corners of the flat barge slide their long poles down into the water, where they eventually met the ground beneath the surface. The men then pushed with all their might as they walked to the rear of the barge along either side, thus moving the vessel away from the shore. As they did so, another two men repeated the manoeuvre, followed by another two.

The three pairs of men continued until they were almost level with a team of workers on another barge. They were driving long beams vertically into the ground beneath the waves, using a large iron contraption, which reminded Wake of a tall cage. They fit the device with a heavy weight at the top and many pulleys and ropes to keep it in place. The men lifted the weight up as high as it would go. A long beam was slid onto ropes and hoisted into place beneath the weight. The timber beam then slid to the sand below, where it came to rest upon its end. The weight then dropped. Carefully, the men then lifted the weight before dropping it again so it drove the beam into the ground, much like a hammer with a nail.

Wake was impressed by what they had accomplished so far. Six pairs of pylons stood in place already. Workers on board the barge with the crane had started construction on the main supports for the boardwalk, setting the cross beams and framing. More carpenters had laid the planks and nailed them in place.

"They've done well," he said proudly.

"They have much more to go," Staiger told him. "At least another twelve sets of pylons before the *Gypsy* can moor here."

"She will," he said, turning to look at the city behind them.

Timber scaffolding filled the scenery, loud hammering echoed through the air and carts laden with building supplies scurried about busily as Newholt was repaired.

"She won't be the same," Staiger said. "No matter how hard they try to make her look like she once did." She turned to look at him, smiling when his eye came to rest upon her. "You look more distinguished with a leather patch," she said, noting the black cow skin over his left eye socket. A tanner had moulded it for him at her request. She was willing to pay for it herself, but the tanner had refused her coins when he realised for whom he was making it. It was hemmed with golden thread and fitted with two long fine strips of leather twine at each corner so he could tie it to his head.

"I shan't take it off," he jested.

"You bloody well will," she told him, jabbing a finger into his chest. "And you'll wash it too. I don't want it stinking."

He sniggered and leant in to kiss her. She, in turn, pulled him into her tightly.

"You're right," he said afterwards. He was looking about them at the people.

"About what?"

"Newholt," he answered. "She won't ever be the same. Even if they try to make it look exactly how it was. She won't be the same again." He sounded sad and distant.

"We could leave," she said.

He looked at her in query. "I can't," he reminded her. "I've responsibility here."

"I mean when yer Commander Brondt returns," replied Staiger. "We could leave together. Go to Dendadia and start a life together there."

"See the marble columns of the citadel," he mused. "Visit the Temple of Four. Swim in the Bay of Dreams. Drink Crystalbridge wine."

"Drink Crystalbridge wine for the rest of our lives," she said, pressing herself against him.

"That sounds glorious," he told her. He looked out to the sea. "But I don't want you giving up what you love for me."

"Silly, one-eyed old fart," she whispered. "I love you."

He kissed her forehead and pulled back to look into her eyes.

"When the commander returns," he said, "I'll tender my resignation immediately."

***

He hoisted another small barrel of ale through the back door of The Petty Beggar. Looking around the room and seeing two men cleaning the benchtops to the side of the kitchen, he placed the barrel on the table in the centre of the room to wipe the sweat from his brow.

"How about you two stop doing that for a bit and help me with this lot?" He pointed to a laden cart outside the door. Neatly stacked barrels of grog and boxes of supplies rested upon it.

"All right, Monty," one of them said, and chuckled.

"That's Mister Monteacute to you," the other snapped with a hint of playfulness.

"All right, Monty," the other repeated as he exited through the door.

Monteacute shook his head and lifted the barrel onto his shoulder. He continued through the kitchen and into the larger room of the tavern. Three women occupied the area, performing menial tasks ranging from tidying tables, sweeping the floor and restocking the bar.

"We should put those down in the cellar," Rose Heron told him, flicking her golden braid over her shoulder as she placed two bottles of wine on a shelf behind the bar.

"This one gets tapped for tonight," the man replied. "The boys will be thirsty after they finish their run. There's two more cartloads over at the Cowardly Soldier." He pointed to the bottles on the shelf. "And, don't put too much of that stuff out. That's expensive, and it's all we have of it until we trade with Dendadia again. We need to make it last."

"No one will drink that," Audrey Mountell, the dark-haired whore of Whitekeep, called from across the room. She continued to sweep dust across the timber floor towards the main door into the establishment.

"No one's got the coin. And they probably won't until the queen returns and gets things organised again."

"Then we should just put it all down in the cellar until they get some coin," Monteacute put in. "Shouldn't we?"

"You're a bloody tight arse, Monty," Audrey scolded.

"I appreciate the value of an excellent wine, thank you very much." He bowed slightly.

"And the taste of an excellent ale," Kateryn Crane sniggered as she wiped a cloth over a table. "And an excellent rum. And an excellent cider. And an excellent mead."

"All right," Monteacute said, returning to the doorway leading back to the kitchen. "So, I like a drink or two."

"Or three. Or four," Kateryn added. "Or five, Or..."

"Oh, shuttit!" He smiled as he waved a hand at her, dismissing her comments. He moved through the doorway and heard all three of them call out.

"We love you, Monty."

"We love you too, Monty," said one man, carrying another barrel through the back door and into the kitchen.

"Shuttit," the other answered with a raised eyebrow. He pointed to the barrel. "Get that down in the cellar and hurry back."

***

Ursula tucked her knees up to her chest as she sat by the fire. The sun was sinking beneath the horizon and a warm, purple glow had spread across the sky. Deeper shades of lavender and strange tones of red and pink swirled through some sweeping clouds that moved like a stream from the north and out over the ocean.

The ships anchored a short distance from the shoreline. She watched as numerous long boats, oars pulling through the water at the hands of many men, made their way from the vessels towards the campsite. Brondt was standing by the water's edge with a few soldiers, ready to greet the allies from Dendadia.

"Here," a gravelly voice said from behind her as they placed a blanket over her shoulders.

"Thank you," she said as Thornton sat on the tarpaulin beside her. "You're not going down there to meet with Commander Zakhar?"

"I met him already," the other answered.

"I know. What do you think?" Alice asked, peering across the flames at him.

"What do I think of what?"

"What do you think of him?" she pressed.

Thornton looked down to the boats, spying Zakhar standing at the bow of the lead vessel, bicorn hat on his head, and appearing as if he was posing for his portrait. *A great conqueror come to save the savage men of the western lands*, thought the captain.

"Bit of a pompous sort," he replied honestly.

"Captain!" Amicia reprimanded. "Remember your place."

"I'm sorry, my queen," he said. "But the young miss asked, and I always tell things how I see them. The man hasn't seen a day's fighting in his life, on land or sea. I wouldn't be surprised if he earned his position by association."

"Earned his position by association?" Ursula queried. "What's that mean?"

"Means the captain thinks that little man got his rank by knowing someone important," Schoenbach told her. His eyes were on the row-boats, watching as they made land. Zakhar climbed out of the vessel and almost tripped, catching his foot on the railing as he stepped out. "I'm inclined to agree."

"The man has offered his help," Amicia reminded them. "He has twelve warships out there. That's twelve more than we have."

"You're right," Alice said, watching the man walk alongside Brondt. His footing seemed awkward, almost as if he had his boots on the wrong feet. "We should give him a chance to prove himself."

Emily put an encouraging hand on her daughter's back.

"Do you think he walks like that because he has been at sea for too long?" Catherine asked.

Commander Zakhar kept his back rigid, but his legs seemed to wobble uncontrollably at the knees.

"Could be from having the yard arm shoved up his bunghole," Jendryng remarked as he watched the man approach.

Catherine laughed out loud, quickly covering her mouth as if to hide her sudden outburst. Others by the fire sniggered. Amicia gave the soldier an incensed glare.

"Shut your trap," Thornton barked.

Sparrow, trying not to laugh out loud, punched Jendryng on the arm. Jendryng, in turn, tried to force the corners of his mouth down as he attempted to compose himself.

"You remember Commander Zakhar," Brondt said as they drew near to the fire. Everyone gave a friendly wave or nod, bearing great big smiles for the most part, caused mostly by Jendryng's comment.

"Hello again," Zakhar greeted them, offering a wave of his hand.

"I won't bother you with reintroductions," Brondt told him. "I'm sure you'll learn everyone's names, eventually. We should eat and talk tactics."

"Of course," the sea commander agreed. He looked across the hearth to Alice. "However, I see a new face. The young dragon rider, I presume." He moved around the fire, extending his hand.

As Alice rose to her feet, Yuri and Nola'ee instantly moved between her and Zakhar. Nola'ee pulled her blade free of its sheath, stepping in front of Yuri, who placed himself closer to Alice.

Zakhar took a step back, clearly shaken by the display, and intimidated by the appearance of the Agrodien.

"I don't like him, Kayl'sro," Yuri said in his own tongue.

"We don't know him well enough to like him or dislike him," Alice replied in kind as she stepped past the reptilian. She placed a reassuring hand on his forearm, urging him to lower his weapon. She then focussed her attention on the newcomer. "Forgive my friends, Commander Zakhar. They are overly protective of me, and they haven't seen me in some time. So, they are even more cautious than usual."

"I understand," the newcomer replied. His voice shook a little. "They seem very loyal."

"You make them sound like pets," Alice said.

"I apologise." Zakhar bowed slightly. "I didn't mean to offend."

"These are my people," Alice informed him. "I am their Kayl'sro. Their leader."

Zakhar eyed her curiously. "You are but a little girl," he said, shaking his head and furrowing his brow.

"Who leads the Agrodien nation," she said, and added, "and who rides a dragon."

"And leads the coven of the Four," Amicia said, rising to her feet. "Of which, I am one."

"You answer to her?" the commander asked. "You're a queen."

Brondt put a hand on the man's shoulder. "There's a great deal you will need to be apprised of," he said. "Alice has proved to be an outstanding leader. Not just to the Agrodiens, but to all of us. She is an excellent tactician and a far better fighter than any soldier I have ever seen on the battlefield."

Zakhar's expression became more and more perplexed. "But she's just a child."

His eyes looked this way and that, as if he had just stepped into a world turned upside down.

Alice smiled and stepped over to the sea commander. She gently placed her hand on the man's upper arm.

"Sit," she instructed him. "Eat with us. We'll talk."

He looked around to the other faces by the flames, pausing on Ursula and Catherine, taking in their piercing blue eyes; the same eyes Alice had. He then turned his face to Amicia.

"If she is the queen," Zakhar said, "and she answers to you, what do I call you? Kayl...?"

"Kayl'sro," Yuri growled in a low voice.

Zakhar looked over at him fearfully.

"No." The girl reached out and offered her hand in a friendly gesture. "Alice will suffice."

Eight

The wind had picked up and howled through the streets and alley-ways of the township. The bodies that had littered the ground had all been removed from sight. Most of her men felt the after-burn ache of laborious work and appeared to dawdle back to their various shelters as if half-dead. They had discarded the white tunics and armour, favouring clothing more fitting for industry. She had put them to work, and they were now caked in frozen mud and muck. They felt cold to the core, courtesy of the constant falling snow and icy breeze accompanying it.

She had ordered the occupants of houses, innkeepers, and whores of Ironfields to run as many hot baths as they could for the men. There weren't enough tubs in town to cater for them all, a little over three hundred men. She had therefore instructed the baths to be emptied and refilled at intervals, and the men to clean themselves according to a roster. Even with almost fifty tubs working, they were still operating until late into the night.

"Some men don't want to give up the tubs," Larson told her, lifting a mug of ale to his lips.

Versel was sitting with her men at a table in their preferred tavern, nursing a young woman on her lap. She had one arm around the wench's shoulders and the other creeping slowly along the girl's inner thigh.

"Can't blame them, she acknowledged. "It's bloody cold outside. Tub is warm."

"The others are complaining because they haven't had their turn yet," Larson informed her, peering across the room to another girl serving behind the bar. She eyed him and gave a playful smile. He waved his empty mug, showing that he wanted her to fill it, and nothing more. Her smile died, and she grabbed a jug from a shelf behind the bar before making her way towards him.

The room was reasonably empty, except for a few soldiers, the bar staff, and those about the table with the general. A quiet night compared to the previous ones.

"Get the lieutenants to warn any who linger in the water too long that my orders state they are to be dragged into the street naked and placed on the ground beside Dakoth Risha and his men," Versel ordered. She pursed her lips and shook her head slightly. "They should have all been finished with it by now."

The bar girl poured ale into Larson's mug. Versel drained her cup and held it out for the girl to fill.

"Some of the townsfolk are complaining about that, too," Larson informed her.

"About what?" the general asked as she nuzzled the lap wench's neck.

"Risha and his mob," he explained. "They don't like where we told the men to—"

"I don't care," she said, waving her hand to dismiss his words. "We had orders from the Maji. We followed those orders. If they don't like what the Maji orders us to do, they can take it up with him."

She planted her lips on the girl's neck before gently biting her ear.

"Small crowd," Willis said, turning to the bar girl, who was topping up the men's mugs.

"Cold outside, my lord," she replied. "The fireplaces would be much more inviting than this place."

"I don't know about that," the young man rejoined, grabbing the bar girl's backside and squeezing his hand around her rump.

She jumped and giggled. "My lord!"

"I'm not a lord," he told her, rubbing his hand up her spine. She smiled to him.

"Hey," Versel snapped at him. "None of that."

He gave her a puzzled look. "General?"

"You're mine, remember?"

He gestured to the young woman on her lap.

"I thought you already had chosen for the night," he remarked.

"So," she said, lifting her mug from the table, "you thought you'd choose one for yourself? Is that it?"

The other men looked at each other quietly. Nervously.

Willis swallowed hard. "I apologise, General," he said sheepishly. "I shouldn't have presumed I could do such a thing."

"No," she replied, offering a stern glare. "You shouldn't have. I am your commander and you are mine to command. Understood?"

"Yes, General," Willis said.

"Good." She gave a wry smile as she looked to the wench on her lap. "You will accompany me and this one to my chamber tonight."

"Yes, General," he said again. The bar girl moved away.

"And you'll bring that one with you."

Willis furrowed his brow. The bar girl stopped in her tracks and turned to stare dumbly at Versel. Suddenly, a broad smile stretched over her face.

Willis grinned. "Yes, my General," he replied.

Larson shook his head in disbelief.

"The rest of you get word to the lieutenants and relay my order," Versel said, urging the wench off her lap so that she could stand. "I want all men washed and in their bedrolls within thirty minutes."

They all stood to attention as she moved away from the table. She led the young woman by the hand towards the stairs to the upper level. Willis took the bar girl by the arm and started after Versel. The girl, in turn, placed the jug of ale on the table and followed closely.

"Orders is orders, lads," Willis said to the others cheekily as he moved up the stairs.

"Lucky bastard," Larson huffed as he eyed Willis starting up the stairs. He reached for his cloak, which hung on a peg by the table, before moving to the door to fulfil his general's command.

"You could have had her," Norris reminded as he followed the other out into the frosty night air.

"Shut your fucking mouth."

"Well, you could have." Norris chuckled. "Just saying."

Larson turned and gave the man an angry glare. Norris continued to smile, as did the other six men behind him.

"He's right," Walters pointed out. "The girl was eyeing you all night. Any of us would have jumped at the chance."

"Has your manhood shrivelled in the cold?" Coogan laughed. "I know mine has."

The others burst out snorting and hooting.

Larson glowered at them all. Then he felt the corners of his mouth turn up slowly. Before he knew it, he was laughing too.

"Come on," he told them. "Let's get this done so we can get back to drinking."

***

Snow drifted past the glass panes, built up upon the exterior sill below and the thin mullions that crossed vertically and horizontally over the portals to the outside world. The fire flickered an orange and yellow glow through the room, casting deep shadows upon the wall behind her.

Several times, she had closed her eyes to sleep, but she couldn't find rest behind her eyelids. Her mind raced and her thoughts taunted her. Each of them involved Takmel and the two girls.

He wasn't with her, watching the fire growing smaller and smaller as the night wore on. He was with them.

He was always with them.

A lone tear built up in her eye, slowly gathering its form and causing the sharp flame tips to blur in her vision. It grew heavy and fell from the corner of her eye and over her skin before being soaked into the pillow.

Let him enjoy his new playthings, she thought. Her hand moved to her face so she could wipe her eyes clear. *He'll come back to you soon enough.*

She considered that for a moment. She wondered if she really wanted him to come back to her.

Part of her had felt a small sense of relief since his interest had moved to the twins rather than upon her. A small sense of freedom had found a home, and she felt some autonomy now that his grip had loosened upon her, if only just a little bit.

Part of her hated him as her mind mended and return to what it once was before he had taken her for his bride. Before he had manipulated her with his gentle words and subtle enchantments.

She remembered.

She remembered John.

She remembered his handsome face, and his scruffy beard covering it all. She remembered his unkempt hair that hung to his shoulders and his broad chest. She remembered making passionate love with him. Unlike the purely physical activity that it had become with Takmel, she remembered it was a deeply emotional experience with John.

She remembered his name; John Barnes. Therefore, she remembered hers also, Isabel Barnes.

She remembered they had no children, and she had felt envious of the others, those of the sisterhood of the Seven who had sons or daughters of their own. She remembered she loved every one of those children as if they were hers.

She remembered who had taken all of that from her, and that she had let him.

A small tap at the door brought her back to her room. She wiped her eyes with her hand and looked into the flames again.

Another tap at the door.

She pretended to be asleep.

If it was a guard, he would leave her.

If it was important, they would knock louder.

If it was Takmel...

She heard a soft hiss emitting from the door.

He hadn't even tried to use the handle.

In her mind's eye, she could see him flowing into the room, seeping through the thin gaps beneath, around the door and through the keyhole. His dark, foggy form amassed together as he entered her chamber. It snaked across the rug at the foot of her bed.

She closed her eyes as she felt the presence move under the covers that draped over the end. Like warm tendrils, he coiled around her ankles and moved along her legs and up to her knees. He reformed there, gather together as he climbed higher towards her torso.

She found the experience pleasing and welcomed it.

Part of him flowed rapidly over her belly and breasts, forcing her onto her back. Another part of him pushed her knees apart.

It was no use pretending to be sleeping anymore. He was determined to get his way. He always got his way.

"Done with your pets?" she asked, opening her eyes.

The black shadow smothering her flesh continued to reshape. She could see him in there, glaring at her with hungry eyes.

"Petsssss?" he hissed. His voice was distant, like a whisper. "Jealoussss, are we?"

"Jealous?" she whispered, offering a feigned smile as she watched his face appear before her. He was already inside her, pushing deeper and deeper as he reformed. "What is there to be jealous of?"

"My pets," he answered, sounding more like his usual self as he became flesh.

She moved her hands over his back, feeling the transformation from mist to skin beneath her fingertips.

"You're here." She arched her back, taking him. "With me. Why would I be jealous?"

He kissed her neck.

She closed her eyes and suffered immeasurable pleasure.

She wrapped her arms around him and pulled him into her tighter.

She remembered.

She remembered she loved him.

She remembered that she always would.

***

Alice rubbed the dragon's jaw. Liana tilted her head, coaxing the girl to rub a little higher. A small smile grew on the girl's face as she complied with the dragon's wishes.

The icy breeze was steady, sweeping from the north and bringing a gentle drift of snow with it. The waves rose and fell about her calmly, methodically, as she stood upon a rocky point that jutted from the coastline before gradually sinking into the sea.

A faint pink glow touched the edges of the clouds to the east, signalling the coming sun. She could hear the call of gulls in the air, causing Liana to look to the sky and follow the birds with her eyes.

The girl peered back to the camp.

Fires, dotted throughout the site, burned strongly. The guards had kept them alive through the night so as to keep warm.

There was movement among the tents; more men packing and gathering equipment. She was too far to tell who they were, but upon seeing the figure of Commander Willard Zakhar approaching, she surmised it was his men preparing to leave.

The sea commander passed two Agrodien, Bein and Varssk. They eyed the man cautiously, gripping their sword hilts as Zakhar moved by. The commander offered them a polite nod and touched the front point of his bicorn hat. The reptilians didn't respond. They simply watched the man silently.

"Good morning, my lady," he said as he drew nearer to Alice.

Liana swung her head around to have a look. Zakhar stopped in his tracks, wide-eyed and full of fear.

"Good morning, Commander," Alice replied, scratching the dragon's neck. "You're safe to approach. She's simply curious."

He did so, slowly, as if not to agitate the creature.

Liana sniffed the air, as if absorbing the man's scent. She gave a dismissive snort and turned her attention to the gulls gathering on the rocks nearby.

"She's an impressive one," said Zakhar.

"Yes," Alice agreed. "She most certainly is."

"I've never seen a dragon," he told her. "Not before yesterday. Are they common in these lands?"

"Perhaps once," she answered. "But, not now. At least, I think."

"You think?" Zakhar looked at her, bemused. "You're not certain?"

Alice stroked Liana's neck. The dragon purred in response.

"The truth is that no one has really seen any dragons since they attacked Woodmyst when my father was a boy," Alice told him. "Before that, no one had, except by pure chance.

"The Haigok are the keepers of dragons," she explained. "They have stayed well-hidden for years and have kept these creatures from prying eyes for all of that time. And those are just the ones they have bred. Who knows how many are living in the wild, if any?

"I'm very lucky to have met this lady," Alice continued. "She is the truest friend I have. Apart from my husband, that is."

"Your husband?" He appeared even more confused. "You're wedded? What are you? All of ten years old?"

"I'm thirteen, Commander," she answered.

"Thirteen." Zakhar shook his head slowly. "You're still very young. Forgive me." He lowered his head. "I don't understand the customs of this land, or its people. I am trying to though."

"It's all right," Alice replied.

"May I ask a question, my lady?"

"Go ahead."

"What sort of man would your mother give you to, and why isn't he here with you?"

"My mother didn't give me away, Commander," Alice corrected. "I took my husband of my own accord, and he took me. My husband, Arthur, is of the same age as I am, and he isn't here because he lost his arm to the Maji. He would be if he could, but I asked him to remain behind with his father." She watched as the sea commander turned the newly gained information around in his head. He appeared to grasp her words. She saw an opportunity to have a little fun with the commander. "My husband's father is my mother's lover."

He seemed to freeze in place.

"What?" His eyes widened as he stared dumbly at the girl. "Wait!"

She nodded assuredly, continuing to scratch Liana along the neck.

"You married your brother?"

"What?" She gave him a look of disgust. "No!"

"But you said, your mother…"

"My father died on the battlefield when I was a small child," Alice explained. "Arthur's mother was…" She considered what words to use. "…taken during an unfortunate incident not too long afterwards. My mother and Arthur's father have only recently become lovers."

Zakhar shook his head. "Your customs are strange to me," he admitted again. "Was there a ceremony involved?"

"Ceremony?"

"For you and your husband's marriage?"

"No."

"So, your mother and husband's father are, by all standards, according to your customs, husband and wife also?"

"Yes."

"Strange," he muttered to himself. "Very strange."

"How do they marry in Dendadia?" she questioned.

He raised his eyebrows as he moved by her to peer out into the ocean. "We have a celebration. Sometimes they are big and costly. They are usually for those who consider themselves important. Sometimes they are small, with just a few people invited. In every situation, we call a magistrate to perform a ceremony. Papers, like a contract, are signed by husband and wife and they live happily ever after. Or, at least that is what we tell children."

"Papers?" she asked. "What do they do with them?"

"One copy is given to the newly wedded couple, and another copy is kept in the citadel with all the records," he explained.

"For what purpose?"

"Authentication," he replied. "If someone wishes to dispute a person's marriage, the contract acts as legal proof of the union. A joining of two, becoming one before the gods and man."

"Sounds complicated," Alice put in. "How many pieces of paper does a man need if he takes more than one wife?"

"He can't," Zakhar said, turning to face her. "A man, or a woman, is permitted to have only one legal partner under the marriage laws of Dendadia."

"That wouldn't go well with some in these lands," she remarked. "My husband's father was married to two women until the incident that took them both. My father had three wives. The Maji has married many."

"And such practices appal no one?"

"I'm certain there are some who find the concept of more than one wife to be strange," she conceded, "if not a challenge."

Zakhar chuckled. He took off his glove and reached his hand out to Liana, almost touching her neck, then hesitated.

"Go ahead," Alice urged. "She won't bite. I promise."

He placed his hand on her coarse skin.

"So rough," he remarked. "And warm. I thought it would be more like a fish or lizard."

"She's no fish or lizard," Alice told him. "There is no other creature like a dragon. That's why they are so special."

"I can see that," he agreed.

"Legal partner?" Alice asked suddenly.

"Sorry?" Zakhar questioned.

"You said a man, or a woman, is permitted to have only one legal partner under the marriage laws," she explained. "Does this mean a man can take a man for a husband, or a woman can take a woman for a wife?"

He nodded.

She shook her head and let out a long sigh.

"And you call our customs strange."

"They are," he reiterated. "At least, to me. As many of the customs in my land would be strange to you, I suspect. But, there are some similarities." She gave him a curious look. "Take the gods, for instance," he continued. "Your people worship the Four, just as mine do. Well, a vast majority do."

"Not all of my people worship the Four," she told him.

"I've heard your soldiers talking," he said. "They say that you, your sister, the queen and the other one…"

"Ursula," she interjected.

"Yes. Ursula. My apologies…The soldiers say that the gods have granted you power. That you are the embodiment of the goddess Gwendra herself."

"I don't know about that," she replied with a smirk, continuing to scratch the dragon. "Not entirely."

"Then, how do you explain the things that you can do?"

"I could do quite a bit long before these gods of yours got involved," she answered. "I don't believe in the Four. At least, not in the same way the worshippers do. I grant you there is something. Something bigger. But, gods? I don't think so." She turned to face the man. "There are no gods, Commander. Just other petty things that make themselves mysterious and secret to us. It is we who give them their power. We set them in high places and make them gods. They didn't make the winter or the summer. They didn't make the north or south. They aren't life, death, or the sky and the earth. We gave them that by bowing to them. That much I know."

"How do you know this?" he asked earnestly.

"Gwendra. This thing. Whatever it is, told me," she replied, shaking her head. "No. That isn't right. The knowledge of Gwendra filled me. It's hard to explain. But, when I was granted these new powers that bind me to my sister, the queen, and Ursula, I understood. I also know that it won't last and that it is already fading. Take my word for it, Commander. There are no gods. Gods wouldn't do this to someone." She ran her finger over the white streak in her hair.

"Not even one god?"

She rubbed Liana's neck again.

"Perhaps." She frowned. "Perhaps there is one. But there aren't many. I don't know." Alice gestured to the Agrodien guards with her chin. "They believe in one god. Q'Sharh. An all-powerful god that controls the earth and sky, and everything beyond. Perhaps Q'Sharh is the only god. I've heard tales of men who worship a god that dwells beyond the stars, and of others whose god sleeps beneath the earth in a bed of molten rock.

"They can't all be right," she said, peering out to the sea. The sky gradually changed its colour. A soft orange glow had yawned over the horizon. "Perhaps none of them are right. Perhaps all the gods are just other creatures, like ourselves, who seek attention from stupid people who will believe in anything they are told to believe in."

"Then, how do you explain why this happened to you?" he pressed. "I mean, the four of you. Why were you chosen? What made the gods decide to give you these powers and not a bar wench, or even the Agrodien girl over there?"

"I don't know exactly," she answered. "My sister was the first to receive her power."

"They say Grolle inhabits her," said Zakhar.

"Something that resembles Grolle," Alice agreed. "She was with Takmel, the Maji, when it happened. Something inside of her at the time drew that thing to her. Whatever it is, choosing her caused the other three to be out of balance. So, they chose us to bring her back."

"She was with the Maji?"

"She was his wife," she explained. "Still is his wife, I suppose."

"And now she is here," he said, "with you. Fighting by your side. So, you and the other three were successful."

"I wouldn't say that," Alice replied. "She came back of her own accord. Perhaps this thing that we call Grolle brought some level of humanity back into her life. She was in a dark place when she was with Takmel."

Zakhar placed his gloves on his hands and thought about the girl's words.

"I still believe in the gods," he told her. "I don't know if these powers you have come from them or not, but you have been given them for a reason. Maybe the gods started it. Maybe it's as you say and there are four other entities that use the persona of the gods for their own means. Whatever the reason, you should use their power before it is taken from you." He looked at the vessels floating offshore. "We leave for the ships soon. My men are loading the longboats now. We can take more supplies on board, if you wish. Your tents, for example. It would lighten your load."

"Thank you," she said, "but, we'll load the wagons as we have always done."

Zakhar smiled politely. He understood that the trust between the two of them had not yet improved.

"In any case," he said, "we'll go on ahead and establish a beachhead at Greyrose. The fires should be burning, and some game roasting, by the time you arrive."

"I think not." Alice smirked.

His face dropped as he expected her to give a new command.

"My lady?"

"Liana and I will be there a long time before you arrive," she corrected him. "I plan to go ahead and scope out the land before anyone else gets there."

"But what if there are hostiles in the region?" he queried. "Shouldn't you wait for support?"

"We'll take care of any hostiles," she assured him. "Safe journey, Commander."

Nine

His cloak whipped about him violently as the strong winds tore across the frozen expanse. Squinting his bulbous, yellow eyes, shielding them as much as he could with his hand, Ganda craned his neck to take in the immensity of the Ice Spires.

They were a strange oddity, at least to Ganda. Not part of the mountain range that stretched into the north a little farther to the east, the spires were a bizarre formation of five tremendous ice towers that had seemed to have grown out of the Frozen Waste like horns would from a ram, only tall and straight for the most part.

The surrounding land dipped towards the spires, like a shallow vale that funnelled towards a cavern that lay beneath them. It too had formed from the ice and the Nrarukh Clan believed it was the lair of the Khadzh.

His dragon snorted loudly from behind him. It was clearly annoyed about coming to rest on the cold ground. Another beside it chirped, its rider rubbing its snout as he passed by. The remaining three watched their Haigok riders eagerly as they gathered by Ganda's side.

"You stay with the dragons," he commanded one of them in their tongue. The other bowed obligingly and stepped back, closer to the winged beasts.

Ganda pulled his curved blade from its sheath and started forward. The four Haigok followed the contour of the land gradually down to the base of the tallest spire. Its twisted form reached far above them, disappearing in the haze of frost and sleet sweeping overhead.

Here, black rock and blue ice intertwined, becoming one where the spire met the earth. The four Haigok scrambled over the craggy surface, finding a large opening; a yawning, menacing mouth with sharp teeth made of frozen stalactites.

"Careful," Ganda instructed the others as they stepped out of the blizzard and into the shelter of the cave. He reached under his cloak and retrieved a short-handled torch tucked into the lining. He poured oil from a small flask, kept in a pouch upon his belt, over the rags tied to one end before sparking a flint stone against the wall of the cave to ignite the torch.

Another Haigok reached his own torch over to Ganda's. With two lights to show the way, the five Nrarukh Haigok moved into the cavern.

The space was immense. The roof of the cave was high above them and the walls stretched out far into the darkness. Here and there, pillars of ice and stone reached up from the ground to touch the ceiling.

The farther the five moved into the dark space, the warmer it seemed to feel. The sound of the wind subsided as they pressed on, making their way deeper and deeper into the lair.

The ground sloped downwards, gradually, barely noticeably. But Ganda noticed.

Just as he noticed the very faint scent of blood.

Old blood.

Stale blood.

Farther and farther.

Deeper and deeper.

Warmer and warmer.

After a long time had passed, and the temperature had risen markedly, he relieved himself of his cloak and flung it to the floor. The others followed suit.

"I can't see the opening," one announced, turning back.

"Our trail is clear enough," Ganda told him, holding his torch close to the ground.

Orange flames lit up the silt and dirt layered upon the surface. Sure enough, the Haigoks' footprints were there for all to see.

"That way," another gestured. "I hear something whisper."

Ganda turned his head and listened.

A long, soft hiss ensued.

He gripped his sword and moved on towards the sound.

The hissing was intermittent. Moments of silence broke the sound into long, drawn-out fragments.

As they drew closer, Ganda could determine that the noise came from more than one source.

The cavern channelled into a thinning passage before them. Thinner and thinner.

Ganda felt drops of water on his face and hands.

The heat was becoming uncomfortable.

The hissing grew louder and louder.

"We should have seen them by now," one of the Haigok said.

The leader nodded as he moved into the narrow passage. He held the torch before him as high as he could, away from their eyes.

The passage twisted and turned tightly to the left and to the right. Their backs and fronts scraped against the rock in some of the more constricted turns. The scent of old blood grew stronger and stronger.

Ganda felt his heart racing. If there was ever a terrible moment to be attacked, it would be now. There was barely enough room to fit, let alone to swing his sword in defence.

He considered turning back.

Then something caught his eye.

"I think I see something," he whispered back to the others.

"Khadzh?" one questioned.

"No," he answered, pushing through a tight opening into a wider chamber.

The area opened up into an immense cavern. Large, dark stalactites and stalagmites stretched out to one another from ceiling and floor. Some had met and melted together, forming pillars throughout the area.

A thick river of molten rock flowed slowly through the centre of the chamber, illuminating the expanse in a deep, red glow.

A sharp hiss caused Ganda to turn his head.

A plume of steam erupted from the floor of the cavern across the glowing stream.

The scent of blood was strongest here.

Bones piled against the base of the cavern walls and stalagmites. Large and small creatures had been devoured here. The leader of the Nrarukh Clan could see skulls belonging to sheep, cattle, goats, horses and rukyul littered across the ground. Claw marks were etched into the bones. Teeth marks showed where the flesh had been gnawed away.

Leaning against the base of a thick stalagmite, near to the molten river, was the half-eaten carcass of something unrecognisable. Its rump was all but gone and the head was missing. The torso was all that remained.

This was most certainly the lair of the Khadzh.

"Where are they?" one of the Haigok asked. "They should be wall to wall."

Ganda shook his head. He didn't know.

"Could the girl have killed them all?" another questioned.

"Not all of them," he replied. "Not from what she told us. There must be more out there still. Or they have found another lair."

He turned for the narrow passage.

"Wait," the other torchbearer called.

Ganda looked at him and saw that the other was pointing with the torch to the half-eaten carcass lying against the pillar.

It moved.

As if breathing.

Ganda stared, perplexed.

The creature had no head.

How can it still be alive?

His grip on his sword tightened as he stepped forward.

The torso rose and fell, as if taking in deep breaths and exhaling slowly.

Rise and fall.

Rise and fall.

"This is bad magic, Ganda," the torchbearer said.

"No," the leader replied. "Not magic."

A wound in the creature's stomach opened slightly, just enough for a tiny, wet, blood-soaked arm to reach out. It gripped the ground with its sharp fingers as another tiny arm burst from the gash. Then another. And another.

"What is that?" another Haigok growled, clearly disgusted by the sight unfolding before him.

A tiny, dark head with long white teeth slipped out from among the tiny claws and emitted a series of rapid clicks. The sound seemed to echo and reverberate from off the walls around the four dragon riders.

"Loud little thing," one of them remarked.

"They're everywhere," Ganda said, peering around the cavern.

Tiny dark creatures, no bigger than cats, appeared on ledges and rock faces all around the chamber. They emerged from deep shadows formed by thin crevasses and overhanging rocks. A number started climbing out of small hollows and deep fissures on the far side of the molten river.

"They left their young behind," the torchbearer surmised.

Ganda realised that their presence had disturbed the infant Khadzh.

"We woke them," he said. His attention moved to the carcass. Seven tiny creatures had crawled out of the body, their skin coated in slick fluid. Another slipped out of the dead beast, followed by another. "Too many to fight."

"What do we do now, Ganda?" the other torchbearer enquired.

"We flee." He pointed to the thin passageway that had led them into the lair. "Go."

They squeezed through the opening, one by one, starting the return journey to the surface.

A high-pitched scream filled the chamber behind them. A hundred more screams chorused it. Then, a hundred more.

Frantically, the four Haigok shuffled and scraped against the rocky walls as they navigated the twists and turns as quickly as they could.

Ganda, at the rear of the pack, heard a loud clicking above his head.

He peered up, only to see a dark figure crawling along the ceiling of the passageway. It clung to the rock and moved at great speed.

With a jab of his torch, he touched the flame to the creature's flesh.

A loud hiss ensued, followed by a loud screech as the creature fell to the ground by Ganda's feet.

He lifted his boot and stomped it down hard upon the dark head of the beast.

The screaming stopped instantly.

"Hurry," he called to the others.

Before long, they were racing through the large chamber.

Their legs pounded the ground as fast and as hard as they could as they advanced up the long embankment. Each of them grabbed their cloaks along the way, all the while aware of how closely they were being pursued.

Loud screams and clicks filled the area surrounding them.

The creatures were on their heels.

Gradually, the light emanating through the mouth of the cavern grew larger, brighter as they drew nearer.

The screams and clicks of the infant Khadzh echoed, reverberated, and filled the cave, sending painful vibrations deep into the dragon riders' ears.

The four Haigok sprinted into the bitter cold blizzard, continuing towards their dragons.

"Fire," one of them hollered to the one that had stayed behind with the winged beasts. "Fire."

"You have fire," the other pointed out to the torchbearer and Ganda.

"Get your dragon to breathe fire into that hole," the leader of the Nrarukh Clan yelled. "Right now."

The guard didn't hesitate.

He looked at his dragon and pointed to the cavern.

"Chakrah," he called.

As the dragon spread its wings and took to the air, countless dark figures appeared on the ice at the mouth of the cavern. Some hesitated and turned back for the shelter from the storm. Others pursued the four Haigok, screaming and screeching as they gave chase.

The dragon skimmed over the ground, forcing Ganda and the other three to dive onto their bellies as it swooped over them. The force of the gust caused by the dragon passing overhead was almost enough to lift them into the air after it.

A great wall of flame barrelled down the gradual slope, engulfing the tiny creatures on the ice. The dragon lowered itself before the mouth of the cave and took in a deep breath before exhaling a long jet of flame into the dark space.

More high-pitched screeches and screams followed.

The dragon took another breath and continued to ignite the cavern. It continued to do so until the sound of screaming stopped.

"They'll return," the torchbearer said. "They left their young behind."

"Then we seal this cavern so the Khadzh cannot return here," Ganda replied.

"And how do you propose we do that?" another asked.

"We bring the Ice Spires down on top of it."

"That will take forever," the torchbearer complained.

"We don't have forever," Ganda told him. "We only have today. We'll take that one down first." He pointed to the tallest spire. "With any luck, it might bring one or two of the others down with it."

Ten

She sat upon the rocks, listening to the methodical sound of water being sucked through the small cracks and fissures, back to the sea before a wave pushed it back again. Liana had curled up behind her and dozed in the morning sun.

Alice found the deep rumble from the dragon soothing, even more so than the ocean's tide. She would have liked to lay her head down to sleep also, but there was much to do.

She scraped her whetstone over the length of one of her swords. A dull ringing resonated with each stroke. Her eyes were on the twelve ships sailing to the western horizon. Her thoughts were on Takmel and his queens.

Alice knew that four of the Seven remained. She understood that their power would never match that of hers and her three sisters. Their loyalty to the Maji, however, was her biggest concern. Just how far were they willing to go in his name?

If the battle of Dweagan was an indicator of what was to come, then future conflicts would be troubling. It wasn't the matter of killing four women, that she'd known since she was born and had once looked up to, that had her questioning her strategies. It was the people of the cities she planned to attack that gave her the most unease.

Just how loyal are they to the Maji? Are they victims, innocent bystanders forced to partake in war for his sake? Are they beguiled, believing that their actions are righteous and will result in reward? Or, are they free subjects who fight for the Maji of their own accord?

She heard the snort of a horse and approaching hoofbeats crunching upon the snow. Liana groaned as she lifted her head to see who was coming.

"We're leaving," she heard her mother say from behind her.

Alice rose to her feet, stretched her sword arm over her head, and placed the blade in a sheath on her back beside the other. She turned to see her sister Catherine, and the Agrodien warriors gathered behind her, all upon their steeds.

"The wagons are loaded, Kayl'sro," Yuri said in his tongue. "The Commander is already leading the troops on."

Alice nodded.

"Watch after my mother and sister," she commanded the reptilians. "Fight by their sides and don't let them out of your sights."

"Are you expecting trouble, Kayl'sro?" Bein questioned.

"What are you talking about?" Catherine asked, peering at the others dubiously, not understanding their words.

"I hope not," she answered the Agrodien. She then turned to her sister, "Nothing to worry about."

"Nothing to worry about?" Catherine said, pointing to Bein. "I may not understand the words, but I detect his tone. He's wary about something."

"He's a soldier," Alice said as she moved to her sister's side. "And we're going to war. Of course, he's wary."

"You know what I mean," the other chided.

Alice put her hand on Catherine's thigh.

"Stay close to them," she said. "I just told them to watch over you and Mama. That's all."

Catherine sighed and nodded.

"Be careful," Emily said, reaching down to touch Alice on the head. The girl responded by reaching up and taking her mother's hand in her own.

"Aren't I always?"

"No."

Alice kissed her mother's hand.

"I'll see you both in Greyrose," she said, stepping back.

Emily and Catherine turned their horses and started away, followed closely by the Agrodien warriors. Nola'ee turned briefly in her saddle to make eye contact with her Kayl'sro. Alice gave her a stern nod, to which she replied in kind before turning away.

Liana gave a small, eager chirp as she watched the horses canter away. The soldiers had formed lines, and the wagons had moved. The march to Greyrose was underway.

"Soon," Alice said to the dragon, reaching her hand to the beast's neck. "We'll leave soon."

She sat back down on the rock, pulled her other sword from its sheath, and applied the whetstone to the blade.

***

Ganda watched eagerly as two dragons took turns breathing a thick jet of flame over the base of the tallest spire. The beasts had clambered onto the rocky mound that the monolithic monstrosities sat upon and made their way to either side of the column. The dragons appeared rather miniscule compared to the spires, like rats to an enormous tree in Ganda's mind.

A large section at the base of the spire had been melted away. Not yet enough to make any conceivable damage. The liquid flowing from the spire ran past the dragons, over the mouth of the cavern below, and into the darkness beyond. It was so cold in the blizzard that the flow became nothing more than a dribble before entering the cave as it frosted over rapidly, settling on the surface as ice.

One dragon lowered its head more and more with each blast of fire. It was tiring.

"Change them over," Ganda called. "Give these two time to rest."

The Haigok were quick to comply. They moved two more dragons into place and took the others aside.

The two replacements continued the work, taking turns breathing fire over the base of the spire. The flames bit deeper into the ice. Deeper and deeper.

Suddenly, a large crack emerged along the side of the column. It started at the hollow formed by the flames and slit open in both directions, upward and around the spike, almost touching on the opposite side.

A great yawning moan accompanied by countless loud snapping sounds followed.

Ganda peered up to the point of the spire. Even with the clouds moving rapidly by overhead, he could see the tip of the column swaying slightly back and forth.

"Get them back," the clan leader called, waving his hands, gesturing for everyone to move away.

The riders quickly climbed onto their dragons and urged them into the air.

Ganda strapped himself into the saddle and urged his own winged beast into the sky.

The spire rocked. First, it moved away from the cavern's mouth, then it swayed back again.

Creaking and groaning filled the air, overpowering the roar of the northern wind.

The clan leader guided his dragon behind the spire. The column was leaning towards him. He feared it would continue to approach, hitting him and his dragon out of the way before coming to rest harmlessly on the tundra below.

But it didn't.

It paused.

Creaking.

Moaning.

Cracking.

It retreated towards the cave's entrance again.

Ganda roared, leaning forward.

The dragon flapped its giant, leathery wings and charged at the spire.

Within an instant, it hit the ice tower with its claws. Using its wings, and all of its strength, it pushed as hard as it could.

The spire continued to tilt slowly towards the direction of the cave. Slowly. Slowly.

Fear gripped the clan leader as the spire slowed too much. He knew it was going to push back and rock in the opposite direction again.

He roared to the dragon again.

The great beast desperately pushed, beating its wings over and over.

The spire slowed more and more.

Moaning.

Creaking.

Cracking.

Ganda reached an unwelcome conclusion.

It was useless.

A noise drew his attention to an area of the spire above, closer to the point. It sounded like a giant blanket being blown around in the wind.

It was another dragon.

One of the other riders had seen what his leader was attempting to do. He joined in, pushing the spire forward.

It was enough to start the momentum again. But, it was slow going.

Another dragon smacked against the tower just below Ganda.

With beating wings and brute force, the three dragons pressed into the ice spire.

The last two dragons found a place near the top of the column. All five pushed with all of their might.

Loud cracks resounded from far below them.

More and more, the tower tilted.

Eventually, it was moving of its own accord.

Creaking.

Moaning.

Falling.

The dragons moved away as the ice spire tumbled to the ground.

It crashed to the surface with a tremendous thud, kicking up frost and ice into a cloud of white, breaking into several giant pieces.

Four of the dragon riders gave a cheer.

Ganda let out a long sigh.

Now came the hard part; using the fallen ice spire to seal the cavern.

***

"There." Takmel pointed to the floor of the drawing-room. Finely upholstered seats and well-crafted timber furniture lined the room. A large rug covered most of the stone floor and a roaring fire crackled away in the fireplace to one side. "Put them there."

Isabel turned her head towards Takmel. A stable hand, carrying a wooden crate laden with little straw dolls, had followed him in.

She sat in a chair close to the fire where she was trying her hand at embroidery. Her aim was to create an image on a cushion, resembling the Assembly Hall of Woodmyst. She thought she had started well, but it looked less and less like the picture in her head the more she stitched. The distraction was unexpected, but a welcome one, nonetheless.

"What's this?" she asked.

"Tip them out there," Takmel ordered the stable hand, pointing on the rug near to where the twin girls were sitting. They watched the White Queen attempt her hand at needlework intently. To them, the image was a masterpiece.

But they had never seen the Assembly Hall of Woodmyst, and for all Isabel knew, they could think that the image was a barn on some derelict farm in any place.

"It's time to play with our toys," Takmel continued.

Isabel peered at the straw dolls being tumbled onto the clean rug. Small bits of stubble spilled in all directions as a hundred straw men rolled and settled on the floor.

"You're going to bring them all in here?" She gave him a troubled look. "You must have thousands out there."

"You're worried about your clean floor," he suggested.

"I'm worried that the servant girls have too much on their schedule without added chores that are unnecessary."

"Unnecessary?" he chided. "You think this to be some game? These are weapons, my love. Besides, I'm not bringing all of them in. Not yet. We'll start small. Give our enemies a taste of what is to come."

He turned to the stable hand.

"One more load, good man," he ordered.

"Yes, my lord." The man bowed and turned to retrace his steps.

Takmel looked to the girls, who were eyeing the straw dolls eagerly.

"This is going to be a lot of fun," he said, putting his hands on his knees to lower himself towards them a little. "You should join us, my love."

Isabel moved her gaze from the miniature straw men to her husband.

"What?" she asked.

He stood upright and moved behind her. His hands reached over the back of her chair and came to rest upon her shoulders. He gave a gentle squeeze. She found it soothing.

"I need you, Isabel," he told her. "I can't do any of this without you. Please, help me."

She heard his words wisping around in her head, like smoke. They calmed her just as his fingers on her shoulders did. She was drawn to him. She didn't want to be, but she couldn't fight his wiles. He was too strong.

"You don't need to plead," she told him, closing her eyes and craning her neck. "I'll help you."

"Thank you," he whispered in her ear, bending down to kiss her skin near her collar. His eyes moved to the unfinished embroidery on her lap. "That's nice, It's..."

He paused.

Too long.

"It's meant to be the Assembly Hall in Woodmyst," she told him.

"An excellent likeness," he decreed, pecking her cheek before standing upright. He turned to the twins, who were both watching the exchange between Isabel and Takmel with interest. "Now. Shall we begin?"

Eleven

Liana flew high enough to weave over and under thin clouds as if they were obstacles in her way. She seemed to enjoy herself, so Alice let her fly as she wanted, as long as they remained on course.

To the southwest, riding on the horizon, the girl could see twelve dark shapes. Commander Zakhar's fleet appeared to make the most of the favourable winds, as did Liana. With the breeze behind them, the dragon barely needed to flap her wings. Rather, she used them like sails to glide through the sky, allowing the air current to push her onwards.

Alice peered at the ground below. She was passing above the marching troops as they followed the coastline. They moved in two long columns. Wagons were at the rear. Foot soldiers paraded just ahead of them. Cavalry led the infantry. Her friends and family rode in front of them all.

A short distance ahead, she could see a pine forest that followed a wide river snaking through the plains to her right and across the ground force's path.

This will slow them down, she thought.

There wasn't much she could do to help. Brondt and his men would need to assist the wagons when they reached the river. She just hoped the current was slow, and the water wasn't too deep.

Liana swooped over another thin cluster of cloud before levelling out. Alice watched the forest pass beneath them. A quick glint of the sun reflecting off the water's surface beneath the trees caught her eye.

It wasn't enough of a view to determine the stream's speed or depth.

She hoped they would be all right.

Her eyes moved to the ships. Liana must have covered more distance than she had thought. Not only could Alice determine the sails; she could see the colour of the flags that the vessels bore.

At this rate, she and her dragon would pass the fleet before she knew it. There was no doubt in her mind that they would be in Greyrose before the sun climbed to its highest point in the sky.

***

Brondt pulled his horse up by the river's edge. The shade of the tall pines was thick, dark and cold. The snow was patchy beneath the trees. Bare rocks and plant litter covered the ground.

The water was slow, but the stream was wide. Brondt was uncertain how deep it was and he needed to be sure it was safe to cross here, or whether he would need to find another place to enter to river.

"I need someone to—" he started.

"I'll go," Lieutenant Brook interjected as he urged his steed into the water.

The horse snorted in protest as the freezing liquid hit its skin. Brook gave it a nudge in the ribs with his heels. Deeper into the stream he went.

The water came up to the steed's belly as Brook continued to the middle of the waterway. On and on, he urged the horse. It clambered up the other side of the stream and stomped its hooves once it reached the bank on the other side.

"It's not deep," he called back to the commander. "A little bumpy in the middle. We might want to get another horse of two on each of the wagons before bringing them over."

"Good idea," Brondt acknowledged. "You stay there. I'll send some men over. Start a fire. I think this will take a while."

Brook waved, signalling that he understood. He dismounted and tethered his horse to a nearby tree.

Brondt turned to Thornton.

"Want me to get the wagons up here?" the captain growled.

"Indeed, I do," the commander replied. "Assign four cavalrymen to each wagon. Two to help pull. Two to ride guard as they cross."

"You expecting trouble?" Thornton asked.

"Doesn't this look like a great place to set an ambush?" Brondt said quietly.

Thornton nodded as he peered at the surrounding trees. He could hear the ocean, not too far to their left, but could not see it through the thick foliage.

Anything could watch them in this mess.

"We had best try to cross quickly, then," he muttered before turning his horse. He pulled up briefly beside Yuri. "Watch the trees."

The Agrodien nodded as the captain started away. Yuri relayed the instruction to the other reptilians in his own tongue.

Instantly, all ten Agrodien warriors turned their steeds, five to the left and five to the right, so they could keep their eyes on the forest.

The infantry moved to either side of their path, joining the reptilian allies in keeping guard as the wagons pulled to the front of the procession. They relieved several cavalry horses of their saddles in preference of makeshift collars formed from twisted ropes and harnesses. They were then attached to the wagons so that four horses, instead of two, tethered to the vehicles.

One by one, they took the wagons through the stream. It was exceedingly slow going. The carts rocked and jumped as they slid over hidden stones and dipped into deep trenches under the surface.

The sun continued to cross the sky, reaching its highest point when they had got three of the wagons across. Four remained on the eastern bank. Most of the infantrymen had waded across the icy stream to stand by the fires that Brook and the wagon drivers had made while they waited. Some men wished they hadn't, as the water came up to their chests in the deepest parts. What was worse was the fact that they wore chain-mail armour beneath their metal plates and had iron weapons strapped to their hips. Climbing out of the stream proved most difficult. Some even opted to strip down to their underclothes and wrap themselves in blankets to allow their battledresses to drain of water.

"Something is out there," Catherine whispered to her mother, peering into the woods to their right.

They were still on the eastern shore, waiting with Brondt for the wagons to cross.

"What's that?" Thornton asked her, not hearing her completely over the splashes emitting from the wagons and horses that pulled them.

"She's right," Amicia told them. "I can feel it. Something unnatural."

"Unnatural?" Jendryng questioned.

"Magic," Ursula clarified.

Yuri scanned the woods carefully, noticing only endless columns of different sized tree trunks. Some thick, some thin. Some straight up and down, others leaning this way or that.

"I see nothing," he told them.

"What about scent?" Emily inquired. "Can you smell anything?"

He shook his head.

"Trees," he answered. "Plants. Small creatures. Rabbit. Only man here is here with us."

"There," Nola'ee called, pointing into the forest.

Everyone stopped to follow her signal.

Some of the infantry guarding the southern side of the procession turned to have a look.

"Keep your eyes on your side," Thornton growled to them. They turned instantly and continued to look for movement.

"I see nothing," Karlena remarked.

Schoenbach shook his head.

"Keep those wagons moving," Brondt hollered. He then called over to the men on the western shore. "Watch the forest."

Brook waved back and pulled his sword from his sheath. The commander watched as the lieutenant started ordering the men by the fires to form a perimeter. The half-naked soldiers dropped their blankets on the ground and started dressing in their armour again.

"I see..." Akasati started. She watched a shadow dart between two trees.

"What?" Emily hissed.

The warrior woman shook her head.

Cracking sounds echoed through the forest ahead of them. At first, it was distant. Then it was very close.

The soldiers moved their heads, following the sound.

Distant crackling, like dried twigs being broken, followed by closer sounds.

"What is that?" Brondt muttered as the last wagon started its journey across the stream.

"This seems all too familiar," Schoenbach said quietly.

Karlena nodded.

A sudden scream down the line caused all heads to turn.

Something hidden in shadow, very fast, dragged one soldier into the woods. A few soldiers gave chase.

"Back to your places," Thornton barked.

Yuri peered after the object. It moved too fast for him to see clearly. It was shaped like a man, but was not a man.

A thick, dark line trailed behind it in the snow. The Agrodien could smell it from his horse.

Blood.

The screaming from the taken soldier stopped; cut off abruptly.

Gurgling ensued.

Then silence.

Brondt cast his gaze over to the wagon. It was a little more than halfway across.

"Hurry," he commanded the driver.

"Going as fast as I can, sir," the man called back. The wagon rocked wildly as the driver urged the steeds to pull harder and faster.

Brondt turned his face back to the woods. He saw something tumbling through the air towards them. It landed smack in a patch of snow on the forest floor.

The taken soldier's head.

"There is nothing out there," Yuri told Emily. "Only dead soldier and forest."

"There's something out there," the auburn woman told him.

"Dark magic," the reptilian grumbled.

She nodded.

"There!" Akasati pointed with her sword.

A shadow appeared from behind a group of shrubs before vanishing behind a tree.

"Over there," a soldier called, pointing to a different section of the wood.

"It's there," another infantryman called, gesturing to another place.

"There it is." Cheyne gestured closer to the river.

"Stop calling," Schoenbach told them. "They're everywhere. Get ready for an attack."

One of the young soldiers peered up at him. Dread had filled his eyes and his body shook with fear.

"W-what are they, s-sir?" he asked, his voice stammering slightly.

The old sea captain stared into the woods, where the shadows moved before his eyes. He heard the answer escape his lips, but he didn't want to believe it.

"Scarecrows."

Twelve

They charged in silence. Hundreds of them.

Misshapen forms with twisted limbs and gnarled fingers, made from broken branches and straw. Faceless figures with hollow sockets where eyes should be.

They ran like men, disjointed and awkward, upright with their arms stretched towards the men along the path. There were no calls from the attackers. No war cries or announcement of their coming. Nothing except the sound of dried twigs snapping and snow crunching beneath their wooden feet.

"Here they come," Brondt hollered. "Be ready."

The straw men leapt over large rocks and closed the distance to their prey rapidly.

The soldiers guarding the path pulled their swords free and prepared to fight.

Their footfalls grew louder and louder as they drew nearer and nearer.

Crunching snow.

Snapping twigs.

Louder and louder, like rolling thunder.

Amicia stretched her hand forward.

"Tremble," she said calmly.

The ground before them lifted and rolled away, like a wave upon the sea.

Dust and snow burst up in places.

The earth opened in small fissures here and there.

Trees tilted one way or another, coming to rest upon others beside them, violently lifting the earth beneath them.

The army of straw men flew into the air.

They landed hard.

But it didn't bring them any harm.

Within moments, they were back up on their feet and charging again.

"You won't stop them like that," Akasati called to her.

"Then how do we defeat them?" Ursula asked with heightened anxiety.

Emily looked along the line of the rapidly approaching straw men.

"Fire," the auburn woman said. "We need fire."

Catherine absorbed her mother's words and looked across the river to the many tiny hearths burning near the water's edge. Some soldiers were preparing to cross back over to assist them.

"Tell them to stop," she called to the commander.

"What?" he asked, keeping his eyes on the enemy drawing closer.

"Tell your men on the other side of the river to stop," she expounded.

He turned to see one man stepping into the water with his sword drawn.

"Stay there," Brondt hollered.

"Are there archers on the other side?" she asked.

"We've archers here," he replied.

"We have," Thornton interjected, gesturing to his lieutenant across the stream. "Lieutenant Brook carries a bow."

"Akasati is the best archer I know," Emily told her daughter.

Thornton shook his head. "We need fire," he said. "Your daughter is suggesting that our archers over there shoot a flaming arrow or two in this direction. Then, we'll have fire."

"By the gods, I am stupid," Brondt spat.

Soldiers down the line met the enemy. Steel blades blocked wooden claws. Straw bellies opened. Timber bones broke.

But no wound suffered by the straw men were enough to stop them from attacking.

Like a wave, the enemy struck the defensive line.

"Brook!" Thornton roared.

"You want us over there or not?" Brook called back.

"Send fire," the captain ordered.

"What?" the lieutenant called, scrunching his face up.

"Send fire," he repeated. "Shoot a flaming fucking arrow."

Brook's demeanour changed. He understood the instruction.

He raced to his horse to retrieve the bow strapped to his saddle. Another soldier, a bowman that overheard the order, took one of his arrows and tied a rag to the dart.

"I wish we had oil, sir," the bowman said, passing the arrow to the lieutenant.

"So do I," Brook replied, placing the shaft onto his bowstring before dipping the cloth into the flames of a nearby fire.

The fighting grew intense as soldiers fought hand-to-hand along the path.

Brook discovered a new obstacle.

Just where was he meant to fire the arrow?

Thornton was engaged in a skirmish with a straw man. It had dragged him from his horse and onto the ground. Before he could get to his feet, he saw a young infantryman fall to the ground farther down the line. The infantryman was screaming as he attempted to crawl away from his attacker. Twisted wooden claws dug deep into the face of the young soldier. The claws then clenched together, mulching the boy's face into a mess of flesh and blood.

Thornton felt another straw man clutch him by the ankle. It pulled him towards the river and away from the horses.

He turned and kicked the figure in the chest. The straw man stumbled back, letting the captain go free. It corrected its stance, preventing itself from falling over.

Thornton rolled to his feet and slashed at the straw man, hacking its head from its body.

That didn't end the attack.

The headless form swung its sharp claws towards Thornton. The old soldier blocked and parried each blow with his blade, taking small pieces of wood from the arms of the straw man with each swipe.

Seeing an opening, Thornton brought his sword across the legs of the scarecrow. One leg snapped free at the knee. The other came away at the hip.

The figure fell to the ground, swinging its claws towards Thornton.

Brook watched in horror from the opposite bank, the flaming arrow still nocked in the bowstring.

"Here," the captain called to Brook. "Shoot this bastard."

The straw man dug its claws into the ground and started pulling its body towards the old soldier.

Brook took aim.

"Now, Lieutenant," Thornton barked.

The straw man moved quickly, scraping over the dirt and snow.

"Shit!" Thornton stepped back as the figure gained ground quickly.

With a loud thwack, the arrow struck the straw man in the back. Its arms flailed as flames took hold, spreading over the figure's shoulders and arms.

Thornton didn't hesitate.

He jabbed his blade deep into the fallen figure and flung it towards the dry litter lying on the forest floor.

The flames bit hard, growing rapidly and expanding in all directions.

Several trees were suddenly alight. The snow-covered pine branches were steaming and smoking in an instant.

"Retreat across the river," Thornton called to Brondt. "We can't fight them here."

The commander signalled for Amicia to ride ahead of him.

The drivers of the last three wagons, seeing their plight, quickly unhitched their steeds from the carts before fleeing on foot themselves.

"Go," he told her.

She turned to Catherine and Ursula.

"We must go together," she told them.

"I won't go without my mother," Catherine replied.

"Go now," Brondt hollered.

The flames were spreading along the edge of the path and over the canopy above them.

"No time to debate. We all go now," Thornton ordered as he climbed upon his steed. He turned to the line of men along the path. "Flee to the river. As fast as you can."

With that, every man, woman and steed remaining on the eastern riverbank, bolted to the water.

The straw men gave pursuit.

Some caught fire.

The infantrymen cut some down.

Some took a few soldiers with them as the flames took hold.

The river burst into white spray as the soldiers raced into the water. The horses bounded through the stream as quickly as they could.

"Get moving," Brondt called to the men watching from the western shore. "We need to get out of this forest."

It was pandemonium.

Wagons, horses, men all tried to escape an enemy that should not exist, as well as an out-of-control blaze that was now stretching itself across the river.

Thornton's eyes grew red with anger as he observed one soldier near Lieutenant Brook trying to douse a little campfire with the heel of his boot. Brook slapped the man over the back of the head, to which the other gave him a shocked look.

"What are you thinking?" the lieutenant asked, gesturing across the stream to the forest fire heading in their direction. "Run, you fool."

The Agrodien warriors surrounded Emily and Catherine during the entire ordeal. They clambered up the embankment together and started through the forest on the western shore at a great pace.

Catherine turned her head to see Ursula and Amicia riding with Brondt and Thornton not too far to her right.

They were still together.

Screams filled the air behind them. Smoke and flames swept over the canopy above, reaching in all directions and crossing the river.

It had not crossed alone.

Straw men, many ablaze, leapt over the wide stream and started after the fleeing men.

The figures fell one by one as the fire ate away their timber bones and straw flesh. Others leapt upon escaping infantrymen and tore away as much skin and muscle as possible before the forest fire engulfed them.

Brondt led them out of the forest and continued the charge onto the open plain beyond for some distance before pulling to a stop. He turned his steed to face the woodlands, watching others burst through the foliage.

"Behind me," he called to them.

The four wagons appeared in the clearing. One of them had lost a wheel in the confusion. Still, the horses attached pulled it with all of their strength to get it and its cargo to safety.

Thornton pulled to the commander's right side, sword drawn and breathing hard. He pointed his blade out to his side and looked about at the men gathering on the plain.

"Make a line here," he roared. "This isn't over."

The cavalry moved to position as more infantrymen spilled out of the tree line.

"They're right behind us," a foot soldier called. He was supporting another soldier, wounded with a gash to his forehead and limping badly. Brondt noticed others in similar predicaments, wounded men giving aid to other wounded men as they fled from the tree line as fast as their bodies allowed them.

"Get those wagons as far from the forest as you can," the commander shouted. "Infantry, behind me." He turned to Amicia. She had gathered with Ursula, Catherine, the small band of Woodmyst folk and Agrodien warriors. "You lot should go with the wagons."

"We'll be fine here," Emily returned, clutching her sword in her hand.

Thick, dark smoke billowed from the forest. The orange glow of approaching flames flickered from deep beneath the trees. Shadows danced between the trunks.

The straw men approached.

Cracking and snapping filled the air, growing louder and louder, caused by both fire and the footfalls of the figures.

Brondt tightened his grip on his sword.

His heart raced so fast and hard, he could hear it thudding in his ears.

His breath became rapid as cold sweat trickled down his spine.

He was afraid.

He didn't know how to defeat such a relentless enemy.

The shadows became clearer, more familiar.

The shapes of the straw men moved through the forest.

One by one, they burst onto the open ground.

Some were ablaze.

Some sent trails of smoke behind them, singed slightly from the fire.

More than a hundred in all.

They ran.

They would not stop until all of Brondt's men, all the women and all those who accompanied him, were dead.

But he wasn't about to go without a fight.

The straw men sprinted over the ground towards them.

Brondt raised his sword and dug his heels into his steed's flanks.

With a great cry, he started his attack.

A great wall of flame filled his vision.

It seemed to burst from the ground, moving from his right to his left.

The heat was immense and the force almost strong enough to knock him from his steed.

A cloud of fire instantly swallowed the straw men.

He pulled his horse to a halt and peered up.

A dragon sped past, low to the ground, breaking through the flames and smoke it had just spewed upon the ground. A great gust followed it, lifting swirling clouds of smoke and fragments of burning straw men after it. The dragon swooped high into the sky and turned slowly to the west.

"Alice," he gasped as he spied the girl riding on the winged beast's back. His eyes welled up, and a lump formed in his throat. A deep, poignant realisation flooded through him. He, the surrounding men, his beloved Amicia; all would have surely perished if not for the girl and her dragon.

Thirteen

Alice leapt to the ground as Liana landed. She started directly for her mother, who sat upon her steed and watched the huge flames tearing into the tree line with ferocity.

"Thank you, Alice," Brondt said as he dismounted. He expected the girl to stop, but she passed him by as if she didn't see him. Instead, she pointed to Ursula.

"Are you all right?" she asked.

"Fine," Ursula replied.

"Good." Alice gestured to the forest fire with her hand. "Do something about that," she snapped.

Ursula, stunned by the girl's attitude, watched Alice walk by.

"What does she mean, do something about that?" Thornton retorted. "I've a good mind to bend her over my knee..."

"Mama," Alice called, increasing her pace as tears filled her eyes. Thornton suddenly realised who they were dealing with.

She was brave.

She was strong.

She was their leader.

But most of all, she was a little girl.

"I'm all right," Emily called, jumping from her horse and running for her daughter. The two embraced in the field.

"Where's Catherine?" Alice looked to the Agrodien warriors. Her sister was among them. The older girl slipped from her steed and ran over to her family.

Ursula lowered herself to the ground.

"She shouldn't have spoken to you like that," Thornton remarked.

"I know," the other replied. "But she was worried. You saw it."

"You're not a soldier in her army. She can't talk to you as I would to one of my men. I should have words with her, I think," he said, peering over to the girl.

"Please, don't," Ursula implored. "Let her have this moment with her mother and sister."

Thornton moved his gaze to her and nodded reluctantly.

Ursula stretched her hands to the sky. As her eyes turned pitch black, thin clouds passing overhead gathered above the forest. They grew thicker and thicker. The darkness in Ursula's eyes spread like tendrils across her cheeks.

The soldiers watched the awesome spectacle unfolding before them. Some started backing away as they observed clouds twisting and spinning overhead like a whirlpool in the sky.

A bright flash of lightning burst from the clouds, and a terrible clap of thunder shook the earth.

Thicker and thicker the clouds became, absorbing every small white puff or wisp passing by.

Liana gave a cry, slinking backwards, farther away from the forest and the swirling cloud above it.

Ursula tightened her fingers into fists, raising them higher above her head.

"Rain."

Water poured from the sky. It fell upon trees and flames in a heavy torrent.

Loud hissing resounded as the fire along the tree line doused.

Thick plumes of steam and smoke filtered through the forest.

Water fell hard, but not a drop upon any of the soldiers.

Ursula continued to hold her stance, focusing her energy on the cloud and the wind, pushing them both to the south.

After some time, she felt a small hand upon her back.

"That's enough," said a gentle voice.

Ursula lowered her arms. Her face and eyes returned to their usual complexion. She turned to see another three sets of piercing blue eyes looking into hers.

Alice, standing between Catherine and Amicia, appeared troubled.

"I'm sorry," the girl said. "I shouldn't have spoken to you in such a horrible manner."

Ursula eyed her warily. She then shot Thornton a suspicious look.

"Did George speak to you?"

"No," said Alice. "Why? Does he need to spea—"

"It's nothing," Ursula interrupted. Her arms wrapped around Alice suddenly and tightly. "Thank you for coming back."

Jendryng shook his head as the two young women embraced. Soon, Amicia and Catherine had their arms around them as well.

"I'll never understand women," he muttered.

Thornton strode by him and clasped him on the shoulder.

"No one does," he growled. "Now, help the wounded."

***

Alice flew ahead of the procession, high above their heads, so she could see what lay before them. She sighted fenced fields littered with snow and tiny farmhouses with thin lines of smoke drifting from their chimneys. Livestock dotted the landscape here and there. The people, she assumed, were tucked inside their homes away from the cold.

She turned Liana about now and then, circling to monitor the advancing army, to keep an eye on her family. The dragon had to exert some energy when retracing her path. The wind, pushing from the north, was almost blowing towards them from directly ahead with each pass over the troops below.

Liana banked to her right as she turned back towards Greyrose, their intended destination. She twisted towards the sea with her wings outstretched, catching the strong breeze in her wings like sails on a ship. Then, she glided.

The wind pushed her to the south. The dragon corrected herself by angling her wings and tail so that she veered to the southwest. She swooped high in the air before levelling out so Alice could take advantage of the view.

The twelve ships were still on the horizon ahead of them.

At this rate, Alice thought, *I won't be able to keep my word to Commander Zakhar.*

He would definitely arrive before her.

Let's hope there won't be any hostiles.

*****

It was dusk before Alice set Liana down in a field by the side of a small farm. A settlement sat nestled by the seaside not too far away.

She removed the saddle and gave the dragon a rub on the snout as a reward for a long day's work. The beast responded with a soft chirp and deep rumbling purr.

True to his word, Commander Zakhar had set fires in place and scrounged up a feast for the hungry troopers. His men had set up their tents by a small hut, to which the door was wide open.

As Alice drew nearer, she saw Zakhar seated on a log by a fire not too far from the cottage door. A few of his ships' personnel sat beside him upon more logs, as well as another man and woman with two small children. They were obviously not part of the crew.

"Alice!" He got to his feet when he saw her approaching. The other men about him lifted themselves from their seats in polite fashion and bowed slightly. "Is everyone safe?"

"Not everyone," she answered. "We have wounded coming."

"You were attacked?" he asked.

"Not I," she informed him. "The ground force was. They said it was straw men."

"Straw men?" Zakhar looked to her in doubt, almost as if he thought she was jesting.

"Believe what you will, Commander. We are not dealing with any ordinary enemy. He is a sorcerer and his wives are witches," she said, moving to stand by the fire and eyeing the strange man and his family. "Who have we here?"

The commander turned to the man. He dressed plainly and appeared lean and wiry. He held a morsel of meat in his right hand and a plate of food in the other. After placing the meat on his plate, he wiped his hand on his trousers and got to his feet. "This is Cedric Bauer. The owner of this property. He has been kind enough to allow us to camp here for the night."

"Pleasure, my lady," Cedric said, extending his hand to Alice. She took it and smiled.

"Alice," she said.

"My wife, Josephine," he said, gesturing to the woman who stood at his side.

"My lady." She curtseyed clumsily as she took Alice's hand gingerly by the fingertips.

"My son, Victor. And my daughter, Freja."

"You have a dragon," the boy, all of five years old, said excitedly through a mouthful. The girl, a little younger, simply waved as she kept her eyes on the flames and used both hands to hold a rib to rip the meat from the bone with her teeth.

"I do have a dragon," Alice replied to Victor.

"Can I go and see?" he asked.

"No," Josephine, his mother scolded. "It looks hungry. I don't want you going anywhere near it."

"Mama," the boy whined.

"Your mother is right," Alice told him. "Liana can be very dangerous. She almost killed me when I first met her. She tried to burn me alive and eat me."

The boy laughed, sensing some exaggeration in the story.

"No, she didn't," the young boy said, chuckling.

The girl grinned, unwilling to share the entire truth, that Liana had once been a weapon that was indeed used to try and kill her. Instead, she sat by the fire to get warm.

She peered around to the other fires where Zakhar's men were sitting. All of them were tucking into some kind of animal that roasted over the hearths.

"I hope we haven't used up any of this man's livestock," Alice said, looking at the commander.

"No, my lady," Cedric said before Zakhar responded. "The township has offered their assistance. Some have donated goats and sheep, so your men will be nourished. Others offered the shelter of their homes, but we are a small village. Not the way we were before the Mirikin. Our people live in dwellings no bigger than my own. All we have to offer is this land for you to set your tents and wood for your fires."

"Thank you," she said, smiling. "It's more than enough."

"Your dragon must be hungry," Cedric said, peering over to Liana, who was watching Alice with interest.

"She may be," the girl answered.

"Come with me." Cedric led her behind the hut where a goat stood, tied to a fence.

"The commander requested I keep this one aside for your dragon," he told her. "I didn't believe him, about your dragon, that is. But, he said you were fighting the Maji, so I kept it aside as he asked me to."

"Thank you, Cedric," she replied. She looked him up and down. His clothes looked worn in places, fraying at the seams. His house was a patchwork of repair with mud, stone, and wood. These people had little, and yet were willing to give so much. "Cedric?"

"Yes, my lady?"

"Please, don't take offence," she began. "But, why are you helping us? Why aren't you loyal to the Maji? He has armies and power. You saw what the Mirikin did. Why not submit to him?"

He let out a sigh.

"We considered that," he acknowledged. "The township, I mean. We don't have a chief or a real leader and none of us are fighters. We're fishermen and farmers. Nothing more.

"If you move along the coast to Pryholt, you'll see more who are loyal to the Maji. Then, if you keep going, the loyalists grow in numbers. It won't be long before you find everyone calling themselves loyal, even if they aren't," he continued.

"We remained true to ourselves. We're not loyal to him. We weren't loyal to his mother and the other witches that destroyed our homes. Why should we be any different now?

"Besides, he sends no one this far south. We see his ships come and go on the horizon. But none have weighed anchor here until your Commander Zakhar. Before him, there hasn't ever been a vessel larger than a fishing boat at our jetty. Not in my time."

She looked to him for a seemingly long time.

"But why help us?" she asked. "You have told me you're not loyal to the Maji. But, you aren't loyal to us either. We have done nothing to earn your trust."

"I remember the march of the Mirikin," he told her. "I don't want to ever see that happen again, my lady. The witches took their armies east and crushed everything in their path. Their armies were in the thousands.

"They don't number anywhere near that right now," Cedric explained. "But we have heard that sellswords have been filling the ranks, and they have become loyal to him, and they do terrible things in his name. Butchering men, burning families in their homes, and raping young girls. For the sake of our families, and our daughters, we need someone like you and your army to stop them before they do eventually come south for us."

As he spoke, the procession arrived, with Brondt in the lead.

"We have wounded," Alice said, gesturing over to the approaching ground force.

"We have an apothecary in the township," Cedric informed her. "I'll send the boy for him."

The farmer left to do just that as Alice untied the goat from the fence. It bleated in protest as she pulled it away from the farmhouse and onto the field where Liana eagerly awaited.

***

Ganda's impatience grew as he watched two dragons breathe fire onto the fallen spire. It was melting, and the cavern was filling, but it was slow going.

"This will take all night," he grumbled as he pulled his cloak about himself tightly.

The winds had picked up, and the temperature had dropped incredibly. Standing near to the spire, where the heat of dragon fire was comfortable, was the only way to keep warm, except when a powerful gust blew in from the north to send shivers over the Haigok riders.

"We could have all five dragons work the ice at one time," one suggested. "It may hasten the progress somewhat."

The leader shook his head.

"We need to be prepared if the Khadzh return to their lair," he replied. "If we have all dragons working at once, we may tire them out and there won't be any fight left in them."

"Do you expect them to return?" another asked.

"I expect they are about their master's business," Ganda answered, peering over his shoulder to the south.

***

The White Queen peered from her bed chamber's window, down upon the courtyard in front of the palace. It was dark and the oil lamps had been lit by the main doors below her and the gates across the way.

Long shadows cast across the snow that covered the cobbles. They moved back and forth, across the ground and around in circles. All sought the attention of one cloaked figure standing in their midst.

She watched as he reached his hands out to them. Their clicking calls were easily audible through the windowpane, even from so high above.

Those that could reach him lapped at his hands with long tongues that slithered over long, white, jagged teeth like wet worms crawling from the ground. Some rubbed their heads against his legs, like cats.

He rubbed his fingers over their clammy skin, over their heads, and along their spines. Others tried to weave their way through the swarm to get to him, but there were too many.

Their numbers stretched over the courtyard, through the gates and beyond.

Isabel believed that every remaining dark creature from the Frozen Waste must have come, answering his call.

He spread his hands out wide.

The creatures lowered their heads and cowered slightly. Their clicks ceased and the air itself seemed to fall silent.

With a swift motion, he thrust his hands forward, to the east.

The creatures instantly took off, bolting out the gate and away into the night.

He is sending them out;; she thought. She could only guess where to. Once they had passed the lamplight by the gate, the darkness of the night swallowed them.

She moved her attention back to the courtyard.

He was looking up at her.

His eyes were cold, and she could feel his icy stare moving through her.

Her heart seemed to stop as a knot formed in her gut.

The breeze picked up about him, causing his damson cloak to drift slightly, and tiny flurries of snow to spin around his boots.

She felt a cold shudder move through her body as he held his gaze.

She wanted to turn, but it was as if he held her there.

His head tilted slightly as a scowl deepened upon his face.

I shouldn't have been watching, she thought. *I should have been minding my own business.*

How she wished she hadn't been looking out the window.

How she wished she hadn't seen him and his dreadful creatures.

How she wished she could shy away and slip beneath the covers of her bed.

How she wished she could close her eyes and pretend none of this was happening.

But she fell transfixed; she couldn't take her eyes from him.

His face changed, turning from a sinister glare to a relaxed composure.

She couldn't tell entirely, not with the lamplight shining from where it was. Most of his face vanished in dull shadow, but it appeared that he was smiling.

A deeper sense of coldness chilled her to the bones, and even with the fire roaring to her side, she had never felt so cold and alone.

He held her there, smiling up at her.

And, something snapped to life within her. A realisation of all that had come to fruition and all that may come to be. She finally saw him for what he was.

He was a monster.

A sixteen-year-old monster.

He was jealous and self-absorbed, deceitful and persuasive; a petulant child who wanted his own way.

He was his mother's son.

A manipulative sorcerer who drained power from those connected to him, using them until he had no more need of them, or until they crossed him.

The smile on his face was a façade, but it didn't hide him as well as he intended. The darkness in his eyes told her that her time was coming to a close.

He had two new brides; young girls, easier to control.

Each was more powerful than she, or any of the last remaining queens of the Seven.

They were discovered by accident and now he had people out looking for more potentials.

Potentials, she thought as she stood by the window, her eyes locked upon his. She remembered the word being used by another who had taken her from her home and subjected her to unspeakable acts.

In time, he would find new queens to replace them all.

As he broke his contact and started for the doors into the palace, she could only guess at what her fate was to be.

Fourteen

Thornton woke with a start.

Something had brought him out of his slumber.

Something didn't feel right.

It took him a moment to remember where he was. The rustling of the canvas roof being lifted and smacked back into place by the wind outside reminded him he was in his tent.

Could it have been that noise that woke me?

He frowned and shook his head, telling himself that it wasn't.

His arm was around Ursula's shoulders as she lay curled against his side. She was comfortable, he could tell. Her deep, soft breaths falling upon his neck and the way she folded her hands over one another against her breast brought a smile to his face.

She draped her leg over his waist, seemingly holding him in place as he stretched upon the bedding, lying on his back. The truth was, he didn't want to move. He was beyond comfortable. He was content.

There was dull light poking through the flaps of the tent; a sure sign that morning had come.

He knew he needed to get up.

He knew he would have to wake Ursula to do so.

A deep sigh emanated from him as he gave thought to how he would do this.

He lay there for a long time, thinking, picturing how he might be able to slip away from her, out from the covers and dress.

Then he heard it; the sound that possibly woke him.

A loud growl, a snap, and strange chirping noises.

Just like Liana, Alice's pet dragon.

But it wasn't her.

He didn't know how, but he had become so accustomed to the beast that he could distinguish the noises that he heard as differing from the girl's pet. It was a different dragon.

A strange moaning, deep and guttural, ensued. It was a different beast. There were two.

Three, if he included Liana.

He sat upright, ignoring the woman by his side. Her head fell from his shoulder and onto the bedding.

"What is it?" she mumbled, fighting her need to sleep as she tried to open her eyes.

"Dragons," he growled, flinging the covers aside as he reached for his breeches.

"What?" She rolled onto her back and wiped her eyes with the heel of her hand.

"I think there are dragons out there," he replied.

"Liana," she groaned. "Come back to bed."

"I need to see," he said, getting to his feet and pulling his pants up to his waist. "Could be the Haigok arriving. I should be up in any case."

She turned onto her other side and groaned some more before forcing herself to sit up.

"All right," she said.

"There's no need for you to come," he told her.

"If you need to get out of bed, then I should get out of bed," she said, flinging the covers away to expose her nakedness.

"Stop tempting me, woman." He smirked.

"Think with your head," she said, reaching for her clothes, "not your manhood."

"Now, that is a tough request to follow when I'm with you, my dear," he replied. He sat upon the bedding to put his boots on as she stood to dress behind him.

"You certainly know what to say to a lady."

"And, who's the lady?"

She reached around swiftly, retrieved a pillow from beside her, and hit him over the head with it.

He fell onto his side in a laughing fit.

Soon after, he dressed, with his sword strapped to his side. He moved to the open ground behind the campsite, where he counted eighteen dragons clustered about. One was Liana.

The dragon towered over the girl, who was accompanied by all ten Agrodien warriors. They had guarded her closely whenever she was in their presence, protecting her like a precious gem, Yuri and Nola'ee even more so than the others.

Thornton knew she didn't need such security. He believed she allowed them the opportunity to protect her, as they were a proud race. It would give offence to deny them the duty of standing guard over their Kayl'sro.

Alice was speaking to a cloaked figure, whom Thornton assumed was Gruloch. The other riders were tending to their dragons, relieving them of harnesses, riding gear, and cargo.

"Good morning," Thornton called as he approached.

Alice turned to see the old soldier drawing near.

"Good morning, Captain," she replied. "You remember, Gruloch?"

"I do," he replied, extending his hand in friendship.

The Haigok took it and smiled, baring his sharp teeth. "Good to see you again, Captain Thornton."

"Are these yours?" Thornton asked, gesturing to the winged beasts.

"No," the Haigok answered. "We have brought nine with us. The other eight come to us by way of the Kazrekh Clan."

Thornton did a quick calculation. Seventeen dragons and twelve riders. He furrowed his brow.

"Perhaps I'm mistaken, but it appears that you haven't brought enough of your people with you."

Gruloch chuckled.

"Erugoth over there is very traditional," the Haigok explained. He pointed to another cloaked figure carrying a saddle away. The magnificent beast he had taken it from shook its back the way a wet dog would to fling water from its fur. "He has trained his dragons to respond to the horn he carries on his belt. That's something my father could do, but something I did not learn to the same level of perfection. Perhaps you will get the opportunity to see his skill."

Thornton nodded as he watched Erugoth turn to another dragon, laden with bags and rolled canvas sheets. The Haigok's cloak moved to reveal the curved horn strapped to his side. It looked as if it had come from a ram, with iron clasped around the bell and a mouthpiece made of steel. Markings adorned the sides of the horn, words or runes that Thornton didn't recognise. All in all, it appeared sturdy and old, possibly passed down through many generations of Haigok.

"They must be hungry," Thornton said.

"The riders?" Gruloch asked.

"Sorry," Thornton said. "I meant the dragons."

"I've already sent a soldier to get goats for our guests, Captain," Alice put in. "Everything has been taken care of."

"Of course," Thornton said. He looked around to all the dragons, impressed by the creatures. "I don't wish to appear ungrateful, but when will the others arrive?"

"We were just discussing that," Alice replied.

"I sent envoys to the other clans. They have all reported back. The Eranak and Traruk Clans will arrive today," Gruloch informed them. "That will give us another fourteen dragons."

"That's good," Thornton said optimistically.

"The Nrarukh are an uncertainty," the Haigok continued. "The representative of the clan leader has informed us that Ganda has taken his dragons to destroy the lair of the Khadzh."

"Khadzh?" Thornton asked.

"Skinny black monsters from Frozen Waste," Yuri told him.

"Those buggers," the old soldier grumbled. "May Ganda have good fortune."

"Indeed," Gruloch replied. "If he comes, we will have another five dragons."

Thornton raised his brow.

"That's a lot of dragons," he said, looking at Ursula, who was approaching them from the tent she and Thornton shared. "We could almost wipe every village from the land with that many dragons. Not that we would want to."

"We could," Alice agreed. "But I don't want that. I'm hoping that the sheer sight, or news of our coming will be enough to discourage our enemies from the fight. I'm hoping to see people lay down their arms and walk away from this with their lives."

"But you're worried about the hold that the Maji might have over them," the old soldier said. "Aren't you?"

"I spoke to Cedric yesterday, the farmer who works these lands," she said. "He told me that the further west we go, the more loyal the people are to Takmel. He also told me that some are loyal by mouth only, afraid to be true to themselves. Perhaps some soldiers we face are the same. Many are sellswords, according to Cedric. Maybe they can be persuaded that theirs is a cause not worth dying for."

Thornton nodded as he turned to face the dragons again. Their size alone was intimidating enough, let alone the sight of their teeth and the fact that they could attack from the air and breathe fire.

"We can only hope," he mumbled.

"Morning," Ursula said cheerily, pulling up to Thornton's side.

"Good morning," Alice replied with a smile as Gruloch bowed politely.

"That's a lot of dragons," she said, looking to the Haigok. "Did you arrive during the night?"

"Early this day," he answered. "Before the sun breached the horizon."

Alice was looking at the other woman peculiarly.

"You and your men should join us for breakfast," Ursula offered. "You must be famished after such a long journey." She stopped and looked to Alice, who was still watching her as if scrutinising her features. "I said *men*, didn't I? I am sorry. I didn't mean..."

"It's fine," Gruloch chuckled. "I understood what you mean. My people and I would be honoured."

Ursula furrowed her brow as she turned to face Alice. "What is it?" she asked, slightly annoyed. "Have I got something on my face?"

"No."

"Then, what?"

"Your hair," Alice said.

Ursula frantically used her fingers to comb some lengths to where she could see, hoping it wasn't falling out or something worse. It appeared dark, as it had always been. Nothing out of the ordinary.

"What about it?"

"She's right," Thornton said. "I didn't notice in the tent."

"What?" Ursula was becoming upset.

"Your white streaks have gone," Alice told her.

Ursula stared at the girl, dumbfounded. "My eyes," she finally said. "What do my eyes look like?"

"Blue," Alice replied. "But, I can see some darker lines by the edges of the colour. They're changing back."

"Yours too." Ursula frowned, placing her hands upon the girl's shoulders to conduct an inspection. "Your eyes were brown before? Right?"

"Like my father's," she agreed.

"They soon will be again," said the other.

"What this mean, Kayl'sro?" Yuri asked.

"It means they won't be bonded together as they are now," Thornton replied. "And, perhaps their power will be taken from them."

"We don't know that," Alice interjected. "The four of us were powerful before all of this."

"You're right," the captain agreed. "I apologise."

"Still..." Alice looked to Gruloch. "We shouldn't hesitate. We should start making a strategy of attack. We have twelve ships, a large ground force, and eighteen dragons at this moment. Let's come up with the best way to use them."

***

Ganda grew more and more concerned as the sun crawled higher into the sky. He knew they should have left for the south long ago, but the cavern was far from being sealed.

Thin plumes of steam wafted from small openings near the top of the cave's mouth, where the ice had not yet enclosed the opening. At first, he thought the heat of the dragons' breath caused it, then after some time, he realised it was coming from inside the lair itself.

He surmised that the runoff from the ice was seeping deep into the cave to touch the molten rock far inside. With nowhere else to retreat, the steam was making its way back to the surface and escaping through the small openings.

No matter how much of the spire the dragons melted, the heat from inside the cavern would be enough to keep the newly formed ice from closing the entrance entirely.

"It's taking too long, Ganda," a rider called from the side of a dragon. The toppled spire was almost depleted, and the dragons were taking longer and longer rests between each flaming attack. "They're getting too tired. Soon, they won't even have the strength to fly."

The clan leader knew this to be true. He was standing on a rise to the side of the edge of the cavern. Two dragons were on either side of what remained of the spire, taking turns to melt it. The other three dragons, including his own, were waiting on the plain across the way from him.

From his position, he could see his plan was failing. He had hoped to build a wall of ice over the cavern's mouth but hadn't counted on the heat inside building up and preventing a total shutting of the way.

"Forgive me," Ganda replied. "I am at a loss. I don't know what to do."

"We should go," another suggested. "Surely we have melted enough to drown those little devils by now. If not, all of this steam would have scalded them. They must be dead."

"We can't be certain," Ganda replied. "Who can tell what the Khadzh can tolerate."

The dragon breathing fire into the remainder of the spire suddenly stopped.

"What is it, Vahnosh?" the beast's handler queried, rubbing his hand over the dragon's cheek. It responded with a low growl as it backed away from the mouth of the cavern, moving its attention towards the remaining spires that still stood high above them.

"Why has she stopped?" Ganda called, stepping towards the dragon.

"I don't know," the other replied.

A soft tremor shook the ground beneath their feet.

Lasting only a moment, it was enough for Ganda to stop dead in his tracks.

The five dragons cowered, peering up at the towering ice spires above them as they slunk away from the cavern slowly.

Ganda looked over the terrain carefully. The newly formed ice blocking most of the cavern's mouth was still holding in place. The thin lines of steam were still drifting through the small openings near to its top.

"What was that?" one rider enquired.

The clan leader felt his heart race as the steam plumes became thicker and thicker, jetting out through the gaps in the ice faster and faster.

The sound of enormous cracking echoed into the air around them as thick lines chiselled their way through the ice.

"The ice spires," another rider called.

Ganda looked up to see the monstrous towers rocking back and forth, slowly at first, but more and more violently.

With a loud snap, one of them broke free and toppled, crashing into another before falling onto the icy surface to the side. The ground shook from the impact, terrifying the dragons and causing them to cry out in fear. They grouped together, looking up at the remaining spires and at their masters.

"The dragons want to leave," Ganda said to the others as he moved towards the beasts. "I'm inclined to agree with them."

Another tremor, more vicious, made the clan leader to fall to his knees.

He turned his head to the cavern mouth, where he saw more and more steam escaping through growing cracks and fissures.

His ice wall was breaking apart.

At the top of the wall, where the steam plumes escaped more freely, tiny dark shadows appeared.

First, there were only a few, but more and more clambered through the gap and down the surface of the ice.

The Khadzh were coming.

"Run," Ganda called to his riders. "Get out of here."

He got to his feet and ran a few paces, only to fall again. The ground shook too aggressively, making his legs useless.

The two dragons by the melted spire spread their wings and leapt into the air with their riders on their backs. Ganda was grateful that those two Haigok were standing so close to their winged creatures. He had deep concerns for the other two, who were trying to clamber up an embankment in an effort to get to their own awaiting beasts.

Ganda had yet to cross the sloping ground that led down into the cavern. He tried getting onto his feet again but fell clumsily.

The ground shook.

The tremor kept him planted to the ground on his hands and knees.

More dark creatures appeared through the small gap at the top of the ice wall.

Seeing them reminded the clan leader of tiny, recently hatched spiders fleeing their nest when disturbed.

They weren't coming for him; he realised. They were simply escaping. Something was forcing them out.

Hundreds of the little creatures scrambled over the ice, up the sides and the sloping ground, over the top and even directly towards Ganda, who was crawling as fast as he could towards the plateau where his dragon awaited him.

He glanced over to see the three grounded dragons cringing together, watching the remaining spires swaying back and forth above them. He saw the other two Haigok riders crawling up the embankment in desperation to reach the top and escape the rapidly approaching Khadzh.

A shuddering loud crack, like a thousand thunderclaps, caused a sharp pain in his chest, as his head snapped around to see what the source of the sound was.

Giant pieces of rock, earth, and ice lifted out of the ground above the cavern. Fire and orange molten stone exploded from the ground beneath it.

The massive ice spires snapped and crumbled slowly as gargantuan flames licked at their thick structures.

The young Khadzh screeched and shrieked as they fled from the mouth of the cave.

Ganda saw hundreds and hundreds of sharp white teeth, long claws and scampering forms fleeing towards him.

Behind the shadows, a dull red glow filled the ice wall. It grew brighter and brighter as more and more steam funnelled through the widening gaps and fissures.

Ganda looked at the two Haigok that were just reaching the flat ground where the dragons waited.

"Run," he hollered to them.

The ice wall exploded.

Molten rock rapidly flooded onto the open ground, engulfing dark creatures and sending thick clouds of white steam in all directions. A loud hiss filled Ganda's ears. The ground beneath him continued to shake.

The heat was unbearable as the glowing wave of rock rushed towards him.

He turned and fell to his back, where he saw two dragons circling far overhead. A thick, dark cloud filled with flames and falling debris to the side of them.

At least they made it away safely, he thought.

He could no longer see the other two Haigok that had accompanied him, or the three dragons on the plateau. The screams of the Khadzh drew his attention back towards the mouth of the cavern.

The molten rock rolled over them effortlessly, turning each into a flame for a moment before engulfing them completely.

Closer and closer the wave drew.

Too fast for him to escape from.

Not fast enough for him to avoid his increasing sense of fear.

Glowing red. Splotches of black. Steam clouds. Hissing and rumbling.

Closer and closer.

Hotter and hotter.

Flames burst to life on his chest.

He screamed as he felt his skin tighten, as if it was being peeled from its bones.

Then nothing.

Fifteen

As the day drew on, the sun had reached the highest point in the sky and more dragon-riding Haigok landed on the snow-covered pastureland belonging to Cedric Bauer. A wide circle had formed around one of the larger campfires, comprising the clan leaders and the officers of the ground forces, where they sat upon blankets, tarpaulins and skins. Casual discussions and greetings were underway as the Haigok leaders slapped one another's backs and shared stories, leaving the small group of people from Newholt, Dendadia and Woodmyst to talk among themselves as they waited for more dragon riders to arrive.

When she noticed how high the sun had reached the sky, Alice rose to her feet. Yuri and Nola'ee rose to her sides, flanking her as excellent protectors should. Gruloch, seated to the other side of the circle, almost directly opposite to her position, held up his hand and signalled for the others to be quiet. The Haigok leaders complied and turned their attention to the girl.

Gruloch got to his feet and smiled at her. "I am ready when you are, Alice," he told her.

She nodded and swallowed hard. She did not need to be nervous, but she was. Seated before her were four Haigok clan leaders, a commander of the Dendadian fleet and several of his captains, the Queen of Newholt, the leader of her forces and several others that she knew all too well. Most of them, she had spoken to regularly and even though they were familiar to her, she still felt a small sense of fear.

"Are we waiting for anyone?" she asked the Lord of the Haigok.

"Ganda," Gruloch answered. "Leader of the Nrarukh."

She let out a long breath, watching the vapour dissipate into the cold air before her.

"We can't wait for him," she said. "We have much to discuss, and the day is wearing on."

He agreed, inclining his head. He quickly relayed Alice's concerns to the other clan leaders. One of them, an older Haigok with many lines on his face, waved his hands as he spoke in a raspy voice.

Alice watched with interest as he gestured to Alice, to the dragons and to the others seated about the fire. The other clan leaders chuckled when the older Haigok had finished speaking. Finally, Gruloch said something in reply and returned his attention to the girl.

"Haildur, clan leader of the Traruk Clan, has motioned that the meeting begin," Gruloch said. "He says that while his thoughts are with those tending the dragons and the others seated about the fire, even with you and your small, skinny frame, he feels the cold more and more with each winter and would appreciate it if we can get into our tents as soon as possible. Ganda will just have to find out our plans later on when he gets here."

Haildur held up his hands, wagged his head and blurted something.

"Just thinking out loud," Gruloch translated.

"Then we should try to get this over with as quickly as possible," Alice replied, offering the older Haigok a respectful nod.

Suddenly, the older Haigok started speaking again. As he spoke, he waved his hand to the dragons, pointed to Commander Zakhar and then to the northwest. Haildur's hand moved to one of his riders, standing a short distance behind him, before turning to Gruloch as he continued to speak.

The other clan leaders fell silent and moved their bulbous yellow eyes to Alice, as if expecting a response. She looked at each of them, dumbfounded. There wasn't one word that was spoken by Haildur that she understood.

"Ah…" Gruloch seemed to take his time to process what they said. The older Haigok waved at him and gestured to Alice, seemingly urging the interpreter to hurry it along. "He said that he sent scouts to the coast before they made their way here. There are ships moored at places man call, Erimoor and Blackshore. The vessels all carry weapons..."

"Weapons?" Brondt interjected. "Blades? Axes? What sort of weapons?"

Gruloch interpreted the question. Haildur shook his head adamantly and spat a long string of words back at the Haigok interpreter. He then held his arm out and made the sound of an explosion with his mouth, making his arm recoil as if firing a blast from his hand.

"Cannons," Thornton decoded.

"Ah!" Haildur pointed to the captain and smiled. "Cah-nonz."

"How many vessels?" Commander Zakhar enquired.

"More than seventy at Erimoor," Gruloch replied. "More than one hundred at Blackshore. Haildur also said that there were some leaving Blackshore and making their way south. That was yesterday. They outnumber the ships we have anchored offshore."

Alice let out a deep sigh.

"There's no doubt that the Maji knows our whereabouts," she told them. "Our encounter with the straw men is enough proof of that. It doesn't surprise me he would send his forces to thwart our advance."

"Where is he getting such a large navy?" Ursula asked. "Surely Newholt or Dendadia would have heard news of such a large fleet from merchants or travellers."

"Pirates," Schoenbach answered. Most of those seated about the fire, who understood his words, looked to him curiously. Only the men of Zakhar's fleet and the Erilian women held their composure. "We've had our fair share of dealings with the bastards of the sea," he continued. "Most of them are just thieves and not much more, but some are utterly vile and behave like animals." He looked at Alice, "Our farmer friend here told you about sellswords being recruited into the army of the Maji. It's not impossible for him to be doing the same to recruit crews and ships for his navy."

"Nearly two hundred vessels," Zakhar mused, shaking his head slowly. "With cannons."

"Cah-nonz," Haildur echoed. He started speaking as he gestured to the dragons again.

"What did he say?" Alice asked Gruloch.

"He said we should send the dragons to destroy the ships moored at the docks," the other replied. "We have thirty-one dragons and they could keep out of the range of the cannons easily."

"Thirty-two," Alice put in, reminding the Haigok of Liana. She turned on her heels and peered over at the dragons. They were all clustered together, some chirping and rubbing up against one another like cats. Some were resting on the ground. Others were being tended to by Haigok riders who rubbed down their dragons with blankets, before covering their backs with large canvases.

Alice kneaded the back of her neck, working at a small knot that had formed near her right shoulder, as she watched Liana sidle up to another winged beast. The other, a larger creature, darker in colour, reached its head under her neck and licked at her jaw with its long, red tongue. The girl furrowed her brow, confused a little at the sight. Then she saw Liana return the gesture to the larger dragon.

Strange, she thought. *Arthur would love to be here to see this.*

"We will march to Dellmoor," she told the others seated by the hearth. Gruloch translated for the clan leaders as she spoke. "On the day we take it, Gruloch will take all the dragons to Blackshore, except for Liana and those of the Kazrekh Clan. They will remain to offer support to the ground forces and Commander Zakhar's fleet. We will need to work out the finer details, but that will be the root of it. And, Gruloch?"

He finished translating before answering, "Yes, Alice."

"Whose dragon is that?" She pointed to the large creature sniffing at Liana's neck.

"I believe that is one belonging to a rider of the Eranak Clan," Gruloch answered before turning to Tarnas, the mentioned clan leader. Tarnas listened to Gruloch and nodded, giving a response and gesturing to the dragon.

"It belongs to Vashish," Gruloch said, and pointed to a rider standing near to Tarnas. "Its name is Rahnk."

"And what is it doing with Liana?"

As she asked, Rahnk placed his mouth around the scruff of Liana's neck and mounted her.

Catherine giggled.

"Oh, this is wonderful!" Gruloch smiled happily. "They're about to mate."

Sixteen

Arthur, kneeling upon the sitting room floor of the cabin, placed his books into neat stacks upon the centre of the blanket spread out before him. He knew they would fall and become a mess once the corners of the blanket were brought together and tied up to resemble a sack, but still, he used care and treated each one delicately.

"Where are the rest?" asked Alan, carrying a few more from the bedroom. "I know you have more than this."

"Still on the shelf in my father's house," he answered. "Back in Woodmyst."

"Will you take them also?" the other queried as he placed the books by Arthur's side.

"That's the plan."

Alan sat in a chair and looked around the cabin. Many of the smaller items, the belongings of both Arthur and Alice, had been packed and loaded onto a covered wagon waiting just off the porch. The larger pieces of furniture remained in place and would continue to do so after they led the wagons away.

"It seems empty," Alan said. "Almost sad."

"It's just a house," Arthur told him, smiling forlornly as he continued placing books onto the blanket.

"But it's her house," the other replied. "She built this."

Arthur breathed a deep sigh. He had helped Alice where he could, sneaking supplies from the timber mill out to the glade when he thought no one was watching. A piece of him was fused into the structure around him, as well. He didn't admit it openly, not on this day, but he had come to know this place as home.

Things change, he told himself.

"Help me tie this up," Arthur said, folding the corners of the blanket over the neat piles of books.

Alan tied knots over the top, using the corners of the blanket, before hoisting it off the floor with both hands. The sound of a few books toppling over one another signalled the destruction of the neat piles that Arthur had meticulously made.

"I'll put this on the wagon," Alan said. "What else needs to go?"

"Only the saddle." Arthur pointed to the leather seat and bridle gear resting on the floor by the door. "I want to ride the stallion back."

Alan stopped as he neared the doorway and peered around the room.

"It feels like we just got here," he said. "And now we're preparing to leave again. I don't want to go back, Arthur."

"Me either," the other agreed.

Alan looked through the door to the glade. Snow was falling gently, adding an extra layer to the frost-covered ground.

"Do you think she knows what she's doing?"

"I don't know." Arthur raised his brow. "It doesn't matter. I would follow her to the ends of the Earth."

Alan's eyes drew to three more covered wagons sitting upon the western edge of the clearing, beside the northerners' cabins, where his father and mother, along with Andris and Sevrina, shared a dwelling. David and Lor were carrying sacks from one hut to an awaiting wagon as Andris and Kygra moved inside to retrieve another load.

"It would seem we are all willing to do just that," Alan observed.

Arthur sensed the other's anxiety. In truth, he felt uneasy about a great many things of late. The primary concern was that his wife was so far away, facing dangers that could bring her to her doom, and he had no way of knowing how she was faring. He missed her deeply and would rather be with her, here in this cabin, than so far apart.

As he lifted himself to his feet and crossed the room to the other boy, he longed to hold Alice with his one and only arm as tightly as he could. Instead, he clasped Alan on the shoulder with his hand and remembered the plans that had been made before she had left on the wings of her dragon.

"Things change," he said again.

***

She carefully moved the needle and thread through the fabric, working her embroidery with finicky attention. The Assembly Hall of Woodmyst had never looked more like a barn than it did on the material in her hands.

Frustration and anger were setting in.

She felt hot, even though the cold winds blew gentle drifts of snow by her window and the fire, way across the room from her, had burned low to glowing embers.

Part of her knew her efforts were in vain. It would never look like the Assembly Hall.

She was desperately trying to keep her mind occupied.

Over and under, she pushed the thread through, adding a slight tinge of grey to the edge of the building. It wasn't working for her.

Her thoughts kept returning to him and the look he had given her as she peeped out of the window, watching him with his dark creatures.

He hadn't come to see her since the night he came to her bed as mist. He hadn't spoken to her since the attack of the straw men.

He had been spending most of his time with other things, most of it with them.

The twins.

Every chance he had, which was becoming more frequent than not, he would keep them in his company.

It was as if he was distancing himself from her to embrace them and their power. And that, she believed, was the heart of why he chose to be with them rather than her.

Power.

She questioned what power she even had now that the Seven were all but gone. Only four of them remained and their prime, who held them together, had been lost.

Was it really any wonder why he chose new queens?

Younger.

Easier to mould.

Powerful.

And since he had taken their innocence, they had become devoted to him.

He was with them now, locked behind the door to his bed chamber down the corridor from her own room.

And why wouldn't he be?

They were closer to his age.

Beautiful.

She was far older and was seeing new lines on her face every time she turned to the looking glass.

Bitches.

She hated them.

At least, a part of her did.

Another part of her kept reminding her they were just two little girls who had been thrust into a situation where they had been manipulated and forced to fulfil the wishes of a monster.

Just as he had done to her and the others of the Seven.

Just as he had done to many people.

She hated him more for that.

His voice echoed along the hall in a call of climactic pleasure.

She pictured him with them. Their arms and legs entwined, writhing and squirming.

A knot formed in her stomach.

Her teeth gritted.

The idea made her sick.

The two little girls should play with dolls, not that.

Not that.

She shot to her feet and threw the embroidery towards the fireplace with brute force.

As she clenched her fists, her knuckles turning white, flames burst to life in the hearth.

The Assembly Hall of Woodmyst ignited in the blaze and was engulfed in an instant.

A large fireball lapped the mantel above the fireplace before vanishing up the flue.

Her fingers relaxed as she tried to control her breathing.

The hearth went dark as the embers turned cold.

Slowly, she sat back in her chair and looked to the window.

Her chin quivered as tears streamed over her cheeks.

His calls subsided. The sound of her heart racing filled her ears instead.

Snow built up around the edges of the window glazing as a breeze continued to blow a gentle drift of frost by her view.

Her hatred, anger, and sorrow grew more and more with each passing moment.

But none of that could ever compete with her loneliness.

**

The Olive Queen made her way down a steep set of stone steps that hugged a retaining wall set by the quaint market square. She was careful to not slip on the icy surface as she carried a wicker basket on her arm, using her other hand to steady herself against the wall. At the top of the stairs sat a large, whitewashed house that overlooked the township. It wasn't a palace, or even a mansion, but it was still large enough for her to consider it too large for one woman to occupy.

Much larger than the house she and Geoffrey had once dwelt in.

That was in a time almost forgotten, before she became a queen.

Before she became the Maji's.

"My lady." A merchant, standing by his stall on a platform by the base of the stairs, bowed politely and offered his hand to her. A tall, broad-shouldered guard brushed by her on the outside of the stairs to stand between her and the merchant.

"This is your queen," he growled. "Show some respect."

"It's all right, Dwight," she said to the soldier, reaching her hand out to the merchant. "He's just being nice."

The merchant guided Claire by the hand, from the stairs and to a boardwalk that ran along the edge of the market, protecting patrons from the slush forming on the ground.

"Couldn't interest you in some fine fabric for making a dress, or a new cloak for that 'usband of yours now, could I?" the merchant asked with a smile.

She thought of Geoffrey.

She thought of how she had loved him truly and deeply.

She thought of how she had slit his throat with a kitchen knife.

"Not today, thank you," she replied.

Dwight the guard moved ahead of her, calling out to the crowd gathered on the boardwalk, "Make way for your queen."

He needn't have bothered, as people fell silent when they saw her olive cloak, allowing her to hear mothers whispering in their children's ears, "That's the queen, that is."

She smiled as she passed people by, said hello and waved to little girls and boys and chatted to stall keepers who offered samples of their stock, she turned down politely and instructed them to sell for coin instead of giving it away to someone who wasn't in need.

She moved on, stopping at another store. A baker was making loaves in the open, cooking his bread in a large iron oven set against a wall behind the counter.

"That smells lovely," she said.

"A fresh loaf on the house," the baker, a largish man with a long bushy beard, said as he held up a steaming cob of bread.

"I cannot accept," she replied, reaching to her purse, strapped to her belt beneath her cloak. "Not unless you allow me to pay for it."

At this point, Dwight's thoughts trailed away from the conversation. He gazed over the crowd, who were all watching her with interest and in awe.

He was not fond of these little walks through the market that the Olive Queen took on occasion. It was unsafe with too many people and too many places for enemies to hide and wait for her to draw near enough to strike.

Still, he had never noticed a moment when any of the people in Dellmoor posed a threat to their new queen. They had taken to her with open arms.

The news of her forthcoming arrival had sparked new life into the town, along with cleaning and repairing, painting and decorating. Not only the house that was designated as the lodging for the queen, but the entire town, particularly the market square, had undergone a thorough transformation.

Dwight recalled a very drowsy fishing village existing around him not all that long ago. Now, it filled with laughing children and cheerful people.

The day of her arrival had turned into a week-long celebration. They greeted each morning with a fanfare of horns to call the morning sun. The townsfolk tied olive and green ribbons along fences and over storefronts. Children danced and sang for her, some kind of traditional pieces taught by old ones that only vaguely remembered the words and movements from their own childhood.

He was so glad when it was over.

Standing by her side with at least two other guards, listening to the whining drone of little voices and watching their clumsy steps and waving hands, was all enough for him to want to cut his own guts out.

He silently thanked the gods when the horns didn't blow one morning. He hoped he could stand by her side, with one or two other guards, by the fucking fire inside rather than come all the way back down those steps to listen to more children sing and dance.

But alas, this was not to be.

Instead, she made it her business to come down every couple of days and partake in the regular banter with every shopkeeper. It was almost as if someone had written the conversation and replayed out with every new rising of the sun. That's how Dwight saw it.

Take this for free, they would say.

Oh no, I couldn't, she would say.

It's a gift, they would say.

I'm rich and I'm a bloody queen, she would say.

Just take it and get moving, silly girl, he would say.

Or, at least, he wished he did.

All in all, he couldn't deny that Dellmoor loved their queen, and she appeared to love them back. But Dwight couldn't understand why.

She had done nothing spectacular, except become one of the Maji's brides. Apparently, she was a powerful sorceress, but he hadn't seen her do much more than brew tea for herself.

To him, she seemed nothing more than a silly girl. She didn't fit the part of a queen at all. Too naïve to understand politics or tactics, and too young to understand the wiles of man.

Or, at least, he thought she was. That was, until she told him she had fought against the White Witch alongside her sisters, the others of her coven.

He then realised that she was not all that much younger than he.

Dwight had been nothing more than a fisherman during the march of the Mirikin. It wasn't until all the fighting men had left to trek to the east that he had found his place as a peacekeeper for his people. He had reluctantly accepted the position of sheriff when it was offered to him, he'd and regretted it when the officers of the north had commanded him to watch over the Olive Queen when she arrived. His position of sheriff dissolved, and they made him Commander of Dellmoor in the service of the Maji.

The Maji, another overrated individual as far as he was concerned, was a little shit who needed his arse kicked.

Dwight was only ever loyal to the people of Dellmoor. The township had no real economic importance, and they could never consider its people higher regarding aristocracy. They were of a tactical significance only.

Physically, Dellmoor sat where two bodies of water met; the Western Sea and the Sea of Lunkhul. It was a prime position to establish a trading post for those from the far east and lands to the west to meet and barter.

The Commander of Dellmoor understood full well that there was no one in his fair village that could represent the boy-master, hidden in his northern palace, when establishing a trading port or a place of valued status. Who better to do that task than one of his own queens?

He would have been called a cynic if he was ever to share his thoughts with others. In fact, he had heard others of his age get laughed at and mocked when they had voiced their opinions of Dellmoor, becoming an important place in the future now that the queen was here.

Most of them kept their mouths shut about such things now. Himself included.

But, with all that put aside, he felt compelled to protect this woman.

There was something about her, a weakness that he sensed deep inside of her; a frailty that was breaking its way through. An old wound that was reopening again.

He could see it in her eyes.

She played happily with all of those around her, but there was an innate despondency that revealed itself when she thought she was alone and no one was watching except for him.

A silly girl. Depressed, confused, and vulnerable.

The sound of an approaching horse drew his attention to the opposite side of the market square.

His hand went to his sword, as did those of the other two guards accompanying him. He relaxed a little when he saw it was one of their own, a uniformed soldier approaching.

"Sound the bells," the rider called.

"What is it, Dwight?" the Olive Queen asked the commander by her side.

He turned and saw the loaf of bread sitting in her basket.

It smelled good.

"I'm not sure, my queen," he replied. He turned his focus to the rider. "What news?"

"Sound the bells," the rider repeated as he drew closer. "An army approaches. They'll be here by dawn tomorrow."

"An army?" Dwight enquired. "What army?"

"They have ships offshore and great flying beasts. I think they might be dragons, sir," the rider continued.

"Dragons?" The commander raised his brow. No one from Dellmoor had ever seen dragons. Tales of them had been told. The story of how Kalibard had become mere ruins and of how Woodmyst burned to rubble were told to frighten children, but they were stories.

At least he thought so before the Olive Queen arrived, sharing the news of how a girl in Woodmyst rode a great flying beast of her own.

Claire covered her mouth and wept.

"My queen?" Dwight looked at her.

"She comes for me, Dwight," the Olive Queen replied. Her voice trembled.

He took her by the arm and led her away, back to the house on the hill.

Tears streamed over her cheeks. The smile she habitually wore vanished, replaced with terror and sincere dread.

Seventeen

They ran on and on, pulled by their master's influence through both day and night. They had climbed over the mountains by Ironfields and followed the length of the range by the edge of the Core Lands.

Eventually, they found the northern coast of the inland sea and followed the shore to the ruins of Redloch and Mallowhill. Onward, to the remains of Strongholdt and Havencrest where they turned east.

Across the great grass plains where the desert began, they ran, following ravines, dried rivers and keeping to brush and coppice cover as much as they could.

They ran.

They were hungry.

So very hungry.

They ignored herds of stag and wild bullock as they made their way over the lands.

He had made them believe that something better awaited them.

Better than stag and bullock.

Something tasty.

Something fresh and sweet.

Through broken villages, discarded huts, isolated abandoned farms, they ran.

And when their muscles ached, and their throats felt hoarse from panting, they ran some more.

Always to the east.

To the east.

***

David drove the wagon slowly, leisurely, along the well-worn road that led between the glade and Woodmyst. They had covered it with a fine blanket of snow, but it was still visible beneath the white powder and easy to navigate as they passed beneath tall, leafless trees and thick patches of pines. He looked around when he could, to see how far the other three wagons were behind him.

Andris gave a polite wave each time the large man turned about, signalling that he was still there. Becka sat alongside him, rugged up in shawls and blankets as Sevrina, Andris' pregnant wife, remained out of sight under the canvas cover of the cart.

Travelling a short distance behind them was another wagon with Lor Verney and his family. Linet, his wife, had opted to stay inside the shelter of their canvas cover, leaving her son to ride beside her husband.

The last wagon in the line belonged to Ruttger and Courtney. He wasn't able to see them all that well through the falling snow. Only the shape of the horse and wagon were distinct enough to perceive.

Arthur, perched high on his saddle, rode the chestnut stallion. He had become quite adept at controlling the beast, or the beast had become quite talented at keeping the boy on his back. David wasn't sure which. He felt the occasional need to call out to his son to be careful and watch what he was doing.

He didn't need to bother, as Arthur displayed no sign of falling from the horse, nor did he believe the horse would put his son in a situation to allow him to fall so easily at such a slow pace.

The memory of Arthur weaving and racing about on the stallion across the glade was still fresh in his mind. He and the horse had become one, so it would seem.

It was almost like the way Alice could interact with animals, creating an unspoken bond that only existed between her and the creature.

David wondered if the connection between his son and the stallion was one that she had put in place.

Was it possible for her to do such a thing?

It wouldn't surprise him if it was.

He had seen her do many things that could not be explained. There were some things that she had accomplished that he believed she didn't realise she was able to do, or else took for granted.

Perhaps this was one of those things.

The rukyul that she had tamed, with all of its ferocity, had aligned itself to Arthur in the end, as well.

Maybe the connection goes out like roots of a tree, considered David. *Maybe the connection Alice makes with the creatures extends to Arthur, because they are connected.*

He pushed the thought aside and looked at the sun above. It was crossing into the western sky.

"Will you stay at our old house," Arthur asked, riding without holding onto the reins, "or with me at Emily's?"

"I hadn't thought of that," his father replied. He pursed his lips and contemplated the boy's words. "I guess, with you. I'm not sure I really want to go back to our house again. There are bad memories there. I had some dark moments in that place."

Arthur listened to his father talk.

He remembered the dark times.

He remembered his father's fear and loathing of Alice when he was chief. He remembered how David had blamed the girl for the death of his wives and daughter.

All of it had been Takmel's subterfuge and manipulation; an influence set upon the chief. An influence that reached deep into all of Woodmyst.

"There were some good times, too, Papa," Arthur told him. "They weren't all dark."

"I know," David allowed. "I still don't feel like going back. It doesn't feel as if I'm returning home. And, in a way, we're not." He looked over at his son. "You go back and get what you want. I'll set up at Emily's."

Arthur agreed with a nod. His father was right. There was no need to revisit and get reacquainted with old places. Woodmyst was just a stepping stone.

It wasn't home anymore.

***

Dwight brushed the snow from his shoulders as he closed the heavy wooden door behind him. His eyes moved to her, but she didn't react to the noise he made as he stepped across the timber floor. She fixated on the flames dancing in the fireplace.

"The night guards are in place, my queen," he said. She sat upon a deep chair before the fireplace with her knees tucked up to her chest, a blanket draped over her and pulled up to her chin. "I'll be leaving for home soon. Is there anything I can get for you before I go?"

He saw the twinkle of tear streaks on her cheeks as she shook her head. Her action reminded him of an upset child, and his heart melted a little.

"I'm all right, thank you Dwight," she answered.

He was about to turn and leave, but his conscience got the better of him. "But you're not."

She looked to him. There was surprise and anger in her eyes. He thought she was about to reprimand him for his statement, but instead, she cried.

He sighed.

Why did I have to open my big mouth?

He crossed the room and knelt beside her chair. Her arms instantly flew out from under the blanket and wrapped around his shoulders as she sobbed.

Not knowing what else to do, he put his arms around her also.

"She'll kill us all, Dwight," she managed. "She'll kill everyone, and she won't even need her army to do it."

"How?" he asked, half smiling, believing that she was exaggerating or overestimating the enemy's abilities. "Is she more powerful than you?"

"Yes." Claire pulled away and locked her eyes to his. He saw terror. "More powerful than even she is aware. She is only a child, and she is the prime of her coven. Even the gods have granted her their favour."

He listened to her words, not sure if he should take them seriously. He still saw her as a silly girl, but he could not ignore her distress. She clawed at his arms as she spoke. He was glad of the layers of clothing he had on, as he believed that she would have peeled the skin from his bones otherwise.

"But none of that matters," she continued. "She won't need to lift a finger against us. Her dragon will devour this village with its breath."

"A dragon can really do that?"

"I've seen it." She nodded frantically. "In my dreams. It destroyed Blackrock Haven. Others burned Dweagan. Now they come here."

He didn't know of these places all that well, except by reports from others. He wasn't able to see their streets and structures in his mind, or understand how she could have seen these creatures attack them. Nevertheless, he believed her.

Her chin trembled as fresh tears fell from her eyes.

"What would you have me do, my queen?" he asked. He did not know how to react to such information. All he wanted to do was to find his tiny fishing boat and let the current carry him away.

"Stay with me tonight," she said. "Don't leave me alone."

He hesitated, giving her a wary look.

"My queen, I don't think it's wise for me to…"

"Please, Dwight," she pleaded. "I just need someone to be near me. I don't want to be on my own."

He saw the girl in her. He saw the vulnerable, confused girl, who was deeply depressed. All she wanted was a friend, and for whatever the reason, she saw him in that role.

Reluctantly, he accepted the position.

"All right," he agreed, nodding slowly.

***

Alice stood upon the edge of a small rocky bluff. White spray broke around her as she watched the longboats making their way from the fleet to the shore.

The sea was rough, and she spotted Zakhar sitting in the lead boat, rather than standing on the bow as he usually would. Yuri stood beside her, growling deeply as the boats drew nearer.

"I don't like this man, Kayl'sro," he said in his tongue. "He's too stiff. As if they have pushed a long stick into his backside."

She smiled, stifling a laugh. He was right. Zakhar stood as though he had a rod inserted along his spine.

"His upbringing was different to yours and mine, Yuri," she told the Agrodien. "Dendadia is a place of culture, education and traditions based in civility."

The reptilian looked to her strangely and shook his head.

"Arthur told me that once," she said. "I don't know what it means exactly. But it was in a book, and that must mean it's true."

"Ink scratches on paper could be just as much a lie as words from a mouth," Yuri offered. "I learnt that from my father."

She looked at him, surprised by the sudden aphorism. He cocked his head coyly and grinned, keeping his eyes on the approaching vessels.

Alice turned back to view the ocean.

"Your dragon is mating with another," he blurted.

This time, she laughed.

"I know," she replied.

His smile dissipated as he looked to the sun hanging low in the western sky.

"The soldiers told me that this place was called Grassbeach," he said. "They say the Mirikin destroyed it."

She nodded.

"I couldn't find any trace of man here," he told her. "I looked and found nothing."

"War brings destruction," she put in.

"This was not war," Yuri replied. "This was senseless annihilation. Blood and flames for the sake of blood and flames."

She reached up and wiped away the tear welling in her eye.

"The Mirikin marched to the east and wiped out village after village," the reptilian pointed out. "We march west and already Blackrock Haven and Dweagan are destroyed."

She swallowed hard, feeling a large lump in her throat.

"The Mirikin need to be destroyed, Yuri," she reminded him. "And two of the Mirikin Queens were each in Blackrock Haven and Dweagan."

"Yes," he agreed. "But, not everybody is Mirikin."

His words were like a great Agrodien punch in the gut. They hurt deeply.

She hadn't considered that their tactic wasn't dissimilar to that of what the Mirikin had employed.

Yuri had.

And he was right.

She took his great, big leathery hand in hers and gave it a thankful squeeze.

"Hello," called the fleet commander, waving his arm at Alice and Yuri from his boat.

Alice returned the gesture.

"I really don't like this man, Kayl'sro," Yuri said again, feigning a smile, which looked more like a grimace to Alice, and waving his arm as well.

Eighteen

David sat at the head of the table closest to the kitchen. It was some time since he had last been in this house. In fact, he couldn't remember when his previous visit occurred.

It smelled dank and felt still, with a sense of stiffness in the air.

Arthur had flung every window open when they first set foot inside the Warde dwelling, even though the chill outside was almost unbearable, just to allow some freshness back into the house. Dust covered everything, and while Arthur returned to the old Gyfford home on the other side of Woodmyst to retrieve some belongings, David and Becka busied themselves with cleaning.

After some time, Lor arrived with a load of wood and piled it outside the back door before setting a fire in the sitting room's hearth. He didn't stay long; just enough time for David to thank him.

"We should have them all over here for supper," Becka suggested. "Our first night back in Woodmyst should be together."

He agreed.

After setting a fire in the stove, he left to invite the others who had come with him from the glade.

The day passed into night, and they served supper. Becka had put together a simple meal consisting of nothing more than a couple of chickens and some loaves of bread.

They sat around the table, speculating about their loved ones who were absent. David, seated nearest to the kitchen, Becka on his left and Arthur on his right, looked around the table to each of the others as they talked.

Lor, Linet and Alan sat on one side. Across from them were Andris and a very pregnant Sevrina, who appeared to be struggling when she reached over her belly and the table for more food. Courtney sat beside her, with Ruttger taking the chair at the far end of the table.

One big, happy family.

"I'm certain they are all right," Becka said, squeezing David's hand, seeing his lonely expression.

He nodded, trying to tell himself that they were.

His heart ached for Emily and the girls. He missed them.

His growing concern, however, was Arthur. Since Alice left, the boy had become even quieter and withdrawn than usual.

Arthur had portrayed the role of a contented lad, smiling when he needed to and talking about things that others wanted to focus upon.

But a father could tell.

His son was miserable. The bond between the young husband and wife was stronger than anything David had ever seen in any relationship. And with each step that the girl took farther away from his son, it stretched the bond more.

David imagined a cord, or a rope, being pulled tighter and tighter to the point of breaking. He felt it too, each and every time he thought of Emily. But Arthur was growing more miserable by the day.

The boy needed the girl. Perhaps as much as the stars need the sky.

A knock at the door broke his train of thought. Arthur moved, so as to answer it, but David got to his feet first.

"You stay there," he said to the boy. "I'll get it."

The table fell silent as David crossed the room. He opened the door to a young, short and scrawny man dressed in the dark garb of a bookkeeper.

"My apologies, Chief Gyfford," the visitor said. "The town magistrate sent me to enquire as to whether..."

"There's a town magistrate, now?" David interjected. He then looked the other up and down. "Who are you?"

"My apologies," the other said again. "My name is..."

"Do you start everything with, 'my apologies'?"

"Sorry?" the young man asked, looking befuddled.

"That's the same thing," David told him.

There was sniggering from the kitchen.

"Stop playing and let him speak, David," Becka called from the table.

The large man smirked as he stepped aside and gestured for the visitor to enter.

"Thank you, Chief Gyfford," the man said politely, stepping into the warm interior. He nodded to the others around the table. "Good evening. Sorry for the intrusion."

"I'm not the chief," David told him as he closed the door.

"My apologies," the other repeated as he turned to face the large man again.

"Son." David glared at him. "If you say, 'my apologies' one more time, I'll give you something to be sorry for."

The young man looked at him fearfully.

"My ah…"

"Go on," David urged him.

"Papa," Arthur growled, standing to his feet and extending his hand to the young man. "Ignore him. He's playing with you. Let's start over. My name is Arthur, and you are?"

"Gilbert," he replied, taking Arthur's hand and bowing slightly. "Gilbert Obelyn."

"Well, Gilbert Obelyn." Arthur moved towards the table, thinking the young man's gesture was a little strange. "Would you like something to eat or drink? Tea, perhaps?"

"No thank you," he answered. "I've come to deliver a message to Chief Gyfford."

"I'm no chief," David reminded him, returning to his seat at the table. "Tell your master he wasted your time."

"Master?"

"Whoever sent you, boy," David said, dismissing the messenger with a wave of his hand.

"The magistrate," Obelyn said.

"The magistrate, then. And who is this magistrate?"

"Stephen Latham, sir," the young man replied.

David looked around the table to see if anyone recognised the name. All shook their heads.

"Where does this Stephen Latham come from, Gilbert?" Becka enquired.

"Oldcastle, my lady," he answered. "He was a magistrate in training at the citadel before the Mirikin attacked us."

"So, you're from Oldcastle as well?" Arthur asked.

"Yes, my lord," he said, bowing slightly.

"How was this magistrate appointed?" Andris enquired as he scrutinised the young man. "And, why are you dressed as a bookkeeper?"

"The magistrate was appointed not long after the Maji was vanquished. There was no one left to oversee the comings and goings of Woodmyst, and we desperately needed someone to fill the void. Magistrate Latham was the closest thing to someone who had experience in a leadership position. I assure you, he has been doing the best that he can, given the circumstances."

"And you?" Andris reminded him. "Why are you dressed so?"

"Oh," he said, looking down at his dark clothing. "I am the only one who was training to be a bookkeeper who isn't currently locked in a cell."

"Why is that?" Lor asked. "Surely, if you were in training to be a bookkeeper, you must have been privy to their discussions with the Maji?"

"I'm afraid I wasn't, sir," the young man told him. "Master Bookkeeper Drayton said I was far superior to him with numbers and keeping books, but I was inept at understanding how people work. In fact, he once called me an arithmetical marvel burdened with shit for brains." He looked sheepishly at the faces around the table, remembering suddenly that there were women present, and blushed. Alan sniggered. Obelyn closed his eyes and lowered his head. "My apologies."

"I told you, boy," David mumbled, warning him again with his mouth full of food.

"What was Magistrate Latham's message?" Arthur pressed.

"He wished to know whether Chief Gyfford wanted a formal meeting called for the Assembly Hall to announce his return."

"No," David replied, tearing a morsel of meat from a chicken leg with his teeth. "Not your chief."

"Then," Obelyn looked to Arthur, "perhaps you would like to address the people about your return, my lord?"

"I don't see how that would be worth the fuss," Arthur told him.

"As you wish, my lord."

"Gilbert?" Arthur spun in his seat to face the young bookkeeper.

"My lord?"

"Why do you call me *lord*?"

Obelyn glanced to the fire in the living room.

"When Alice defeated the Maji and sent him away, people started calling her many things. Some, not many, said she is a witch, just like one of the Seven. Others thought she was like the White Witch of the Mirikin or even the Sovereign. Most of us call her our queen. Some call her the Queen of Fire, because she brought dragons with her and burnt the tree into the ground."

Arthur listened to the young man speak and heard the opinion of a child. It made him smile a little.

"Most of Woodmyst just say that she is Queen Alice Warde, because they still love her father, Tomas. And then there are some who call her Queen Alice Gyfford, because she is your wife.

"That's why I call you *my lord*, my lord," Obelyn continued. "If she is my queen, then you are my king."

Lor and Alan burst out laughing.

"Hush," Linet snapped at both of them.

David snorted, trying not to choke on the chicken in his mouth. Ruttger forced the corners of his mouth down and sat rigidly still. Courtney simply let loose and fell into a laughing fit. Andris wheezed out a long hiss as Sevrina held her breath. Becka covered her mouth and turned away.

A great, beaming smile spread across Arthur's face. He tried not to laugh. Tears were welling in his eyes as he fought tooth and nail to keep his composure. He stood and extended his hand to Obelyn.

"Did I say something wrong, my lord?" the young bookkeeper enquired, peering around at the others confusedly.

"No," Arthur replied. "Please tell Magistrate Latham that we will not require an audience with the people of Woodmyst. Tell him we would rather keep a low profile and that I would like to see him myself in due time."

"Yes, my lord." The other bowed.

Arthur showed him to the door before returning to his seat at the table.

"Queen Alice," Alan laughed, "and King Arth—"

"Don't say it," Arthur chuckled. "Not ever."

***

Alice sat by her mother. The campfire felt warm against her skin as she stared across the flames to the others seated about the hearth. Amicia was leaning into Brondt. Ursula snuggled against Thornton. Schoenbach had his arms around Karlena. And Alice missed Arthur more than ever.

Emily reached her arm around the girl and pulled her against her side. She planted a kiss on her daughter's crown and held her tightly.

Alice tilted her head against the auburn woman's shoulder and breathed a long sigh. A long, comfortable silence followed, and Alice felt the urge to close her eyes and drift away.

Yuri plonked himself down on the ground next to her, unwittingly ruining the moment. His tail scraped over the canvas they were resting upon before coiling around his body.

"Where have you been?" Alice asked in his tongue.

"Walking the perimeter," he replied, looking into the flames. "The night watchers are in place. Everyone has been fed."

"What about you? Did you eat?"

"I'm not hungry," he replied quietly.

She looked at him doubtfully.

"I need you strong," she told him.

"Do you know any stronger than me?"

She smirked and shook her head as her mother started running her fingers through her hair.

"What are you two talking about?" Emily questioned.

"Nothing," Alice replied. "Except, Yuri believes he is too strong to need food."

"I no eat," he told the girl's mother, using his best common language.

As he spoke, Nola'ee and Nakrah emerged from the darkness. Nakrah carried two long, steaming packages. They were flat pieces of bread, rolled up with meat wrapped inside. The Haigok were cooking them up in their campsite a stone's throw away from where they were sitting.

Nola'ee sat down on a canvas across from Alice before taking one parcel from Nakrah, who then sat beside her. They engaged in conversation as they ate.

"I think those two are in love," Catherine said with a smile.

"Those two mating," Yuri corrected her.

Upon hearing the Agrodien's words, Commander Zakhar almost choked on the tea he was drinking, sending William Vawdrey into a laughing fit.

Alice stared wide-eyed at the large reptilian, uncertain that she heard him correctly.

"He get her food all the time," Yuri clarified, keeping his voice low. "I watch them."

Catherine leant over her mother's lap towards the Agrodien.

"You watch them?" she asked, perplexed.

"I see him get food all the time."

Alice raised her brow.

"So, you haven't seen them mating?" she pressed.

"No," Yuri answered, giving each of the girls a strange look, appearing disgusted at the concept.

As he spoke, Bein appeared from the shadows, carrying two parcels of Haigok food.

"Yuri," he growled, holding one roll out to the other. The large reptilian took it and thanked Bein in their native tongue.

"So," Zakhar started as Bein sat beside Yuri. "How long have you two been mating?"

Vawdrey suddenly fell onto his back, hooting with amusement.

Yuri glared at the fleet commander angrily as the laughter spread around the campfire.

Nineteen

Dawn.

Claire Staunton, the Olive Queen, stood by a large window that overlooked the Western Sea. Her fear-filled eyes fixed upon the twelve ships that had sailed in to view from the south, now anchored some distance from the shoreline. Compared to the tiny fishing boats moored to the short piers below her house, the tall vessels were like monsters swaying slowly upon the ocean.

She saw the blue banner on each of the ships, flaunting the golden eagle with down-turned wings, carrying a war axe in its talons. Her eyes moved to the men on board, rolling up their sails as anchors lowered.

The vessels sat turned side-on to Dellmoor. Their gun portals opened and their cannons pushed into view.

The Olive Queen had no defences to match them.

Fish hooks, nets and farming implements; what were these to the black powder and projectiles that could tear her new home apart?

Her thoughts turned to the children she saw every day, to their smiling faces as they danced for her when she had first arrived.

She envisioned the pedlars in the market. The man at the bottom of the stairs who sold fine fabrics. The baker who made possibly the best loaves she had ever tasted.

"My queen," Dwight said from behind her. "We have spotted a large army to the east. Should I assemble the guards?"

She frowned as she turned from the window to face the soldier, dressed in his armour and ready for battle.

"How many men do we have?" she asked.

"Only fifty," he replied.

"And they?"

"We estimate anywhere between three and five hundred."

She took a deep breath and let it out slowly to calm her nerves.

"We should go out to meet them," she said, starting across the room towards him. "Don't you think?"

"I'll stand by you, whatever your decision, my queen."

She stopped beside him and locked eyes with his. Tears were building up.

"I know." She placed her hand on his arm and offered a brave grin before moving towards the door.

Together, they moved down the steps, into the market square, where the soldiers of Dellmoor waited.

"My queen," the fabric stall owner said, and bowed. "We can gather more men and assist you with this fight."

Several other men, either too old to combat or unfit for battle, gathered about to support the merchant's statement.

She shook her head and smiled gratefully.

"No," she said. "Go home to your families. Stay inside where it is safe."

As she spoke, a loud ripping sound tore through the sky as five dragons raced over the township.

"By the gods," one soldier gasped.

Claire followed the giant beasts with her eyes as they climbed gracefully into the air before turning about. Even from such a far distance, she could see that one rider was much smaller than the others. She felt the energy emitting from that individual form.

She knew it was Alice.

Her chest hurt as her heart thudded rapidly, loudly.

Her chin quivered, her knees felt weak, and her hands shook.

Dwight took her by the wrist, placing her hand into his own.

"We'll go together, if you wish."

She nodded, silently thanking him.

Hand in hand, the Olive Queen and the Commander of the Dellmoor guard moved through the small village and onto the snow-covered pastureland to the east.

A multitude of armoured men waited for them some distance away, stretching across the expanse to the left and right. Cavalrymen and infantry covered the ground, swords already in their hands. Horses pawed the ground eagerly.

Above, high in the sky, several dragons flew in wide circles over the army and the township. One of them swooped lower and lower. It appeared as if it was going to plummet into the earth, but it pulled up at the last moment and hovered a few feet above the frost before landing.

It roared.

The ground beneath Claire's feet shook, and her ears rang.

The rider slid down the left side of the beast and landed elegantly on both feet.

Claire felt her fear grow as she watched the rider approach. The stride was purposeful, aggressive.

She eyed the two sword hilts poking over the figure's shoulder.

She caught the glint of the morning sun striking the iron claws hanging over the bearskin cloak.

As the rider drew closer, and the covers over the face removed, Claire noticed the piercing blue eyes staring directly at her menacingly.

Alice.

A lump formed in her throat.

A knot tightened in her stomach.

She thought she was about to be sick.

Dwight instinctively pulled his sword free and stepped before his queen. His fifty men followed suit.

Alice reached her arm over their head and lifted one of her blades from the sheaths strapped to her back.

The Olive Queen knew the girl and her combat capabilities. It was all the soldiers of Woodmyst ever talked about.

The fact that none of the men that supported Alice had moved an inch, even after Dwight had shown his sword, informed Claire that the girl intended to fight them all on her own.

"Drop your swords," the Olive Queen instructed.

Dwight shot her a puzzled look.

"My queen?"

"Tell your men to lower their weapons, now," she reiterated.

"We can defeat one girl," he told her.

"Not this one, Dwight," she replied. "She will slaughter you and all of your men on her own. Do as I say. Drop your swords."

Reluctantly, Dwight tossed his sword to the ground.

"Drop them," he shouted to his men. They complied instantly, even though they were just as perplexed as their commander.

"Give me your knife," Claire commanded, holding her hand out to him.

Dwight furrowed his brow and did as he was told, taking his dagger from his belt and offering its hilt to her.

She took it and stepped towards the approaching girl.

"Stay here," she said, moving away from him.

"My queen?" he called after her.

"We surrender, Dwight," she replied, keeping her eyes on Alice. "We can't defeat them."

He watched on, stunned, as she moved across the snow towards the girl.

"What is she doing?" one of the other men asked him.

"I don't know," he replied.

The Olive Queen wiped tears from her eyes with the back of the hand that held the knife.

"Put the knife down, Claire," Alice shouted.

"No," she replied, coming to a stop. She saw a few horses approaching from behind the girl and recognised Emily, Catherine, Queen Amicia and Ursula. "I relinquish my position as Queen of Dellmoor, hoping you would spare its people."

"We have no wish for bloodshed," Alice assured her. "But, you have joined with the Maji and we have come to bring his influence to an end."

Claire nodded.

"You have weakened him," she said. "Without your Aunt Joanne, we have lost our ability to keep connected to one another. At least, in the way it once was. I could feel it when Joanne and Tricia, and Gilda were taken, but that's all. It isn't like before. Something has changed." Claire cried. "I want to go home."

Emily pulled to her daughter's side, listening to the Olive Queen's words.

"Come back with us," the auburn woman pleaded.

Claire shook her head.

"I can't. He continues to draw strength from us," she said. She looked at Catherine. "He will always be a part of us. And we will always be a part of him."

Catherine understood and sobbed.

"We can protect you," Alice offered. "We can send you with an escort back to Woodmyst."

The Olive Queen shook her head as she lifted Dwight's blade to her own throat.

"He can reach me anywhere I go," she sobbed. "There is only one way to stop him."

"Wait," Alice yelled, dropping her sword and moving forward a step.

"It's the only way, Alice," Claire told her. "I'm not strong enough to defeat him on my own, but this might help you."

She plunged the dagger into her neck, just below her jaw.

A fine spray of blood pumped out at intervals as she fell to her knees.

Dwight let out an almighty, painful cry as she fell onto her face into the snow.

A crimson puddle spread over the white ground and through her hair.

He raced forward, sliding over the frost, dropping beside her to lift her into his arms.

Her body was limp, and her eyes were already glazed over. "You silly girl," he wept. "You silly, silly girl."

Twenty

Takmel felt short of breath. A sharp pain shot through his temples. His hands moved to his head, as if he was trying to keep his aching brain from escaping.

His brow throbbed and the backs of his eyes burned hot.

He leapt from the bed, almost knocking one twin to the floor. With his eyes squeezed shut and his teeth grinding against one another, he pressed his cheek to the cold stone wall, hoping to ease the agony.

The two girls sat up, pulling the covers to their necks as they watched him with uncertainty. Fear gripped them as Takmel groaned.

He dropped to his knees and breathed shallowly. The agony was too much to bear.

He fell onto his side, curling into a ball. His voice was shaky as he cried.

One of the twin girls climbed out of bed, feeling compassion for him, and lowered herself to his side. She pressed herself to his back and wrapped her arms about his shoulders.

Her sister remained in place, blankets up to her neck and staring with wide eyes at the shivering, moaning boy on the floor. She was petrified.

He was a figure of power and strength, suddenly brought to a weakened state by something she didn't quite understand.

As she watched, his breathing slowed. His body relaxed, and he became less tense.

Her sister, lying on the floor, started running her fingers through his hair, hoping to calm him, to soothe him. His moaning stopped,

169

and his hands slowly moved away from his temples. His eyes remained closed as he became tranquil.

The moment of torment had passed.

For now.

Outside, in the corridor, another had felt a disturbance. She had not experienced the pain that her husband had undergone, but nevertheless, she sensed loss.

A sister had been taken.

Isabel had an idea of how it happened, but not completely. Claire was gone, she was certain.

A tear slid over her cheek as she remembered the Olive Queen.

A smirk grew upon her lips as she stared at the twins' chamber door.

She had heard his cries.

She knew he felt pain.

She wiped her eyes on the back of her sleeve as she turned and walked away. Her head felt a little higher than it had been of late. A sensation she hadn't felt in a long time suddenly filled her.

Delight.

Part of her felt guilty for the sudden emotion. She loved Claire, as much as real sisters do. She would miss her dearly.

Nevertheless, the Olive Queen's death had brought an unexpected outcome.

It had brought strategy.

***

As the Maji underwent his moment in agony, the dark creatures far to the east paused upon the open ground. They exchanged glances, as if confused.

Some took to squabbling, scratching, hissing, shrieking and growling for no apparent reason other than they felt afraid and lost.

Others sniffed the snow, knowing that they were in search of something that would ease the hunger they felt.

A few turned their heads towards the north, feeling an instinctive pull towards their home far, far away.

Slowly, a score or so at a time, as the Maji came out of his painful episode, the dark creatures resumed their flight to the east.

The mountains were in sight.

Soon, they would see the forest.

Then, not long afterwards, they would feast.

***

The black ships burned brightly upon the sea. Others moored by the wharves were being set alight as the Haigok dived their dragons for the vessels before circling them about for the sky so that they could make another run.

Screams of men, women and infants wailed into the air as waves of orange, red and white heat rolled over buildings both tall and small, falling silent as the flames ate into their flesh.

The ground troops, vastly under-prepared for such horror, did their best to fight back. Arrows were loosed and projectiles shot from catapults. It was all in vain as dragon after dragon swooped over the town, setting the archers and mechanised slings ablaze.

The monolithic stone tower, the palace of the Lilac Queen, toppled onto several smaller structures as two winged beasts used their strength to push it over. The barracks, a single-levelled building made mostly of timber, was instantly covered in grey and black stone.

She gripped her chest as her city crumbled and scorched.

The sensation of loss had hit her as her personal guards guided her through ravines and clefts. They climbed into the hills to Blackshore's east, up steep embankments and always keeping to weather-worn troughs and gullies where they could.

Tears streamed over her cheeks and caused her vision to blur. It wasn't the destruction behind her that caused the emotion. Nor was it the sound of horses, men, women, or even children screaming that made her feel this way.

Claire, the Olive Queen, her sister of the Seven, was dead.

"This way, my queen," one of her men said, taking her by the hand and leading her up a steep embankment.

She put her hand out to steady herself, pressing the bare skin of her palm to the icy snow covering the ground. Her frame of mind was so confused that she barely recalled how they had made it through the streets of Blackshore and onto the open ground between the township and the rugged hillsides.

Shadows passed overhead, and she feared the dragons had found her.

"What was that?" she gasped, pulling back.

"Trees, my queen," the guard answered, understanding her apprehension. He saw the moisture covering her face. Reaching into his pocket, he retrieved a kerchief and wiped her tears away. "Just trees."

She moved her gaze over the features of the man. Four long scars stretched from his forehead on the left side of his face to the jaw on his right. His untidy black hair reached over his shoulders, a rebellious lock filtering over his right eye to touch his cheek.

Behind him, tall pine trees stretched high into the sky as they followed the terrain into the sharp hills that overlooked Blackshore. She turned to see dragons, at least twenty, circling through the smoke clouds that drifted from the city and out to sea. Several of the flying monsters dived towards the ground, spewing long jets of flame into untouched structures to the southern end of the township.

It suddenly reminded her of stories that the old custodian of Woodmyst, Richard Dering, had told her when she was a younger woman. Stories of how the Haigok, the Night Demons he had called them, brought two dragons and destroyed his city.

The tale had frightened her then. Cloaked figures maliciously and relentlessly brought death with them from the air and on the ground. Fire from above and blood from the earth. Attacks when the sun had gone below and the dark had risen.

The Night Demons, she thought.

Only here they were in the day.

She felt just as afraid as she did when she had heard those stories.

"We must flee, my queen," the guard told her. "There's nothing we can do here. Our only hope is in Erimoor."

She nodded, finding new courage.

"Lead the way, Braden," she said.

***

Magistrate Stephen Latham was a tall, lean man with a leathery face and a thinning crop of hair sprinkled with silver flecks. He reminded Arthur of a well-travelled saddle. Every time he smiled, or frowned, the lines around his cheeks deepened and his brow creased like furrows in a field.

"This is an excellent tea," he said to the boy as he placed his mug on the table. Arthur sat across from him, facing towards the sitting room where David and Becka had taken up position, keeping in his view.

"Thank you, Magistrate," Arthur replied with a grin.

"Stephen," the other offered. "I don't much like titles."

"You don't?"

Latham shook his head, clearly taken aback by the question.

"It's just that I have heard people talk about my wife, referring to her as their queen. I was under the impression that you may have had something to do with that."

"Sorry." The other shook his head. "That was the action of the people, not I. I have never met your wife. I saw her from a distance when she swooped over the city on her dragon, but that was it. I have no opinion whether she should be queen or otherwise."

Arthur nodded. "I don't believe she likes titles much, either. She would probably prefer to remain simply as Alice than to be called queen. I will let her decide when she returns." Arthur sipped from his mug and put it down on the table before him. He thought of the dank prison cell in which he had once been kept. He remembered the sour stench of sweat and blood, the sound of incessant dripping as moisture built upon the ceiling and walls, the clang of gates and jingle of keys. "Tell me, Stephen. How do the prisoners fare?"

"Truthfully," he answered as he lifted his mug from the table, "I don't think they will last the winter. Our food stores are just enough to get Woodmyst through the hardest months ahead, the prisoners included. But there's a shortage of timber and linen."

"We can cut down more trees," David called from the sitting room. "That's easy enough."

"Yes," Latham agreed, "but we can't spin yarn and sew fabric fast enough to make extra blankets and clothing for the fifty people in the cells."

"Fifty?" David queried.

"Mostly bookkeepers loyal to Takmel," Latham replied. "Some officers of the guard. I dare say there are more, still walking the streets of Woodmyst, that gave their ear freely to the Maji. It's impossible to know who. In any case, we don't have enough blankets in store for the prisoners we are keeping in the cells."

"Takmel sent supplies to the glade," Becka added. "There was plenty of blankets and linen."

"That's true," the other replied. "But I don't believe the Maji thought it possible that he would be overthrown and his followers put into prison." He placed his attention upon Arthur. "Perhaps we could send word to the people of the glade that we require some stores that are kept there."

"No," Arthur answered abruptly. "The people of the glade need those supplies. There are younglings out there. We do what we can with what we have here."

"I saw tapestries in the Assembly Hall," David informed his son.

"Enormous sheets of fabric," Arthur agreed.

"Wait—" Latham shot glances at both of them. "You're not suggesting what I think you're suggesting? They were the last cultural remnants of both Oldcastle and Belburn. They signify Woodmyst is a city that a union of diverse people have built. They announce we welcome others from far and wide. We had planned to continue to add to that gallery as more and more come to live here."

Arthur felt the magistrate's anguish. Since his early childhood, he had loved reading and absorbing information about history and distant cultures. He enjoyed learning about how civilisations had been formed under the coming together of differing peoples.

Yet there was a need that had to be met.

"Woodmyst was here long before those tapestries were hung in the hall," the boy started. "It was here long before that hall was constructed, and even before the first walls stood and the Great Hall was opened.

"This city has weathered much change over time. It has grown from a small village to a large, fortified township. Then the Haigok brought their dragons, and it was all turned to ruin. Only the children survived and they lifted it from the ashes and start over again.

"In such a short time," Arthur continued, "my father has seen a tiny settlement grow. People came from far and wide to escape the Mirikin. They didn't go to Newholt, or flee over the sea to Dendadia. They came here, to a place with a few huts and crude farming implements with men carrying chipped blades that their fathers once used. These remnants had survived trials unlike any have seen since the Realm Wars.

"Together, these people built new walls, a new hall, paved streets and stronger houses to live in. We are creating a new history.

"I don't want to see those relics of old destroyed," Arthur assured the old man. "But I don't want to be held accountable for anyone perishing because we couldn't supply them with blankets.

"We can make new tapestries. We can try to recreate those hanging in the Assembly Hall at a later date. But, for now, they are cloth that can be distributed for the sake of keeping people warm. Perhaps, by making such a sacrifice, these prisoners may see that we intend to keep them safe and alive. Maybe they may recant their allegiance to the Maji and turn away from him."

Latham looked at the table and pursed his lips. The lines in his cheeks deepened.

"You're right," he said. "I'll order the lowering of the tapestries and have them divided into adequate portions immediately."

"Thank you." Arthur got to his feet and extended his hand to the magistrate, signalling that the meeting was over.

After seeing the older man to the door, Arthur returned to the kitchen. David and Becka were clearing the table.

"You know," Becka said, "some people here may not like the decision you have just made."

"If they are willing to give up their blankets to save the tapestries, then they can go right ahead," the boy replied.

"I think you did well, son," David offered. "It's a tough decision, but I think it was the right one."

"Thank you, Papa," Arthur smiled. "I hope you're right."

Twenty-One

They set a pyre upon a rocky outcrop that stretched a short distance into the sea. Flames spiralled in the wind and quickly took the Olive Queen, whom they wrapped delicately in linen before being placed on the wood.

Alice felt a deep sorrow as she watched women and young children among the gathered crowd wail and sob. She noticed the odd despising glare being shot in her direction from men who held onto their loved ones tightly, mourning the loss of their queen.

The girl had left her own people on the ground that overlooked the outcrop. She could sense them watching her, concerned for her safety. Emily, Akasati, Amicia, Brondt... all of them. Alice would have attended the pyre on her own, but the others had demanded that she take an escort. So, there she was, paying her respects with Nola'ee and Yuri by her sides.

The Dellmoor army, if that is what they could be called, lined up as neatly as they could, dressed in their fatigues and standing at attention. Their commander was a few paces in front of them, weeping profusely.

Alice felt an immense amount of guilt, believing she was responsible.

She had forced Claire's hand.

What other choice was there?

If the Olive Queen had fought, the whole town would be in ruin and many innocent people hurt, or worse, dead.

If she had surrendered herself and joined Alice, she would have Takmel taunting her and torturing her relentlessly through her thoughts and dreams.

Claire didn't have the same protection that Catherine had experienced. Catherine was blessed with the joining of the Four. The guidance of her younger sister covered her.

Sadly, Claire had lost her prime. There was no longer any provision such a safeguard as the Four had been.

Alice understood that the Olive Queen had been connected to the remaining three sorceresses of the Seven. However, their power was vastly subsiding without Joanne to bring focus. The Maji spread his brides far and wide, hoping to build his kingdom through them. His scheme was failing. Claire's act of sacrifice was proof of that. She was, essentially, on her own.

As Alice pondered this, the commander of the Dellmoor army turned and stepped towards her. He unsheathed his sword.

Yuri tensed and placed his hand on the hilt of his blade.

The commander lifted his sword and carried it in both hands, arms outstretched and palms up with his fingers splayed.

Alice signalled the Agrodien with a wave of her hand, to be at ease.

The commander lowered himself to one knee before the girl and bowed his head.

"My name is Dwight Ryall," he said. Tears stains covered his cheeks. "I know little about the formalities of surrender. I'm just a fisherman. I don't know why you came here, or what you had against our queen, but she is gone now. We don't have enough men to fight against you and to stand a chance of winning.

"Take what you want from our stores. Claim whatever it is that you came for. But, please, don't hurt any of my people. We aren't warriors. We won't resist. We surrender."

He offered his sword by lifting it to her.

Alice felt a tear spill from her eye.

"Sheathe your sword," she said. "We didn't come to take anything from you. What is yours will remain yours."

He looked at her, his brow furrowed.

"Then, why did you come?"

Alice turned her face to the pyre.

"For her," she told him. "For the one that she represented."

"The Maji?" Dwight shook his head, confused. "He has never been here. I don't believe he has ever seen this place. Not even from a distance."

"She gave him strength." She looked back to the man kneeling before her. "He took power from her. They were joined."

"She loved her husband," said Dwight.

"Takmel," Alice put in.

"No," he replied. "There was another. Geofrey. Before the Maji. She loved him, right until the end."

"I don't understand," Alice said, confused. "What are you telling me?"

"She can't have been joined to the Maji all that well, if she loved this Geofrey, could she?" Dwight sobbed. "I heard her say his name all the time. She would sit by the fire and whisper words to him when she thought she was alone. Like a wife to a husband. Geofrey, not Maji or Takmel. Geofrey. Geofrey."

Dwight had become a blubbering mess.

Several men standing behind him had also wept.

In such a short time, Claire had truly become the beloved Queen of Dellmoor.

Alice felt a lump in her throat grow and tears stream down her face as she watched the kneeling man drop the sword upon the black rock with a clang. He fell upon his hands and cried.

***

The army marched onward to the north. There was no reason for them to dally. The people of Dellmoor appeared unwilling to accommodate them after Claire's demise. Alice did not want to upset them any more than they had been already, so she ordered them to continue their journey.

Ostford was the next settlement along the coast, at least a full day's march away. She could reach it with the Haigok and their dragons quickly enough, but after the episode with the straw men near

Greyrose, she thought it best to stay within sight of the ground forces and the fleet upon the sea.

The sun was already past the highest point in the sky. Alice knew they wouldn't make Ostford before dusk was upon them. They would need to set up camp for the night.

Alice guided Liana high into the air. The chill of the northern wind seeped through her thick layers of clothing to touch her skin. The dragon gave a friendly chirp as eight more flying beasts swooped after her, carrying their Haigok riders.

The girl turned her head and peered over Liana's side, where she saw the multitude of infantry and horsemen moving along the coast. She looked out to the sea, where twelve ships tacked through the waves.

Far ahead, barely visible through the haze of cloud and drifting snow, were several wide clearings surrounded by many thickets and groupings of wooded lands. There were no hills of any decent size. No place to really take shelter from the weather.

The ground was mostly flat and exposed.

She signalled Erugoth, leader of the Kazrekh Clan, and gestured to an area ahead of them. It was a large glade bordered by a thin stream on its south and a thick pine forest on all other sides.

The clan leader waved his fist in the air to draw the attention of his fellow riders and dived for the ground below. Eight dragons fled for the clearing as Alice turned Liana around to retrace their course.

Eventually, the dragon landed a few yards ahead of the marching army. Emily and Catherine galloped alongside Brondt and Amicia so as to meet her.

"We saw the others lower to the ground," Catherine called to her sister. "Is everything all right?"

"Fine," Alice replied from Liana's back. She looked to Brondt. "We found a place that I think will be suitable for the night. Go directly north and through that woodland. You will find a stream with a clearing on the other side. We will camp there."

"What about Commander Zakhar?" he asked. "Can he reach the campsite easily enough?"

"No," she answered. "The forests cover the coastland. I will go out to him and let him know the situation. He will need to anchor his ships and have his men stay on board for the night."

With that, she urged the dragon back into the sky and took off to the west.

"It must be marvellous to be up there," Brondt said as he watched Alice and her dragon lift into the air. "I can't imagine what the world would look like from so high."

"Good enough to see our next campsite." Emily smiled. "We should keep moving. The light won't stay this good forever."

***

Gruloch returned with the rest of the dragon riders as the sun vanished below the horizon. They had set the campsite up and many fires were already burning with game set over the flames on spits or grills that the soldiers had brought with them.

"Blackshore is gone," the Haigok leader said as he joined the group seated with Alice. The girl offered him some venison, holding out a portion of meat attached to a skewer. He held up his hand and shook his head. "I'll sup with my clan's folk. Thank you all the same."

"Did you see the Lilac Queen?" Catherine asked.

"I did not. There were none that could have survived the attack. We burnt all the ships in their harbour and sank those that were already underway. She could not have escaped."

"She is still alive," Alice told him before tearing a piece of the skewered meat away with her teeth.

"We would have noticed," he assured her, giving the girl a confused look.

"We would have noticed if you had killed her," Ursula informed him. Gruloch shook his head in disbelief.

"It's impossible," he said, looking around at the faces gathered by the fire. "Nothing survived in the city. Nothing."

"She escaped," Amicia put in. "It's that simple. She found a way out."

The Haigok appeared shattered. He looked to Alice apologetically.

"I am so sorry," he said.

"Not your fault," the girl replied with her mouth full.

"Alice," Emily reprimanded. "Wait until you swallow to speak."

The girl forced the food down her throat.

"Sorry, Mama," she said before turning her attention to Gruloch. "It's not your fault. Don't be so upset about it. We'll catch up with her soon enough. Besides, you took out their fleet. That was your objective. You did a good job, my friend."

"Some of it," he interjected. "There are still more ships in the north."

"We'll get to them soon enough."

"What of the path to the north?" Thornton asked. "Is the land clear ahead of us?"

Gruloch nodded.

"As best as we could see," he replied. "There is a narrow stone bridge, with stone towers on either end, reaching over a wide gorge with high cliffs on either side."

"The Griralith Pass," Schoenbach put in.

"We circled it a few times to see if we could spy any defences," Gruloch said. He shook his head. "There were none that we noticed. The bridge looks strong, but only wide enough to take one wagon at a time. It will slow our progress. There is a settlement a few leagues north of the pass. It is empty and falling to ruin, but it will suffice for shelter."

"That must be Meadowmoor," Akasati told them. "Not much more than a seaside village. It has probably been empty since the time of the Mirikin."

Alice looked into the flames and pondered what the others had told her.

"We'll leave at first light," she informed them. "Commander Brondt will lead the ground forces for the bridge over the Griralith Pass." She moved her attention to Gruloch. "The clans will offer support from above and circle the ground forces, especially when they are crossing the bridge. That will be when we are at our most vulnerable." Keeping her eyes on Gruloch, she pointed to him with the skewer of meat. "You and I, however, will go north to Meadowmoor and take a closer look just to see how suitable it is to our needs."

"Kayl'sro," Yuri growled from her side. Alice turned to face him. He spoke to her in his tongue. "I must object to you going alone with Gruloch. One of us should accompany you."

She hesitated and pursed her lips.

"I don't have a saddle that can take another on Liana's back," she replied in kind.

"I can press myself against your back and hold on to the straps by your sides," he suggested.

She shook her head and looked to Nola'ee, seated with Nakrah across the fire from her.

"I'll take my personal guard," Alice told the other.

Yuri looked over at the female Agrodien and nodded.

"Yes, Kayl'sro."

She turned to the others and spoke so they could all understand.

"We had best inform our people that we leave at first light."

***

Slowly, one by one, the stars twinkled to life.

A harsh, stiff wind blew down from the mountains. The dense forest grew quiet as darkness crept over the land, drawing thicker shadows beneath the pines and making the bare limbs of oaks and maples look more and more like gnarled, twisted fingers stretching into the cloudless sky.

The sound of trickling, bubbling water drew them away from their run. They were parched, exhausted, and ready to drop where they were.

The desire to feed upon the flesh of man, placed upon them by their master, pulled them towards the forest. They sensed their journey was nearing its end. The image of mountains and trees had haunted their thoughts and drawn them to this place.

The road through the woods was right beneath their feet. The forest reclaimed most of the passage, covering it with vegetation, but the old divots made by many wagon wheels during many journeys over many years were abundantly discernible.

It wasn't very far now.

But it would have to wait.

The master would have to wait.

Thirst, a stronger urge, drew them to the water's edge. They swarmed and pressed against one another there, clicking and screeching as they lowered their heads to drink.

Darkness grew, and the light dissipated quickly.

One by one, the creatures had their fill and moved away from the river's edge.

One by one, they regrouped. Hundreds of them.

One by one, they placed their thoughts back upon the promise that their master had made to them.

One by one, they felt the urge to feed build up again.

As one, they ran into the forest, following the road to the east, the road to Woodmyst.

Twenty-Two

Stalekk Rank'sku walked across the quarterdeck, gesturing to the stack of barrels positioned on the newly constructed pier next to the *Gypsy*. They were the first crew to have their ship moored to the dock.

"I need those barrels of water loaded into the hold before we knock off for the night," the tall, dark man shouted.

"Come on, Stalekk," one of the younger crewmen whined. "It's already night and we're all tired. There's got to be fifty of those things there."

"Well." Rank'sku put his hands on his hips and turned to face the complainer. "I could light some more lamps for you. Or perhaps you would like me to fetch you a blanket and sing you a lullaby."

Some of the crew laughed as they started towards the awaiting cargo.

"Sing us all a song, Stalekk," one of the older men called back.

The first officer smiled, his large white teeth almost glowing.

"Sorry, sir," the younger crewman offered.

Rank'sku slapped him on the back.

"It's all right, son," he replied. "We're all tired. We're all cold. But this is the last of what we need to put on board today. The sooner we get it done, the sooner we can rest."

He stepped down from the quarterdeck and made his way to the gangplank that stretched from ship to pier. Joining the queue of crewmen, he waited his turn to help with the work. Two by two, the men shuffled barrels or struggled to carry them back onto the *Gypsy*. Rank'sku, however, hoisted a whole barrel onto his shoulder with a loud grunt. On his own, he carried the load across the plank and onto the ship.

"That's a crewman's job," Captain Davine Staiger told him as he passed her on his way across the deck. She was leaning against the wall by the door that opened to a set of descending stairs. She folded her arms across her chest and her cavalier hat sat askew upon her head.

"Have me whipped if it pleases you," he said as he passed her.

"I just might." She smirked and started across the deck towards the pier.

"Captain on deck," someone shouted. All the men froze in place, some plonking their barrels down upon the deck or wharf to stand at attention. She looked over at all of her men, puzzled.

"Get yer arses moving," she hollered. "I don't want to be out here all bloody night."

"Ay, Captain," they shouted, resuming their work instantly.

She moved to lean her rump against the banister next to the gangplank. She watched the men move back and forth for some time before moving her gaze towards the sound of hammering and sawing a short distance away.

Another pier was being constructed beneath the glow of lamp lights and the watchful eye of Sub-Commander Landon Wake.

She wanted so much to be there with him.

Anywhere with him would be better.

The truth was, she wouldn't be able to drag him away from his work, no matter how much she tried. An obsessive behaviour had overtaken him and he had made it his personal mission to complete all five piers before the return of Queen Amicia and Commander Brondt.

I need to do this;; he had told her. *I need to.*

She knew he felt responsible, if not entirely guilty, for what had happened to Newholt during the Black Queen's short, but terrible, reign. He had suffered sleepless nights and barely touched his food during their suppers together.

Using her wiles and charms, she had distracted him long enough to give him some relief. It was only temporary. He would always return his thoughts to how he had failed the city, and how he could atone for his failure.

They had constructed three new piers. Finishing touches would need to apply to the other two before more vessels could dock alongside them. The *Gypsy* was berthed to the only fully operating pier.

For five whole days, construction had increased and kept underway without ceasing. Teams had taken shifts, three per day, and Wake had been there, overseeing it all, for a little over two days without rest.

Staiger went to him to draw him away, just long enough to sleep for a while. He had insisted that he stay and complete the task. She was growing more and more concerned for him with each passing moment.

In desperation, she had turned to the Whores of Whitekeep for help. She had asked them to speak to him and convince him to come home. They declined to intervene directly, but implored the newly appointed Sheriff of Newholt to act instead.

Monteacute agreed.

He offered to speak to Sub-Commander Wake as a friend, offering assistance on the worksite by overseeing some of the minor tasks. Surprisingly, Wake took up the offer and, after seeing how much the people of the city respected the man after his demonstration of leadership during the uprising, placed Sheriff Monteacute as second in charge.

That had been three days ago.

Still, Wake remained on the worksite. He had not returned home, nor had he visited Staiger while she worked on the *Gypsy* a short walk away. She thought she would need to order her crew to kidnap him, and tie him to her bed, just to force him to take a rest.

The incessant hammering echoed across the water.

The biting, grinding sound of hand saws continued to ring into the darkness.

"He needs time," a deep, soft voice said from her side. Rank'sku had returned from below deck.

"I know," she replied. "But, I need him. I can help him if he would let me."

The first officer placed his hand gently on her shoulder.

"Work sometimes helps a man with his thoughts," he told her. "He may be trying to spare you from his pain."

"I don't want him to spare me, Stalekk." She felt a lump form in her throat and fought the urge to cry. "I want him to talk to me."

"He will," the other said. "But, he needs time."

***

Monteacute waited at the land's edge of the fourth pier. Wake was at the far end, making his way back towards the sheriff, stepping across the newly constructed boardwalk to inspect every inch of it.

The sub-commander pointed this way and that, speaking to men positioned along the length of the dock, no doubt telling them what needed more attention before the work was done. Now and then, he stopped his approach to stamp his boot against a plank. Monteacute saw the other crouch several times, and remove his glove to knock his knuckles on the timber before standing back to his full height.

It seemed that Sub-Commander Landon Wake had become a bit of an expert at carpentry since taking on this task. However, Monteacute suspected the man had never laid a finger upon a hammer before he had ordered the construction of the wharves.

A thud drew Monteacute's attention away for a moment.

Two barges waited offshore, only a stone's throw away to his right. A large machine linked the two vessels. It rose high into the air with tall timber columns reaching up from the decks of the floating platforms. Two thick cross beams joined the top of the columns, long enough to keep the two barges set far enough apart so that construction on the fifth and final pier went unhindered.

The fifth pier was nothing more than a frame that stretched a few yards from the water's edge. Apart from the two barges, there were no other workers to be seen.

A winch nestled at the centre of the cross beams, linked with chains and pulleys that moved along in both directions to the timber columns and down to the deck of both barges. There, the chains attached to massive crank wheels, which were each operated by two men. As the men turned the wheels, the winch emitted a series of loud, repetitive, almost melodic clinks.

Monteacute watched as the chain retracted, lifting a giant iron weight out of the water. The weight had a flat base and, from the sheriff's viewpoint, could have easily weighed as much as a hundred men. Maybe more.

Slowly, it lifted until it almost touched the cross beams. A loud metallic clunk resonated from each of the barges as the workers locked the weight into position.

"Set?" one man called from the vessel closest to Monteacute.

"Forward," another on the other barge shouted, gesturing with his hand out to sea as he looked up to the weight, then down to a timber pylon sticking out of the water. Two men, one on each barge, lifted long poles from the side of the decks and used them to push the vessels away from shore. "Whoa!" the second man called, holding his hand up as his eyes lined up the weight and the half-submerged pylon.

"Swinging," another shouted. The sheriff looked up to see that the weight was rocking back and forwards.

"Wait," the second man ordered, watching the weight as it slowed. "Wait."

"How are your teams faring?" a voice asked from Monteacute's side, causing him to jump a little. He turned to see Wake standing beside him. He had been so entranced by the barge operation that he hadn't noticed the other at all.

"Fine," the sheriff answered. "They're just waiting for your men to finish on four so they can get back to work."

Wake gave him a perplexed look before wiping his eye with the heel of his hand.

"You've finished the others already?"

"All done," Monteacute told him. "You can go and see for yourself. Moorings are all in place. We've put guard rails at the ends and entrances. They'll take any of those ships out there." He pointed to several vessels that were anchored offshore.

"These men are almost done here," Wake said, gesturing to the men on the fourth dock. He yawned. "When's the next shift change?"

"Soon," the sheriff answered. "You should take this one for yourself."

"You say that every time," the other smiled. "We have one more to go."

"Let me take it," Monteacute said.

"Now!" came a shout from the barges.

Both men turned in time to see the massive weight fall from the crossbeam. It hit fair and square against the top of the pylon with an almighty crack, knocking it deeper into the ground beneath the water. The weight then fell to the side to plummet beneath the waves.

"Pull it up," one man hollered.

"I can get a team started on the planks for number five," Monteacute told Wake as the rhythmic clink of the winch resounded. "Another to finish the work on four. And you can go and lie in the arms of that beautiful sea captain of yours. She's over there right now." He pointed to the *Gypsy*, moored not too far from where they stood. "I think she stays on board to work, just so that she can be close to you."

The sub-commander stared at the incomplete framework of the fifth pier.

"There's still a great deal that needs to be done," he said.

"And these men will do it," the sheriff assured him. "Even if you aren't here to see it."

Wake looked at him, offering a wry smile.

"You know how to make a man feel needed," he said. "You know that?"

Monteacute grinned, placed a friendly hand on the other's shoulder and gestured to the *Gypsy* with his chin.

"Go on," he whispered. "Get out of here."

Pursing his lips, Wake gave a nod and simply walked away, towards the *Gypsy*, without saying another word.

"Well, that was easy," Monteacute said under his breath, moving his gaze back to the men on the barges. "Only took three days."

***

His step seemed lighter, a burden lifted from his shoulders, as he walked briskly along the waterfront. The sound of hammering and sawing faded away slightly as his mind focussed upon her.

He passed by pier three, where two men were whitewashing the tips of the pylons which jutted above the boardwalk to knee height. Shortly after, he passed by pier two.

From there, he could see the large hulk of the *Gypsy*. The crew was busying themselves with cargo, heavy barrels that needed two men to move along the gangplank between the dock and the ship.

He followed their movement from the wharf to the vessel and held his stare when his eyes reached the gangway.

There she was.

Captain Davine Staiger.

His heart skipped a beat, and his feet froze in place.

It was almost as if he was seeing her for the first time. Seeing her for the first time in a long while, at least.

The cavalier hat pulled slightly to one side, hiding her eyes from him. The long, dark braid draped over her shoulder. The coat hung to her ankles, pushed back by her hands resting upon her small waist. The hilt of her rapier attached to her hip glistened in the lantern light as she supervised the work.

A giant of a man, tall and dark, stood at her side. Wake knew him to be Stalekk Rank'sku, the First Officer of the *Gypsy*. They were speaking together. As Staiger pointed and barked something to some men gathered on the dock, the sound of her voice reaching Wake's ears but not allowing him to hear her words clearly, Rank'sku peered over to him.

A wide smile grew upon the first officer's face.

Rank'sku nudged Staiger, who gave him a stern look of reprimand in return. The tall man, still grinning, gestured with a nod towards Wake.

Staiger turned, misinterpreting the first officer's signal to be aimed more towards the sound of construction. She looked past Wake with an expression of urgency, hope. Wake felt his heart sink as he watched her face turn to disappointment as she turned and scolded Rank'sku, punching the first officer on the left shoulder.

The big man flinched, stepped away and brought his hand up to his shoulder and offered his captain a foul look. He then pointed to the sub-commander of Newholt.

By this time, Wake had started walking towards them again. He could hear the exchange given from Rank'sku to his captain.

"Down there, you silly bitch."

Staiger turned and saw him this time.

A broad smile spread over her face. From Wake's position, she appeared to be laughing. Suddenly, she turned with fire in her eyes and punched Rank'sku again, this time in the face.

"Never call me *silly*," she hollered as the first officer collapsed on the deck. As quick as that, her countenance changed, and her smile returned.

She pushed past the crewmen and started down the gangplank. Once she had reached the pier, she started running. Within moments, she was in the sub-commander's arms with her lips planted firmly against his.

The crew of the *Gypsy* stopped what they were doing to applaud and cheer at the spectacle.

Staiger pulled away from Wake and turned to them with a scowl.

"Get back to work," she hollered. And they did, instantly.

She pressed herself against Wake again and kissed him again.

"Let's go home," he suggested after a moment.

She nodded and offered a sweet giggle in reply.

First Officer Stalekk Rank'sku pulled himself back to his feet, with the help of the guardrail, just in time to watch the couple stroll away hand in hand.

The smile returned, but it was only temporary as his jaw throbbed painfully. Stars started spinning around and his eyes rolled back into his head. Within moments, he came crashing back down to the deck again.

Twenty-Three

David stood rigid. His heart was racing and a cold sweat had trickled down his spine.

The fire in the stone hearth was ablaze, and the room appeared untroubled. Arthur, making a pot of tea, looked at him with curiosity and urgency at the same time.

Becka, seated on a chair beside David's, looked up to the big man. To Arthur, she appeared as frightened as he did.

It was the distant clanging sound of a bell in one of the guard towers that had set them on edge.

"It couldn't be," she whispered, peering towards the door. "Could it?"

David shook his head and moved away towards the bedrooms.

"It couldn't be what?" Arthur asked as he left the steaming pot on the bench by the stove. He exited the kitchen and moved into the sitting room to peer towards his father.

"Night Demons," Becka replied.

Another tower chimed. Then another.

"They are our friends," Arthur said. "The Haigok are not our enemies."

"It's not the Haigok," David told them as he emerged from his room. He held his sword in one hand and his leather breastplate in the other. "It couldn't be them. They have gone to the west with Alice."

"Then who?" Becka wondered out loud.

David leant his sword against the wall so he could put his armour on.

"You stay here," he told Arthur. "The wood axe is still by the back door. Fetch it and protect Becka."

Arthur retraced his steps into the kitchen to retrieve the weapon.

"He's only got one arm," Becka said quietly, reminding the big man. "How will he be able to wield such a heavy thing?"

"He chopped all that wood you've been throwing on that fire today," David said, nodding to an enormous pile of timber set neatly by the hearth. "He'll be fine with flesh and bone."

Arthur shut and locked the door behind him as he carried the axe back inside.

"Where will you be?" he asked his father.

"The east tower by the river," David answered. "It's the closest, I think."

"The chimes sound as if they're ringing to the west," Becka supposed.

More towers joined the resounding clangs and peals. Louder and louder. Closer and closer.

"Whoever is out there is moving around the walls," Arthur put in. "They're trying to surround us."

"Protect Becka," David told his son again as he lifted his sword. "And barricade the doors as best as you can." With that, the big man opened the door. The sound of the bells intensified and filled the room. With a quick turn of his head and a nod to the two others, he left the house and moved into the dark street beyond.

Arthur immediately leant the axe against the wall and moved to the doorway, where he watched his father disappear into the night. He then closed the door, locked it and moved to a large cushioned chair positioned against the wall.

With great difficulty, he started pushing the chair towards the door. It wasn't easy for him, manoeuvring such a large piece of bulky furniture with one arm. He struggled, trying to line the back of the seat up with the door, twisting it to the side and thudding against the wall with each step of progress.

"Let me help," Becka said from his side, placing her hands against the armrests and high back of the seat. Together, they propped the heavy seat in place before moving to the kitchen. There, they both pushed the long dining table against the back door.

The ringing of bells was all around them now.

The enemy, whoever it was, had surrounded the city.

***

"Commander," called a crewman, resting his elbows against the guardrail. He held a spyglass to his eye, aiming it carefully towards the shoreline.

"What is it, sailor?" Zakhar asked, walking swiftly down the stairs from the quarterdeck. He pulled his own spyglass from his coat pocket as he stepped up to the rail.

"Movement, sir," the other replied. "There are people on the ground."

"Probably just our friends out for a hunt," the commander offered, lifting the short telescope to his eye.

"I don't think so, sir," the other answered. "They don't move like people. Not really."

"Agrodien, perhaps?" Zakhar said. Then he saw them.

The thin, gangly forms seemed to have a stiff motion. The sight was odd indeed.

They appeared as mere shadows moving through the darkness beneath the trees. If it wasn't for the contrasting snow piled on the ground and weighing the limbs of the pines down, they might have gone unnoticed, disappearing into the darkness of the night.

"I think I saw the dragons land in the direction that they are heading, sir," another spotter announced.

"Should we fire a payload, sir?" called another.

"And risk injuring our friends?" Zakhar answered. "I think not."

A deep silence ensued. Every man with a spyglass watched on helplessly as the figures continued to move through the forest by the shore.

"I can't keep count," a spotter stated. "They just keep coming."

"Lemme see," a young lad pleaded.

"Master Gunner," shouted Zakhar.

"Aye, sir?" an officer called from farther along the rail. He quickly stashed his own spyglass into his coat pocket and stood to attention.

"Pack powder and two empty barley sacks into a port-side cannon," the commander ordered.

"Aye, sir," the officer saluted and moved away.

"Make it ring loud, Master Gunner."

"Aye, sir," the officer replied as he moved below to the gun deck.

***

"What was that?" Catherine queried as she peered into the sky, expecting to see lightning.

"I don't think it's a storm," Amicia told her.

"That wasn't thunder you heard," Schoenbach explained as he got to his feet. He turned towards the west, towards the direction of the coast. Tall trees stood between the campsite and the ocean. "That was a cannon."

Alice and the Agrodiens were on their feet, peering to the north. The sound of tapping and crunching echoed through the trees towards them, growing louder and louder.

The dragons, nestled together at the eastern edge of the clearing, started growing restless. They growled and hissed, turning their faces towards the tree line that surrounded them. In turn, the horses tethered a little farther to the south snorted and pawed the ground nervously. Their agitated state alarmed the soldiers.

"Have the Dendadians engaged in battle?" Jendryng enquired.

"I only heard one shot," Sparrow put in. "That doesn't make a battle in my way of thinking."

"That was a warning," Alice told them.

"Something is coming." Ursula pointed to the edge of the clearing to the northeast. "There."

All turned their faces to where she was pointing.

There, standing silently between two trees, stood a lean figure with twisted limbs of timber, and sinew and muscle formed of straw and stems. Gnarled wooden fingers with sharp claws bent and stretched as the figure stared blankly, with hollow sockets burrowed into its tightly wound grass face.

"Gruloch," Alice hollered.

"I see it," the Haigok roared as he started towards his dragon.

"There are others," the girl called out.

Gruloch stopped to see.

More figures stepped into the clearing near to where the first had appeared. More followed closely.

The sound of tapping and snapping grew louder and louder as more and more thin figures stepped onto the clearing's edge.

Soon, the campsite was completely surrounded.

Suddenly, the sounds emitting from the forest ceased, and the air grew silent and heavy.

Hundreds of faceless forms stood motionless, leering towards the inhabitants of the clearing. Hundreds more waited in the shadows beyond.

Alice tightened her grip on the swords in her hands. The leather on the hilts creaked beneath her fingers. Her knuckles cracked slightly.

"What do we do?" Gruloch asked. His voice shook slightly. It was the first time that Alice had sensed any fear in him.

"Well," William Vawdrey replied. "I don't know about you, but I think I'm going to shit my britches."

**

David climbed the ladder inside the tower, listening to the tolling bell above him and the clicks and screeches of the creatures gathering outside the walls. He stepped upon the platform, about halfway up the tower's interior, and through a doorway that led to the parapet.

Men of similar age to himself were peering through the battlements to the sight below them. He started along the walkway, moving towards the river.

"David," a familiar voice called from behind him. He turned to see Andris holding a bow in his hand, a quiver of arrows over his shoulder.

"How long have you been here?" the older man shouted over the din of the clanging chime.

"Just got here before you," the other replied. "Come. Lor found us a place closer to the stable house."

The wall walk was filling as more and more men emerged from the towers, and still more moved through the streets to aid in the defence of their home. David had to sidestep past a small crowd of soldiers gathered to the north of the tower he had climbed.

"You should spread yourselves out a little, lads," he told them politely.

They stood in place as he brushed by them, offering sour looks.

"Move your arses," Andris barked, stepping towards them aggressively. "Do what you're told."

"Sir," one of them replied, instantly recognising the commander of the Black Forces. The group instantly disbanded.

"This way," Andris said calmly to David. It was as if a different person had surfaced, a gentleman suddenly taking over from the assertive soldier.

The clanging bells continued to ring out across the city. Each strike was setting David's teeth on edge.

Following, he moved with Andris, dodging others who were trying to find their place along the wall until they came to Lor. He had half of his body leaning over the edge of the wall so he could peer down to the ground directly below. Andris tapped him on the hip, causing him to turn about.

"What do you see?" the younger man asked.

"Those strange animals of Takmel's," Lor answered. "A lot of them. We should get hot oil up here and scald the bastards."

"No time," Andris replied. "They already have the city surrounded."

"We should stop those bloody bells," David remarked.

"Agreed," the other nodded. He placed two fingers in his mouth and let out a sharp whistle. He started waving his arms at the men on the tower. They didn't notice him.

Others standing near Andris joined him, waving their hands and shouting to get the tower guards' attention. Within moments, they were chorusing together, "Stop the bells. Stop the bells."

The sound of their voices must have reached the guards, as the tolling from the closest tower ceased soon after. The chanting agitated the creatures below, who started screeching louder and louder.

The towers by the East Gate fell silent. The three men turned their attention towards it in time to see many arrows being fired towards the ground, directly down the side of the wall.

"There." Lor pointed to the closest of the two gate towers as he leant over the edge of the wall. "They're climbing."

David peered over the edge and saw numerous dark forms clambering up the stonework in great haste, like insects. He grabbed Lor by the scruff of the neck and pulled him back onto the wall walk.

"Swords," he called as he and the other man fell to the platform just as two menacing white grins appeared above the battlement.

Two other men leapt forward and hacked into the creatures, severing their dark heads away from their slender necks.

"Here they come," Andris hollered as he loaded an arrow onto his bowstring.

Lor looked at David and let out a loud huff.

"Thank you," he managed.

"Save it for after," the big man told him as they both pushed themselves back to their feet.

Several more creatures appeared along the length of the wall, climbing through the battlements and snapping their razor-like teeth. Sword and arrow stopped them and sent them back over the edge to plummet to the ground.

There was no time for celebration as more and more arrived.

"Push them back," Andris called. "Don't let them get by you."

Spears and blades, arrows and axes, hammers and hoes were used to keep the creatures out.

David stabbed and slashed his sword at every dark form that appeared at the wall's edge. One after another, they kept arriving. One after another, they continued to fall.

He knew their numbers were great.

He knew Woodmyst's best fighters were away in the west.

He knew those on the walls were mostly older men who had passed their prime.

It would only be a matter of time before one of these creatures broke through the defences.

***

A steady silence had ensued.

The men of Newholt and Woodmyst kept their gaze fixed upon the figures at the edge of the glade.

The straw men hadn't moved or made a sound since they appeared.

They simply watched with their empty eyes.

None of the troop were willing to move. They were afraid of what might occur if they did.

"Commander Brondt," Alice said in a low voice.

"I'm here."

"Tell your men to arm themselves."

"What?" he asked, turning his head slowly to see most of the soldiers staring at the straw men with nothing more than a morsel of bread, or some other useless item in their hands. "Bloody heck," he snorted before turning abruptly. "Weapons at the ready," Brondt shouted. "You won't beat these bastards with harsh words."

Alice turned to Gruloch.

"Blow the horns," she called. "Get the dragons in the air and command them to burn the tree line."

He nodded and called to the other clan leaders. Within moments, trumpet calls rang out through the clearing.

Several dragons, including Liana, spread their wings and lifted themselves into the sky. The remaining dragons that didn't understand the commands of the horns, soon followed the other flying beasts.

The straw men reacted immediately. They set off at great speed, bursting from the forest and spilling onto the grassland.

"You plan to burn them?" Amicia asked.

"It's the only way," Alice replied.

"You will set the forest alight," the queen put in, a small sense of alarm in her voice. "We'll be trapped."

"We'll be fine," the girl assured her. "But we will need to fight."

The straw men raced over the field towards the camp.

They spread their claws wide.

Their limbs rattled, creaked, and rustled noisily with each step.

"I hope you have something spectacular planned, Kayl'sro," Yuri said in his tongue. His eyes grew wider and wider as countless figures moved from the shadows beneath the trees into the clearing.

Alice raised her brow and cocked her head slightly to the side.

"No," she replied. "Not really."

Twenty-Four

Erugoth of the Kazrekh Clan pressed the horn to his lips and blew a long, single note. The sound trumpeted through the air, signalling the dragons above to circle the edge of the clearing.

He watched the flying beasts carefully as the lead dragon swooped by the southern edge to move over the eastern tree line. Gruloch, standing beside him, pointed to the shadows beneath the pines and made a remark in their tongue. The trumpet sounded again, dipping twice in tone.

The lead dragon, a larger beast than the others, tucked its wings and angled towards the trees. A long jet of flame burst from its mouth and set the trees by the eastern edge alight. The other dragons followed the actions of the first, setting the forest ablaze all around the open ground.

Forms like those of men moved among the flames beneath the burning trees. They continued to move unhindered as the fire engulfed them.

The straw men that had evaded the assault continued charging towards the awaiting army.

Closer and closer they drew as more and more stepped into the clearing with their limbs aflame.

With both hands filled with her swords, Alice charged. She had no intention of waiting for them to come to her.

The Agrodien followed obediently, raising their blades high as they let out an almighty roar.

"What are you fuckers waiting for?" Thornton hollered. "An invitation?"

With that, he charged after the reptilians. His men were close behind.

"Stay here," Brondt instructed Amicia.

"Who will stay with me?" she asked, her eyes darting around to the multitude of straw men emerging from the blazing forest. She gripped Ursula's arm tightly. "Who will protect us?"

"I will," Emily announced, freeing her curved sword from its sheathe. "I will stay to protect my daughter. I will stay to protect you, as well."

Brondt nodded, accepting the offer, and charged after Thornton with many men in tow.

"Why don't you strike them with lightning?" Akasati asked, turning to Ursula.

"I could hit one of the dragons," she replied. "I can't risk it."

She was right to be concerned about using her abilities with the beasts in the air. They were unpredictable, changing altitude and whooshing by one another. But the truth was that she felt less and less confident with her power since the four of the coven started to physically revert to their old selves. She wondered if she truly had any control of the sky.

The horn blew again. Twice.

The lead dragon sent a barrage of flame over the trees to the west, setting more of the woods and many straw men hiding within alight.

At that moment, Alice had reached the closest of the attackers, just to the north of the campsite. She leapt high into the air, over the first few straw men, only to land in the midst of a large pack of them.

In a fluid motion, she swung her swords around her in a wide arc and hacked the legs off all of them.

The enemy fell to the ground, but remained undeterred.

They swiped out at her with their sharp claws and crawled upon their bellies to reach her.

In quick succession, she cut their arms from their bodies before jumping into a few to break their timber ribs into pieces.

They continued to writhe and roll in an attempt to gather themselves together again, to reform.

Nola'ee was first to arrive behind her, followed closely by Yuri. Both Agrodien warriors moved to either side of their Kayl'sro to even the odds.

"Keep them off me," Alice commanded them as she watched Liana fly by. She placed her fingers in her mouth and let out a loud whistle. Liana heard the call, tilted her wings, left the train of dragons circling the clearing and started towards the girl. Alice pointed directly north with one of her swords, hoping that Liana understood her intentions.

The dragon straightened her path and glided over the ground towards the northern tree line, passing over Alice's head and causing the snow to lift in swirling clouds beneath her. It knocked several straw men off their feet. Others blew apart and scattered to the wind.

Liana opened her jaws and thrust a large blast of flame over the woodland.

Alice quickly placed her swords back in the sheaths upon her back and stretched her hands towards the newly formed fire still spilling from the dragon's mouth.

She could feel the intensity and heat flowing through her veins.

She could sense the ripple of the flames upon her flesh.

The fire was in her.

She was the fire.

"Devour," she whispered, closing her fingers into tight balls.

The flames surrounding the clearing moved as one. They swept from the southern edge, moved around in both directions as if it was a torrent wave, and came together directly before the girl.

Intense white light, filled with immense heat, gathered and grew.

The Agrodiens and men engaged in battle shielded their eyes from the bright glow.

Loud hissing ensued as the snow gathered on the ground by the northern tree line melted and steamed away.

A terrible cracking followed as trees directly to the north of them were obliterated.

The straw men kept coming.

***

"What was that?" a crewman on the galleon murmured.

Zakhar and his men had been watching on helplessly as dragons circled above the site where their allies were located. They became mere onlookers as flames leapt into the sky from the forest. In all earnestness, the commander feared the worst had happened as he and the other spotters had continued to witness more and more figures moving towards the battle.

None had emerged, run in the other direction or had escaped to his knowledge.

And now, a bright wave of light, enveloped in flame, rolled towards the north before suddenly vanishing into the night.

Steam and smoke lifted into the air.

The dragons continued to circle.

The straw men continued to advance.

"I hope that was something that our people did," Zakhar remarked.

***

"Gather what you can," Alice called over her shoulder.

Brondt's eyes focused again. He turned to see the girl in time to pull her swords free as she moved towards the north. Glowing cinders rained down around her like red snowflakes. She hacked into a straw man on her left, breaking it to pieces with three quick blows before another attacked from her right. It, too, smashed apart with a few swipes of her swords.

His vision grew clearer, allowing him to see the open ground beyond. The forest to the north had opened like a channel.

The straw men in that direction had all turned to blackened chaff and ash. There was no longer any threat before them.

To the west, east, and south, however, was another tale.

"This way," the commander hollered, pointing his sword after Alice. "This way."

While most of the infantry were engaged in battle, the cavalry quickly tore down tents, threw what they could onto the wagons, and prepared the horses for travel. The Haigok gathered the saddles and bridles for the dragons and tossed them on top of what cargo they had loaded on the carts before joining in the fight.

Warriors on foot and men on horseback surrounded the wagons as they started after Alice. She was already moving into the channel that fire had cut.

Smouldering trees lined the wide corridor on either side. Bare rocks hissed as a light drift of snow fluttered down upon their hot surfaces.

Charred forms crawled upon their bellies, scraping themselves over the blackened ground, stretching out their gnarled fingers.

A quick swipe with one of Alice's blades broke them apart easily enough. A shower of red embers erupted from their bodies as the chaff and burnt timber was smashed to pieces.

Erugoth clambered onto the unsteady cargo of one wagon. He blew his horn as he watched his dragon and pointed to the southern edge of the clearing, hoping that the great beast would see.

A vast mass of straw men had gathered together and raced across the open ground towards them. There was no way that the warriors surrounding the carts could fight the attackers off while keeping those closer to the vehicles at bay.

"Faster," one horseman shouted to the wagon driver.

The wheels rattled loudly. The wooden frame creaked and groaned. The horses huffed and snorted as they pulled the cart as fast as they could.

"This bloody thing will fall apart if I try," the driver snapped back. "You just keep those fuckers off me."

Erugoth blew the horn again.

The straw men advanced at great speed, closing the gap between the mass and the retreating army rapidly.

The attackers beside the wagon continued to swipe at the infantry, who mostly protected the vehicles.

Occasionally, one or two contacted a soldier, tearing torsos open or stripping flesh away with their sharp claws.

The dragons turned towards the advancing straw men that charged across the open ground.

As Erugoth watched, he judged the distance between his position, standing upon the last wagon in the line, and that of the approaching attackers. The gap was closing, closing, closing too quickly.

The lead dragon tilted his wings and dived towards the ground, towards the straw men. His great jaws opened and a bright orange glow filled his mouth.

Erugoth gave a wry smile as he considered they may just survive.

Suddenly, a faceless form stood before him.

One of the nearby straw men had clambered upon the wagon.

It dug its fingers into the Haigok's belly and twisted its hand, tearing a great gash open.

Feeling pain, but not deterred, Erugoth reached up with his hands, dropping the horn onto the cargo by his feet, and tore the figure's head from its neck.

There was a loud crack as the head came free. A great deal of straw and chaff fell for the wound on the scarecrow's neck.

But it wasn't enough to stop the straw man from sinking its other claw into the Haigok's belly, creating a fresh wound beside the other.

A warm flow of blood ran down Erugoth's crotch and legs.

The straw man recoiled its fingers and raised them above its shoulders.

The Haigok saw small, wet pieces of himself dangling from the ends of the figure's sharp fingers. He let out a soft grunt as he dropped to his knees.

At that moment, a great fireball expanded across the clearing just to the south of the fleeing wagon.

The straw man's arms came down violently, aiming towards Erugoth's face.

A sharp glint of a steel blade flashed between the Haigok and the straw man, knocking the figure to the ground in the wagon's wake.

One infantryman stood upon the unstable cargo, peering out to the fallen figure, then out to the multitude of straw men engulfed in flames.

"Your dragon did a good job on those buggers," the soldier remarked as he turned to face Erugoth.

The Haigok was lying upon his back, reaching for something just out of his reach. The infantryman saw the horn resting on an untidy pile of canvas sheets. He reached down and handed it to the other.

"Is this what you want?"

Erugoth gave the soldier a thankful nod. He pressed the horn to his lips and blew.

A pitiful sound resonated, not clearly loud enough to be heard by anyone else but the soldier by his side.

He dropped the horn to the cargo again.

The soldier knelt beside him and placed a hand upon the Haigok's shoulder.

Blades continued to hack into straw men around them. Flares of dragon breath swept over the southern end of the clearing. Erugoth, leader of the Kazrekh Clan, closed his eyes and saw the Spine Mountains one more time.

One last time.

He let out a long sigh and was gone.

Twenty-Five

Dark blood smeared over David's face and dribbled into his mouth.

He let out a cry as he pushed the creature lying on top of him farther away, using the edge of his sword. The blade had cut deep into the chest of the dark beast, cracking through ribs and slicing open blood vessels inside its chest cavity.

"Help!" the big man called, pinned in place against the wall walk.

The creature shrieked, opening its jagged teeth wide and sliding its long tongue towards its intended victim. The thick, pink organ bent and swayed like a serpent. Oozing bubbles of dark saliva stretched down in long web-like formations.

David filled with an intense urgency to get out of this situation.

"Somebody help me," he hollered.

A sword flashed into view, the blade's edge sticking into the creature's forehead.

The dark figure fell limp.

David was saved, but not before another splash of blood, accompanied by a good portion of drool, smacked against his eyes.

He felt the weight of the creature lift away before he was pulled to his feet.

"Thank you," he said as he wiped his face on his sleeve, "whoever you are."

"It's me, you idiot," Lor told him. "And you're welcome. Now hurry up. There's more to be had."

David heard the screams of more creatures advancing over the wall. He quickly cleaned the mess away from his face as best he could.

A quick look along the parapet showed him they were faring better than the dark beasts. Scores of dead creatures were piling up along the top of the wall. A larger number had fallen to the ground on either side, but there were a growing number of slain men among them.

Shrieks from within the walls, far to the western edge of Woodmyst, echoed across the rooftops.

"What's that?" David asked, peering into the distance.

"A greater number of these fell things are attacking the western wall," Andris replied as he swung his blade at another creature that clambered through the battlements.

"I think some might have made it into the city." David started towards the tower, feeling an intensifying ache in his thigh. A complaint from a recent wound he got when an arrow pierced his leg in the glade. He stopped to rub it with his hand.

"You can't go," Andris called after him. "I need you here. We're barely keeping them back as it is."

"If they get through over there, it will only be a matter of time before they make their way through all of Woodmyst," Lor put in.

"There are more of our capable guards over there than there are here," Andris informed them. "They all made their way over when the first bell sounded."

Another creature appeared on the wall a short distance from David. He plunged his sword into the beast's chest. It fell lifelessly back over the wall, the thud on the ground below.

"We stay here then," he agreed. "We can chase after any inside the walls after we're done with this lot trying to get in."

***

Glaun was first to race from his hut and into the clearing. He armed himself with a wood axe, the only thing he had at his disposal besides a broom leaning against the door. Lilen, his wife, had taken that for herself as she stepped through the door to stand behind him.

"You should stay inside," he whispered to her, listening for the sounds again.

"I don't want to be on my own," she replied, her eyes wide in fear as she scanned the tree line.

Their heads snapped around to face the hut next to theirs. Kygra pushed the door open a little too hard, making it thud against the wall.

"You heard it?" he asked.

Glaun nodded.

"Terix?" Lilen enquired about the other man's wife.

"She's in there," he gestured with a wag of his head. "Under the covers."

"Go to her," Glaun instructed.

With a quick nod, Lilen started for the open door to Kygra's hut.

"Leave the broom," Kygra said, reaching for it as she passed by. "My axe is down by the stream." He offered a sheepish look as she handed it to him.

As Lilen closed the door behind her, Kygra walked over to his friend. Snow crunched under his feet, seeming to echo across the glade as he moved.

"Maybe they're gone?" he asked.

"You think your loud door slamming and heavy feet scared them off?" queried Glaun.

More footfalls approached from their left.

It was Porf, carrying a long blade, a double-edged sword that glistened with a silver sheen as the moonlight struck it.

"Where did you get that?" Kygra questioned, pointing to the sword with the handle of the broom.

"Found it near the livestock," he answered. "I think one of those soldiers that got swallowed up by the ground might have dropped it."

"Not fair," Kygra grumbled. He looked at each of the men beside him. "You got a sword. You got an axe. I got a fucking broom."

"That's my fucking broom," Glaun reminded him, "and there'll be hell to pay if you break it or lose it. Now, shut it. I'm trying to listen."

The three men fell silent.

The air whistled softly as the northern wind swept over the glade.

They could hear cattle calling in the distance. The livestock sounded nervous, as if something disturbed them.

Some hounds sleeping near the herds barked, sending their echoing calls towards the huts on the higher ground.

Glaun peered towards the east.

Rustling from their left. Movement among the trees.

Clicking.

Clicking.

A single creature hid in the shadows.

Glaun felt his heart race in his chest and heard it thunder in his ears.

A chorus of clicking arose as more and more creatures joined the first in its song.

"The Agrodien," Porf whispered. "Those things are right by their dwellings."

Glaun shook his head.

"We can't get to them," he said. "Listen. There's too many."

A sudden rattle and thud drew the men's attention to the open ground behind them. They tensed, lifting their weapons in haste, ready to battle.

Hygo lay upon the ground, face buried in the snow and one bare leg sticking from his trousers.

"Shit," he bellowed.

The clicking stopped suddenly.

Silence again.

"Bugger me, Hygo." Kygra lowered the broom and approached the fallen man. "You're meant to get dressed before you come outside."

"Sorry," the other replied, rolling onto his back so he could pull his trousers on. He then reached for his boots, lying on the snow next to him, and slipped them over his feet.

"Where's your weapon?" Porf enquired.

"Weapon?"

"Bloody heck!" Kygra snorted with disbelief.

Porf shook his head.

"Shut up," Glaun growled. His eyes fixed upon the northern tree line, where the Agrodien dwellings were located. "There's movement over there."

The others turned to see shadows moving beneath the trees.

A roar ripped through the stillness. It thundered across the valley and rippled through the air.

An ear-piercing shriek immediately followed it.

Moments later, several dark creatures burst into the clearing and started towards the stream.

Glaun tensed and readied himself for a fight.

The creatures didn't get far. Smaller figures with long tails leapt from the tree line and gave chase. The fleeing creatures were tackled to the ground and torn asunder.

"Bugger me," Kygra muttered as he watched in awe.

More dark forms emerged from the trees, at least thirty by Glaun's count. They got about half the distance to the stream, starting down in a south-easterly direction, towards the path to Woodmyst.

"Come on," he called, charging after them. There was no way that he would catch them. The snow was too thick. His clothes were too heavy. The creatures were too fast.

Nevertheless, he had to try.

From his left, more figures burst from the trees, larger and smaller together.

They were much faster than he.

They bounded over the frost-covered ground with ease as they overtook him.

Some held kitchen knives in their hands. Others carried the blades of their fallen husbands and fathers. Still, some went with nothing but what nature had given them, teeth and claws.

They leapt upon the dark creatures, preventing them from escaping.

Terrible shrieks and screams filled the vale as the Agrodien females and younglings wreaked havoc upon them.

Glaun stopped running.

The other three men pulled to his side.

Each of them buckled over, hands upon knees, as they caught their breath.

"I thought you told Alice that *we* would remain here to protect the Agrodien," Kygra said between puffs. "Doesn't look as though they need much protecting to me."

Glaun pursed his lips and gave a shrug.

The cattle called again. Glaun could see the herds moving together towards the south, suddenly parting in the middle as something moved among them.

"Come on," Glaun instructed, starting for the livestock. "This isn't over yet."

***

Alice had led the charge through the smouldering channel formed by dragon fire and onto open ground. The dragons continued to circle overhead and take turns diving for the attacking straw men pursuing the fleeing army. Streaks of flame filled the night sky behind the army as they moved northward.

"That way." Gruloch pointed a little to the right.

"That way will take us away from the coast," Brondt argued. "Away from the fleet. We should head for Ostford."

Alice looked to the Haigok for his reasoning.

"The crossing over the water is that way." He pointed again. "Ostford is a ruin with no protection. We'll have water on all sides and these creatures on our backs. The ships cannot help us."

"Gruloch is right. Osford is no place to make a stand, even with dragons helping out. We should make for the crossing," Schoenbach urged the girl.

Alice peered back over her shoulder to see the flying beasts burning the trees. The wagons were emerging onto the open ground and the last of their people were in the clear.

"Lead the way," she told Gruloch.

The Haigok set off on foot at a great pace. Alice was right on his heels.

"It's not far," Gruloch shouted as they climbed to the top of a ridge.

The area opened wide before them. A vast plain of snow-swept land with a thin, dark line winding through the centre from east to west.

The Griralith Pass.

"Down there," the Haigok gestured.

Alice could see it, far away, a stone bridge with a tall, forbidding tower at each end. It appeared as if guards should occupy it, but there were no men to be seen on the platforms of either fortification. No light twinkled from the windows.

Both towers appeared abandoned.

Alice called to the others, still climbing the ridge. "It's just down the other side," she said.

She weighed her options, taking their current situation into account.

The straw men outnumbered them tremendously. The enemy also had a means to regenerate and keep coming without tiring or truly dying.

Her people, on the other hand, were exhausted and ready to drop in their places. She needed to get them across the Griralith Pass safely and she couldn't accomplish that on the ground.

Placing her fingers in her mouth, she let out a long whistle.

From among the beasts in the air, one turned and pitched itself towards the girl.

"You will need your saddle," Gruloch told her.

"No time," Alice replied as Liana settled on the ground nearby. Emily, upon hearing her daughter's words, offered a worried look. "I'll hold on tightly," the girl promised with a hearty smile.

She leapt upon the dragon's back and gripped with her thighs and hands as firmly as she could.

"Let's go, girl," she told the beast.

Liana bounded across the snow, flicking clouds of frost and spirals of swirling white dust in all directions as she took to the sky.

The army looked on as the girl and her dragon sped overhead towards the pursuing straw men.

"Come on," Gruloch shouted, beckoning the others to follow him over the ridge and onto the plateau.

Across the plain, they raced.

The men on foot were aching all over.

The horses panted and puffed.

The wagons rattled and creaked loudly.

The drivers feared their vehicles would fall apart at any given moment.

As the last of the troop clambered over the ridge to follow the rest onto the open ground, the straw men burst from the burning forest.

Some were ablaze. To douse themselves, they simply dived upon the snow-covered ground and rolled once or twice before rising to their feet before continuing the charge.

The dragons circling in the sky continued diving towards the forest, focussing their efforts upon the thousands of straw men moving through the trees. Alice saw the need to transfer the effort on the ground between the trees and the ridge.

She urged Liana to sweep along the tree line.

The dragon spewed a barrage of scorching flames over the emerging straw men. As she lifted into the air, the burning figures lowered themselves to the snow and put out the flames.

A vast number of the straw men started across the open ground towards the ridge. There were too many for Alice to take down in one pass, and with the new counteraction taken by the straw men bitten with flame, there was no chance that she could prevent them all from reaching her people.

She needed the other dragons, but they were not hers to control.

The straw men piled out from the smouldering tree line. Hundreds. Thousands.

Several had reached the rising ground and had ascended the ridge.

From high above, Alice could see the last wagon bouncing down the other side in great haste to reach the flat ground of the plateau.

The straw men were moving faster, however, closing the distance rapidly as they spilled out of the forest as far as she could see along the tree line.

She urged Liana to make another pass, closer to the ridge this time.

She hoped to keep her people safe.

She hoped the other dragons would see the urgent need to move their attack to her position.

She hoped to stop the straw men in their tracks before they reached the open plain beyond the ridge, but a small part of her told her that her fight would be a lost cause.

She was losing hope fast.

Twenty-Six

Brondt led the charge to the bridge, urging Amicia and Ursula to keep up with him as they galloped across the plain. Behind them were Emily and Catherine, followed closely by Akasati and Karlena. The Agrodien warriors flanked them tightly on either side.

They were nearing the first tower at the southern end of the bridge. Schoenbach peered up at the dark monstrosity that loomed menacingly over them.

Dark stone walls stretched high into the air, with small, square portals just wide enough for an archer to pitch a shot at unwanted visitors. An archway that passed through the structure reminded him of a yawning mouth. It was wide enough for the wagons to drive through, but only just.

Across the top of the arch were metal spikes, the lower section of a heavy iron gate that hung concealed inside the tower.

Beyond, was the long, narrow bridge to the other side of the Griralith Pass.

The wind howled as it passed through the gorge. The faint sound of water sloshing about from far below carried on the breeze.

"This is going to take some time," Thornton growled from his side as he looked to the bridge, then back to the number of men behind him.

"Women cross first," Brondt hollered. "The Agrodien go with them. The rest of us stay here to defend our position until the wagons have crossed over."

"The towers?" Lieutenant Brook pointed. "Could be someone inside."

Thornton peered up to the dark windows.

"Looks abandoned," he remarked. "Best to check it out, just in case." He turned to his men. "Cheyne and Jendryng. Go and see. Sparrow and Vawdrey. Ride over the bridge to the tower on the other side and see if anything still dwells there. Quickly."

The four men raced off. Two went across the bridge on horseback, while two dropped to the ground to climb a ladder to the right, just inside the first tower's archway.

"You should get going," Brondt told Amicia. He lowered himself from his horse and offered the reins to her.

She hesitated, offering a look of concern.

"I want you to come with me," she said.

He smiled in an attempt to soothe her fears.

"Now, what sort of commander would I be if I left the men behind?" He took her by the hand and planted a kiss on her fingers. "Go. I'll be along shortly."

She frowned and urged her steed through the stone archway. Ursula followed closely, turning briefly to look at Thornton. He responded with a stern nod.

Catherine and Emily rode side by side, with Karlena and Akasati in tow.

"I stay," Yuri said to Thornton as the other reptilians entered the arch. "I fight here with you."

"No," the other said with a shake of his head as he alighted from his steed. He gave the leads to the reptilian. "Protect the women. That's what Alice ordered you to do."

The Agrodien gave a reluctant nod as he steered the horses for the tower.

Thornton watched the large warrior lead his horse through the passageway. Part of him also wanted the Agrodien, his friend, to fight by his side. The reptilian was a far superior warrior than any of the men. They could use his help, but each of them had his own part to play. And Yuri's was to protect his Kayl'sro's family and coven.

"Commander," John Cheyne called from inside the tower.

"What is it?" Brondt peered up to a window just above the archway. Cheyne had his face pressed through the narrow hole.

"The tower's empty," he yelled. "Nobody's been here for a good while. There's some mouldy bread. Black through and through."

"Couple of mushrooms growing on it," Jendryng hollered from inside the structure. "Smells like shit."

"We found the mechanism for the gate up here," Cheyne informed them. "Looks a little rusted. We could try it, if you like."

"No." Brondt looked to the army racing over the plain towards his position. The last wagon was at least halfway across the expanse. "I don't want that thing getting stuck where it could hinder our escape. Don't touch a thing. You understand?"

"Yessir," Cheyne answered.

"Yessir," Jendryng echoed.

As they spoke, he saw one dragon sweep from east to west, spewing fire on the other side of the ridgeline. Several silhouettes appeared on the crest.

The straw men were coming.

Sparrow and Vawdrey were already moving through the northern tower's interior as the women and Agrodien warriors raced through the archway on horseback beneath them. Like the twin structure at the other end of the bridge, it was empty.

Emily led the others to the left. They pulled to the side of the tower and peered back across the chasm to where the army was forming up in a defensive line.

The first wagon slid through the passage in the southern tower and began its approach across the bridge.

"I can see the fleet," Vawdrey called from one of the top windows.

Amicia turned to face the sea, but the ridge on the other side of the channel obscured her view, as it swept a little to the north where it followed the twisting trench.

"Where, soldier?" she yelled.

"Directly west, Your Highness," the other replied. "I think they must have followed us."

"Watching the dragons, no doubt," Ursula put in.

"Why don't you cause the ground to shake and swallow those bastards up?" Sparrow asked from a portal closer to the ground.

"With our people between them and us?" Amicia shook her head. "It's too risky."

"Then you could strike them with lightning instead," he urged Ursula.

"Not with the dragons in the sky above them," she answered.

"Then we'd better hope those bloody wagons move a little faster," Vawdrey said. "The sooner we're out of here, the better."

Alice glanced to the bridge, where she saw the first of the wagons making its way over the crossing. It was nearing the centre as the second wagon passed beneath the southern tower's arch. The third was racing over the plain, closing upon the defensive line of infantrymen upon the ground.

The last and final wagon was still in the open. Numerous men surrounded it on foot and ran as fast as they could, spurred on by the straw men now racing down the ridge towards them.

She directed Liana to the ridge. Her legs tightened upon the dragon's flanks and she gripped with all of her might as the beast tilted to the right.

Every muscle in Alice was aching. The amount of work she had to put in just to stay on Liana's back was tiring. She wished she had her saddle, that her legs were strapped in so she could sit upright instead of belly down against the dragon's coarse skin.

Liana dived for the straw men and let out a jet of flame over them. As she rose back into the air, Alice looked over her shoulder to see the figures rolling in the snow to douse the flames.

Smouldering and steaming, the scarecrows lifted themselves back to their feet to continue the pursuit. As they did so, a flood of straw men flowed over the top of the ridge and down the other side.

Alice cursed and urged Liana back around for another attack.

"Hurry," Brondt called to the driver of the third wagon.

The cart rattled and bumped over the frosty ground and onto the stonework of the bridge. The horses were panting loudly, echoing each breath as they passed under the archway, before racing after the other two wagons.

"I don't like the looks of this," Brook announced, pointing to the wave of straw men spilling into the plain.

Thornton eyed the last wagon, still a long way from their position.

"They're not going to make it," he growled.

A line of fire ignited along the base of the ridge, swallowing hundreds of the figures speeding down the embankment.

"Good girl," Schoenbach remarked, watching on proudly.

"Where are the other dragons?" Brondt asked, turning to Gruloch.

The Haigok's bulbous eyes widened as he offered a look of surprise. He suddenly blurted something in his tongue that only the others of his kind understood, before speaking directly to some of the others. He gestured to the ridge and pointed to two Haigok in dark cloaks. The Kazrekh riders.

The two Haigok responded by pulling curved horns from beneath their cloaks. They lifted them to their lips and let out an almighty trumpet call that echoed in the night sky.

The army watched as Alice and her dragon passed over the straw men, spilling fire over the ground again. The figures charged through the flames, rolled upon the damp snow, and ran onwards.

They were gaining on the last wagon, drawing too close for Alice to attack.

More and more straw men charged over the ridge and onto the plateau.

Too many to count.

Brondt pursed his lips and gritted his teeth as Liana breathed another assault over the scarecrows racing across the plain.

Countless straw men burst into flames and fell to the earth. Some struggled to get back up. Others stayed down and burned, too broken to rise again.

Some had managed to escape the fire and catch the men by the wagon, tackling them to the ground and tearing into their flesh.

There were two that climbed upon the cart, leaping over the cargo to reach the driver.

Their claws dug into the poor man's face, peeling skin from bone.

His ear-shattering cries echoed across the icy ground and into the ears of every man and Haigok watching on.

"Across the bridge," Brondt ordered. "Everyone across the bridge."

Soldiers and horsemen filed onto the long, narrow stone crossing. They fled as fast as they could from the approaching straw men.

It was a slower process than Brondt would have liked. Trying to get nearly five hundred men onto the bridge simultaneously, and under such conditions, caused his heart to leap from his chest and into his throat. The sound of its rapid beating thundered inside his head.

Another barrage of flame spilled over the ridge as Alice and Liana swooped past again. The fiery assault barely made a difference as flaming scarecrows continued down the embankment, following the hundreds that were already charging over the plateau.

"Come on," Thornton roared to the gawkers who stopped to watch the dragon speed by.

The enemy drew nearer and nearer.

Brondt was certain that he could hear their wooden arms and legs creaking, their feet crunching in the snow, their straw innards rustling.

Louder.

Louder.

The Haigok followed the men over the bridge, leaving Brondt and Thornton by the tower's arch alone.

The straw men raced forward, their empty eye sockets glaring, their sharp, gnarled fingers outstretched.

The commander and the captain stepped backwards, swords raised, ready to fight. Their feet moved from the soft ground to the stone roadway of the bridge.

Another flare of fire filled the sky, illuminating the hundreds of figures charging over the ground.

Closer.

Closer.

Brondt stepped beneath the arch with Thornton by his side.

The straw men were almost within reach of their blades.

Closer.

Closer.

The sound of an enormous clunk and the sudden clanging of chains caused Brondt to look at the roof of the archway.

The heavy iron gate fell to the floor with a deafening clunk.

The scarecrows smashed against the bars, pieces of straw spilling harmlessly onto the stonework by the two soldiers' boots.

Stabbing wooden claws abruptly jutted through the gate, reaching for the men. Thornton and Brondt stepped further back, out of reach.

Cheyne and Jendryng appeared on the ladder to their left.

"That won't hold them for long," the younger man said. "I saw a few of the fuckers climb around to this side. They'll come back up onto the bridge and cut us off if we don't get moving."

"Then we'd better get moving," Brondt suggested, gesturing with a nod towards the army already crossing the bridge.

A trumpet call sounded ahead of them as they emerged from the tower. One of the Kazrekh riders had stopped momentarily to summon the dragons again.

"Maybe we're too far for them to hear him," Cheyne offered.

"Or they're too busy," Thornton replied.

"Just how many of those things are there?" Jendryng queried, peering over his shoulder to the claws reaching towards them through the iron gate.

"Come on," Brondt shouted, ignoring the question as he raced after the rest of his men.

He peered out to the side of the bridge and saw the deep gorge fringed with sheer cliffs of rock. A powerful wind moved through the trench, bringing the scent of saltwater from far below. Moving his attention to the far side of the crossing, he saw the army regrouping on the open ground to the left of the tower. They lined the remaining three wagons up, ready to proceed. The archers were lining up on the cliff's edge. Torch bearers had lit fires by the side of the northern tower and carried flame to each of the bowmen. Amicia, Catherine, and Ursula stood hand in hand, ready to do battle in their own way.

A great orange glow lit up the scene before him.

He turned to see a long line of dragons flying over the ridge, bearing down upon the plain with mouths agape, sending forth a wall of fire.

Many straw men ignited instantly, but many more remained unscathed, enabling them to continue their approach to the southern tower.

It was then that Brondt saw five straw men clamber from the sides of the bridge and onto the crossing behind them.

"Move," he hollered, picking up his pace.

Flaming arrows shot through the air towards the southern end of the walkway, below the waist-high walls that hemmed the sides of the crossing. Brondt was unable to see what the targets were, but he could hedge a guess.

The five straw men on the bridge charged towards them.

"Hurry," Vawdrey called from one of the tower windows.

"Get ready to close that gate," Thornton barked.

"What gate?" the other shouted.

"The fucking tower gate," Jendryng replied.

"There's no gate," Vawdrey answered.

"Shit," Jendryng spat.

More straw men appeared on the bridge, flames spreading over their forms from fiery darts protruding from their bodies. Pretty soon, pursuing figures filled the southern end of the crossing, racing towards the northern tower.

"Get out of the tower," Brondt called. "Hurry."

They reached the archway and turned to face the first of the straw men.

More fiery arrows swept over the bridge to stop the attackers. They struck a few so severely that the flames became overwhelming, causing them to drop to the stone path and burn away. Others continued on, closing the gap between themselves and the men beneath the arch.

"I don't like these odds," Lieutenant Brook said as Vawdrey and Sparrow emerged from the tower.

Loud tapping, rustling and knocking filled the soldiers' ears as the straw men drew nearer and nearer, their wooden feet striking the stonework of the bridge.

Brondt braced himself for the attack, tightening his grip on his sword.

"Get out of there," he heard a familiar voice call. He pivoted around to see Amicia standing on the ground by the arch. The men stared at her blankly. "Now," she barked.

"You heard her," Thornton growled.

As the men raced out of the archway, a great jet of fire engulfed the crossing, swallowing the charging straw men in flame.

Brondt peered up at the sky.

It was Alice.

She was gripping tightly to the back of her dragon, hovering above the bridge. The dragon spewed a long jet of flame over the crossing, devouring the straw men making their way to the northern tower.

The bright flare from the flames illuminated the flying beast's form. Liana's wings stretched and furled, casting the flaming straw men to the wind as bright embers that rained like a thousand falling stars into the dark chasm below.

Brondt had seen nothing so terrifying, so horrific, as he did then, staring at the magnificent beast with the little girl upon her back.

Amicia stepped past the men and crouched by the archway, placing her hand upon the stone floor in the arch beneath the tower. She closed her eyes and took a deep breath.

"Fall," she said in an emotionless tone. Her voice rumbled through the air like thunder as the bridge cracked and crumbled.

Alice steered Liana away, turning the dragon towards the awaiting army. She passed over their heads as the bridge broke into large pieces and tumbled away into the darkness below, leaving only the northern tower in place.

Liana landed softly and lowered her belly to the ground. Alice slid from the beast's back and winced as she stretched her arms above her head. She had been holding on so tightly that her muscles had formed into tight knots. The dragon gave a soft, apologetic chirp as she brought her head around to face her rider.

"It's all right, girl," Alice said, giving Liana a rub on her snout. She peered over the gorge to the plateau on the other side. The dragons were continuing to swoop and pour fire over the countless straw men making their way to the northern ledge. "Call them back," the girl shouted to Gruloch.

He was standing by the cliff face with the other Haigok, proudly watching the dragons attack. A look of surprise fell upon his face when Alice gave her instruction. He looked at her, confused.

"They're wiping the enemy out," he told her. "Why would we call them back now? We're safe here. We can just sit and wait until they're done."

"We need to keep moving," she told him as she approached. "We don't have time to sit and wait until they're done. Who knows what awaits us over here? We're closer to the Maji than ever, now. Call them back."

Reluctantly, he translated the instruction to the Kazrekh riders. They, too, offered puzzled glances before raising their curved horns to their lips.

The trumpets blew, and the dragons retreated, swooping over the Griralith Pass to land on the frosty ground by Liana's side.

Alice looked to the witch from Whitekeep. A silent reckoning passed between them. Ursula's eyes turned from piercing blue to pitch black as she lifted her hands to the sky.

A strong gale swept up through the deep trench between the army and the straw men. Dust, vapour, and smoke lifted high into the air as dark clouds formed above the open plain.

"Here we go." Vawdrey smiled, peering to the sky. He then moved his gaze to the straw men on the other side of the canyon. They were standing still, silent, staring blankly towards the army on the southern ledge. "You bastards are in for it now," he shouted to them.

Great clouds swirled above the southern plateau. Growing. Growing.

Flashes of light.

Booming thunder.

The dragons cowered.

The horses stamped their hooves.

The men almost fell to the earth.

Ursula stretched out her fingers and focused her attention.

"Strike," she muttered. Her voice filled the air.

Thick shafts of jagged light erupted from the clouds. They broke into hundreds of smaller lines and struck the ground hard. A boom emitted from the swirling mass above as jets of steam from snow instantly turned to vapour, and chunks of dirt and flint ejected from the ground.

Still, the straw men didn't move.

"What happened?" Vawdrey asked, disappointed.

"Nothing," Jendryng replied, just as disenchanted as his friend. "Absolutely nothing."

"Are you sure?" Thornton said, pointing to crumbling rocks along the face of the southern cliff.

"It's as if someone's using a hoe to loosen the earth," Schoenbach remarked as more and more rocks tumbled away from the cliff face.

Amicia crouched by Ursula's side and touched both hands to the ground. Her eyes had turned dark.

"Shatter," she said.

It was as if the ground beneath their feet shivered slightly.

A thick spray of white foam lifted into the air, rising from the deep trench between the straw men and the watching army, as the tremor passed beneath the water far below.

Puffs of dust and cracks appeared across the southern cliff.

The newly formed fissures widened suddenly, making the ground fall away beneath the straw men standing along the ledge. The fractures opened wider and wider, spreading beneath the southern plateau, opening the surface and causing the ground to break apart.

Large segments tilted this way and that, spilling the straw men into the darkness below. Plumes of soil and dust burst into the sky as the entire landscape churned over and over violently. A great and terrible rumble could be heard as a gentle tremor vibrated beneath the feet of the army on the southern side of the widening canyon.

"By the gods," Schoenbach huffed, dropping to his knees.

Straw men were flung about like rag dolls as the surface broke apart beneath them. Like a wave, the ground opened up and crumbled away until the chaos reached the ridge.

Amicia rose to her feet.

Her eyes returned to their piercing blue.

Her breathing was rapid and short. Her legs shook, and she reached out her hand towards Ursula. Catherine and Ursula took the queen under the arms, resting her frame upon their shoulders.

"We don't have long," Catherine said to Alice.

"I know," she replied, looking at an exhausted Amicia. She peered over to Yuri and spoke to him in his tongue. "Make a place for her on one of the wagons. She needs to rest and we need to get moving."

"Yes, Kayl'sro," he replied, bowing before moving away.

Alice put her attention on Gruloch.

"Saddle the dragons and prepare them to leave," she ordered.

He responded with a nod, then he turned to speak to the other Haigok.

"We need to press on," the girl said to Brondt. He focussed completely upon Amicia, missing Alice's words. "Commander," she barked.

"Yes?" He turned to her, looking shocked.

"Your wife will be fine," she assured him. "Mount up and tell the troops to prepare to move out."

Brondt swallowed hard before replying, "Of course."

Emily moved to her daughter's side, concerned. She watched the commander move away to fetch his horse before placing her gaze upon Catherine and Ursula, helping Amicia away to the wagons.

"Are you all right?" she asked.

"A little sore," Alice admitted. "Riding Liana is a lot easier with a saddle."

"I don't mean that," Emily told her. She gestured to Brondt with a jut of her chin. "I think you might have been a little harsh towards him. He worries for his wife, after all."

"I know," the girl answered, peering over to the monstrous dust cloud covering what was once the southern plain. "But we can't linger. We're changing back."

Emily gave her a perplexing look.

"Changing back?"

Alice searched her mind for the correct words.

"The four of us are turning back to what we were before," she explained.

"Your hair and eyes," Emily said. "I have noticed."

"Our strength also," Alice put in, looking to Amicia. "We're not as strong as we were when we first came together. I fear we will lose it all before we reach Takmel."

Emily gave her daughter's words some consideration.

It would be a setback to have come all this way and face the Maji only to be beaten in the end. It was true that Takmel was indeed powerful. The Four appeared to be even more so, but now the power they possessed was drifting away.

"You were already stronger than him," Emily replied. "The four of you together will be more than enough to defeat him, with or without your blue eyes and strange hair."

Alice thought about that for a moment. She then leaned over and kissed her mother on the cheek.

"Thank you, Mama," she whispered as she wrapped her arms around Emily's shoulders.

Emily gripped her daughter and kissed the crown of her head.

Twenty-Seven

His hands shook, resting on his knees, palms open and facing towards the ceiling. He sat cross-legged on a rug by the fire in the white marble throne room.

The twins had recoiled, pulling away from him slightly, shuffling a short distance on their rumps. They had taken their hands away from his when they felt a sudden, uncomfortable surge make its way through his body and into their arms.

Something terrible had transpired.

Something devastating.

Countless straw dolls, scattered across the floor, surrounded them.

A large number were scorched. Others turned into ash. Still, more lay torn asunder and filled with soil that had not been there before.

A soft giggle emitted from the seat to the side of the throne. The woman in white put her hand to her mouth. She hadn't intended for her laughter to be so loud.

His eyes were like fire, boring into her.

"You think this is funny?" he huffed.

The two girls got to their feet, frightened by his demeanour.

"It's your fault," he growled at them. He slapped one across the face before returning the back of his hand to the cheek of the other. Both fell to the rug hard and cried.

"Takmel," Isabel reproved, standing up. "Don't blame them for your weakness."

"You!" He snorted. "You wanted me to fail. You want Alice to win."

He glided across the floor towards her, feet dangling inches from the surface, over the stairs leading up to the dais.

His hands wrapped around her neck. His fingers squeezed tightly.

"Please," she hissed. "Kill me."

He stopped suddenly, glaring at her.

"No," he said, balling his hands into fists as he lowered himself to the floor. He took a deep breath and repeated the word more calmly. "No."

"Because you can't," she told him spitefully. "You need us. You need me. My life gives you power. But with each one of us taken, your power diminishes."

"Close your mouth, woman, or I will sear it shut with a hot iron."

"Just what will you be if we are all taken from you?" she questioned viciously.

"More powerful than you," he replied.

"Not more powerful than her," she sneered.

Like a flash, he turned and smacked her in the face with his fist, sending her falling over her chair, down the side of the platform to crumple in a mess upon the stone floor.

"I told you to shut your mouth," he hollered.

Tears filled her eyes.

Her hand went to the wound in her lip, a widening split as swelling quickly took hold.

Blood spilt into her mouth.

She touched the wound with her tongue and laughed.

Takmel turned away from her and was confronted with the angry eyes of two ten-year-old girls.

"Weak," he heard Isabel's voice whisper behind him.

He gritted his teeth and marched down the stairs and towards the door, kicking angrily at the straw dolls in his path.

When he had moved from the room, the girls raced to the White Queen's side to offer assistance. They helped her to her feet and back to her seat by the throne.

"Thank you, ladies," she said, pulling a white kerchief from her pocket and dabbing it on her lip, mopping small splotches of blood and wincing slightly from the pain. She looked at both of them with care. "Be wary. He is not what he says he is. He doesn't love you as he says he does. He is weak, and he is growing weaker. And this is making him more dangerous than ever. You aren't safe with him."

Both girls responded by touching their faces where Takmel had struck them. They peered at the blood seeping from the White Queen's lip and placed their heads upon her breast, embracing her.

Isabel put her arms around them both. As they sobbed quietly, she looked at the large door to the throne room where Takmel had just passed through and grinned.

***

Three hounds sniffed the stone path, eagerly pulling their handler by their leashes. The man, a thin and wiry boy not much older than Arthur, turned and smiled.

"I think they've found something, my lord," he said.

"I told you not to call me that," Arthur reminded him, holding a flickering torch over his head. Behind him were David, Lor and his son Alan, and Ruttger Harrow. All were carrying weapons.

A screech emitted from somewhere deep inside the city.

"Another one," Alan murmured. He was nervous.

The streets were dark and the few creatures that had found their way into Woodmyst had also found the darkest corners to hide in. Andris had instructed the kennel master to gather all dog handlers. It wasn't long before a few groups of men formed to accompany the handlers. The hunt began shortly afterwards.

The three hounds paused at the entrance of a thin alley between two houses. The passage was barely wide enough for a man to fit down.

The dogs sniffed at the ground, a little to the left, a little to the right.

Alan quietly hoped they would move on. The alley was deep and thick, and black shadows filled it.

The hounds entered the passage, tugging their handler forwards.

Alan felt his heart sink and a cold sweat dribble down his spine.

Arthur followed the handler, lifting the torch high above his head.

The men moved in single file, Ruttger taking the rear of the line.

"I hope there's only one in here," he muttered. "There's no room to fight if there are more."

"I hope there's none," Alan admitted.

The thin passage opened into a small yard. The dogs stopped in their tracks and growled.

Arthur moved to the handler's side, allowing the torchlight to illuminate the enclosed area. The others filed in after him. Their eyes fell upon a lone creature huddled against a wall on the far side.

"By the gods," David huffed.

The creature held something to its mouth. The object was covered with matted, blood-soaked fur and no longer resembled anything that could be recognised.

"What's it eating?" Lor queried. "Is it a cat?"

The creature emitted a clicking sound and cowered lower as one dog barked.

"Shuttit," the handler snapped. The hound offered an apologetic whine and closed its mouth.

"Why doesn't it attack?" David asked.

Arthur considered that for a moment as he watched the creature. It looked to them, nervously. It clenched the bloodied object tightly, defensively.

It was afraid.

"Takmel has severed his bond," Arthur stated.

"What?" asked Alan.

"Look at it," Arthur gestured with the torch. "It's nothing more than a lost animal."

"So." David stepped forward, his sword clenched in his hand. "You're saying that Takmel has no control over them any longer."

"No." Arthur shook his head. "Just that he has no control over them right at this moment."

"Why?" Ruttger asked. "Why would he leave them on their own?"

"Because they were being defeated," Arthur suggested. "Because he simply doesn't care."

"Because he's Takmel," Alan put in.

David stepped forward and thrust his blade into the creature's chest. It let out an ear-shattering cry before falling to slump against the wall.

The big man stepped back and peered at the creature despondently. Something about it appeared helpless and vulnerable to him.

"Don't tell Alice I did that," the large man requested. "I don't know if she would be too happy with me if she knew I had just killed that poor creature."

"Poor creature?" the dog handler queried, with a puzzled expression. "Those things attacked us."

"The Maji attacked us," David explained. "That thing was the device he used to do so."

"Much like your dogs there," Arthur added. "You have trained them to do your will. He used these things to do his. What we saw just now was a creature at its true nature. It didn't want to attack us any more than it wanted to be attacked."

The handler seemed to understand, peering at the body of the dark figure as he mulled over David's and Arthur's words.

"I don't think Alice would think less of you for that, Papa," Arthur offered.

"Don't tell her anyway," David said, looking at each of them. "I suddenly feel... I don't know."

"We won't," Ruttger assured him, placing a comforting hand on the man's shoulder.

***

"This way, sir," the guard said, leading Andris through the long corridor of the prison.

He had to step around a guard or two here and there as the men were engaged in cleaning up after a small skirmish. They had placed sheets and blankets over dead prisoners. Bars and cage doors had been bent and broken on almost every cell. Blood stained the floor in thick puddles, running over steps in places like thin red streams.

A few bodies of armoured men were lying on the floor near those of dark creatures. The dead soldiers bore wounds of deep gashes caused by the sharp claws of the beasts. The creatures had marks of their own caused by axes or swords. Some had arrow shafts sticking from their flesh.

"Down here." The guard stepped over a fallen comrade as they neared the cells of the imprisoned bookkeepers.

Andris saw the blood first, covering the entire floor like a small lake.

He lifted his gaze to the bars of the cells, where he saw entrails and pieces of flesh sticking to the iron.

Red covered the entire walls inside the cells. Some of it was bright, while some was splotchy and dark.

Andris tasted bile as the stench hit his nose.

There was nothing identifiable as once being a man. Nothing.

"None of the bookkeepers...?" he asked, picturing Master Book-keeper Lewis Drayton among the chaos before him, wondering just which pieces belonged to the old man.

"The beasts got in here." The guard pointed to the bent and broken bars covering a small window inside the last cell. "The bookkeepers were the first to be attacked. If I might speak freely, sir?"

"Speak," Andris replied.

"I think these men were targeted," the guard averred. "What if this was the intention of the attack all the time? To get to these men."

Andris frowned and nodded, silently agreeing with the other.

"Clean this up as best as you can," he ordered, turning on his heels and retracing his steps back along the corridor. "And burn the bodies."

***

General Saruun Versel, First Garrison Commander of the Maji, sat upon her steed, dressed in her dark armour, ready for battle. Her nine lieutenants positioned themselves behind her in a neat line. An army of three hundred men stood in formation farther back.

They were on top of a rise that looked down upon a frozen river, deep blue in places as it snaked across an open plain from the mountains and out of sight towards the sea. The easterly wind blew bitterly across their flanks, kicking up small wisps of snow and ice that stung when it hit bare skin. A soft light had spilled into the sky from behind the mountains and a white haze had spread in all directions, making it hard to see anything in the distance clearly.

Versel kept her eyes fixed to the south. Shadows had been seen moving from the coast, so a scout reported.

"A large mass," he had said. "An army."

Leaving Ironfields behind, the general had taken the entire detachment stationed in the township and marched them a few miles through the snow.

Now, they waited and watched for the shadow, the mass that approached.

"There," Willis called over the gale, pointing directly ahead.

"I see them," Larson announced. "There're some horses among them."

Versel noticed a dark blur at first. Bit by bit, she could distinguish objects. People on steeds led the rest of the troop. A moment later, she was able to determine that at least two women rode near the front of the pack.

"Who are they?" Norris queried. "Is it the girl from Woodmyst?"

The general shook her head. "No. It's the queen."

Each of the men squinted and tried to focus their sight.

Sure enough, two women rugged in thick apparel rode among the cavalry. A gold banner flapped wildly in the wind, carried by one of the horsemen.

"Erimoor has fallen," Norris remarked. "The Gold Queen is coming."

"We know nothing," Versel corrected him. "We'll wait to hear from them what has happened before we make any claims."

"Who is the other woman riding beside her?" Norris asked. "I don't see any other banners."

"I don't know," the general replied, "but I think it's the Lilac Queen from Blackshore."

"What makes you say so?" Willis questioned.

Versel turned in her saddle to face him. "Just a hunch."

The figures drew nearer, becoming clearer in the haze. The army following didn't look even half as large as what Versel had at her disposal.

"What do we do with them all?" Larson asked, as he quickly estimated their numbers. "That's a lot of mouths to feed and shelter to find for them. We might be hard-pressed to accommodate them in Ironfields."

"We'll do what we can," Versel told him. "Floor space in the tavern and in the upstairs rooms. No whoring or drinking until we can figure out something more fitting. Understand?"

"Yes, General," they all replied.

She watched as the riders carefully navigated their way across the frozen stream. The men on foot lined up neatly behind the cavalry, stepping only where the horses dared to tread.

When the bulk of the forces had crossed safely, Versal edged her steed slowly forward.

"Norris. Larson. Accompany me," she commanded. "I need to formally welcome the ladies and offer assistance. The rest of you stay here."

Twenty-Eight

Commander Willard Zakhar closed his eyes, soaking in the warm light from the rising sun. The northern wind was bitter cold, but the yellow rays flooding over the skin of his face were a welcome feeling compared to the frost and sleet they had endured during an endless night.

From their position offshore, they had all witnessed fire flowing over the land beyond the coastline, like a bright orange wave sweeping to the north. They had watched through their spyglasses as the straw men burned away. They had hedged bets and made commentary when the dragons swooped over the trees, swinging around over the water's edge when they turned for another attack.

All the while, they felt fear, excitement and concern for their allies upon the ground.

All the while, they felt helpless and useless as they could not contribute to the battle.

The fleet had tacked north during the night, trying to keep up with their comrades as they fought fiercely against the wind.

Eventually, they had reached the Griralith Pass, sealed with fallen debris for a decade, allowing the water in the channel to rise and cascade over fallen boulders. So cold the water was, it had frozen in places on the rock face, clinging tightly as it formed into giant spikes that hung precariously over the bubbling water below the falls. Large enough to crush a galleon, Zakhar thought as he gazed at them.

A great, thick cloud of dust and smoke rose in the east, far behind the waterfall. The crew of all twelve ships passed messages around, hoping that someone could see what had happened. There was no sign of battle, no sight of the dragons and no more rising fire.

Zakhar had commanded the fleet to tack onwards, to continue north. All the while, he kept a watchful eye on the land and waited, and hoped.

Hours had passed by before the sight of a winged creature emerged a little to the north of the dust cloud. The sun was only just starting to send a fine, golden glow over the horizon, letting the world below know it intended to show itself soon.

Alice instructed the fleet to sail to Meadowmoor, the next point to the north of the Griralith Pass on any map. There, they would regroup and discuss the next move.

The fleet continued to tack into the wind for a long time.

It was slow progress and arduous work, but the crews of all the Dendadian vessels were disciplined and well trained. Their patience was one of their strongest qualities, according to the commander of the fleet.

They were steadfast and driven by their duty.

The sun was well into the sky when they caught their first glimpse of their destination.

"Meadowmoor," a lookout called down from the crows-nest.

Commander Zakhar, still appreciating the warm glow of the sun, opened his eyes and peered up the mainmast, past the sails and rigging to a crewman pointing northward.

"Make a bearing for that location, sailor," he shouted to the wheelman.

"Aye, Commander," came the response as the crewman turned the wheel to shore.

Suddenly, a loud horn sounded from one frigate further to the west.

The commander peered out to sea where the signalling vessel was located. It appeared fine, not in distress.

"What's that all about, First Officer Grady?"

Grady, a stocky man with a thick, dark beard, tilted his head to the lookout and shouted, "What's that all about?"

It took a moment to get a reply as the man in the crows-nest scanned the horizon with his spyglass.

"Four black frigates off the port bow," the lookout reported. "Gun hatches open. Another two flee to the west. All at full sail and have the wind at their backs. Gold flags hoisted."

"We're about to be attacked," Zakhar muttered.

"Four against twelve?" the first officer queried.

"They might think they have the upper hand with the wind in their favour. Nevertheless, we need to defend ourselves."

"What of the two fleeing out to sea?" Grady asked.

"Leave them," Zakhar replied. "Cowards on the run. Prepare the cannons and change course to intercept."

"Aye, Commander," the first officer saluted and then relayed the command.

They blew horns to signal an attack. All twelve ships loaded their cannons and opened the hatches, ready to engage the enemy.

Zakhar's galleon rocked wildly as they turned towards the four black ships.

"You hold on up there, boy," Grady hollered to the lookout.

"Aye sir," the other called down as he wrapped his arms around the rope net, connected from his post to the mast. The ship lifted itself upright as it careered over the peak of a high wave. The lookout felt his stomach lift and drop suddenly, causing his grip on the rope to tighten as his rump momentarily left his seat. "Shit," he hissed.

"Cannons ready," the gunner shouted from beneath the deck.

Zakhar weighed up the situation, observing the approaching black frigates closely as the space between them grew more and more narrow. The vessels were travelling in pairs. Two in front, two behind.

"Bring us between the lead ships," the commander ordered.

"It'll be bloody tight with the waves tossing us around like this," Grady offered.

"Just do it," Zakhar told him. "And signal the rest of the fleet to form a blockade behind our position. I don't want any of those frigates escaping."

Horns trumpeted. Distinctive patterns and notes informed the captains of the other eleven vessels what the commander wanted them to do.

The response was almost instantaneous.

The Dendadian vessels formed a wide line behind the galleon.

White spray broke over the bow of the ship as it burst through wave after wave.

The distance between the four black frigates and Commander Zakhar's galleon closed rapidly.

The two enemy vessels in the lead parted slightly, intending to let the galleon come between them. All ships had their cannons ready. It would just be a matter of who fired first, who had the thicker hull, and who survived in the end.

"Here we go, lads," Grady called, making a fist around some rigging, his knuckles turning white.

Boards creaked loudly.

The galleon's bowsprit passed between the frigates.

"Get ready to fire," Zakhar yelled. His eyes met with those of the enemy captain on the vessel to his left. They were drawing closer to one another.

The commander looked to the frigate approaching on his right and saw infuriated hatred on the face of the captain there.

Closer.

Closer.

On all three men, nostrils flared.

Teeth bared.

Closer.

So close they were in earshot of one another.

Closer.

Closer.

"Fire!" they all shouted at the same time.

Alice was first on her feet.

"What's that?" Catherine asked. "Thunder?"

They huddled around a small fire; Alice, Catherine, Ursula, Amicia, Emily, the two Erilian women and the Agrodien warriors. Others were out counting their numbers, calculating the losses from the battle with the straw men. The Haigok were tending to the dragons on a patch of open ground nearby.

The ruins of Meadowmoor laid only a stone's throw away from where the army had set up camp. Some men had explored the toppled buildings, finding broken trinkets and empty jars among the rubble.

It didn't appear as if any violence had occurred in the township. It had simply been abandoned and left to fall into disarray. Slowly, over the years since the Mirikin, the forest had reclaimed the bulk of the structures, causing walls and roofs to collapse as roots took hold and expanded beneath the earth.

There was a long road, twisting through the trees, covered with snow, that led to rotting dockyards by the sea. It was well hidden from sight, shielded by tall pines and thick growth on the western edge of the campsite.

This wall of trees wasn't of any advantage, as Alice had pointed out to Brondt and the other military-minded men. While they prevented enemy vessels from seeing their position from the sea, they also hindered the view of those on land from seeing any approaching ships, including their own allies.

The location had its advantages and disadvantages as far as Alice could tell. She hoped that the need to linger would be only for a short time. The sooner everyone rested, the sooner they could move on.

"Not thunder," Ursula said, shaking her head and peering to the cloudless sky. "I would know."

"Then what?" Catherine queried, standing beside Alice.

"Cannon fire," Akasati told her, rising to her feet with her bow in her hand.

The Agrodien contingency stood, watching their Kayl'sro eagerly.

"Wait here," the girl instructed, turning to approach the Haigok.

Liana bucked her head excitedly as Alice lifted her saddle from the ground.

"The dragons need rest, Alice," Gruloch said.

"Our allies need assistance," she informed him.

He frowned and shook his head.

"That's just the sound of waves breaking on rocks," Gruloch told her.

A long rumble of cannon blasts ensued. It was far away and could easily be mistaken for what Gruloch had taken it for.

Alice pointed to the west.

"Do you see?" she asked. "Above the trees there."

He squinted his bulbous yellow eyes.

Sure enough, a thin line of smoke rose into the air.

"I apologise," he said with regret. "I had no reason to doubt you."

"It's all right," she assured him, slapping him gently on the shoulder. "Help me get Liana ready. I need to go out to them."

"I will accompany you," he replied, summoning two other Haigok to assist both of them with their riding gear.

A thick cloud of dark smoke wafted around the galleon, obscuring the view of their surroundings from the deck. Shrill cries mixed with the sound of splitting timber and splashing water reached the ears of the galleon crew. At least one of the enemy vessels was in peril.

Zakhar peered up to the lookout.

"What do you see, lad?" he shouted.

"One frigate is sinking fast," came the reply. "Her guts have been torn open and her crew is on fire."

"We must have hit the black powder," Grady surmised.

"Bloody lucky shot is all it was," the commander replied before returning his attention to the lookout. "What else?"

"The other still floats, but she's aflame," the crewman offered. "The other two are turning wide to avoid us. One to starboard, the other to port."

Commander Zakhar quickly considered what action to take.

"First Officer," he said, signalling that he was about to give an order.

"Aye Commander." The other stood at attention.

"Prepare the port guns," Zakhar said. "Turn the ship to starboard. Bring us alongside the frigate heading towards shore. Signal the fleet to sink the other one before it escapes."

"What of the other black frigate burning to our aft, sir?"

"Let it burn," the commander replied emotionlessly. "We'll come back to finish it when we've dealt with its friend."

"Aye, Commander."

The orders were relayed, and they turned the galleon towards the shore.

"Dragons," the lookout called.

"Where?" the commander inquired.

"Directly ahead." The young man pointed. "Two of them."

Zakhar raced to the forward deck with Grady in tow. The smoke thinned out just in time for him to see two large winged beasts flash through the sky just above his tallest mast.

The dark cloud wisped and turned around him and the large ship rocked wildly as a loud noise, like something tearing the sky open, erupted in the air.

The men gave a mighty cheer.

The commander felt his heart leap for joy.

"Where are they?" he shouted to the lookout.

"The dragons are climbing into the sky and continue westward," the crewman reported. "The black frigate is off our port bow and continues to shore."

"Maintain course," the commander instructed.

"Cannons ready," came the call from below deck.

The galleon moved clear of the thick smoke. The black frigate was much closer than Zakhar had expected, almost within boarding distance.

"Bugger me," Grady huffed, his eyes wide with surprise. The rest of the crew froze in place momentarily.

"Prepare to fire," Zakhar said, not missing a beat.

Grady stood in place, watching as they drew nearer to the frigate.

"First Officer?" the commander said, nudging the other man with his elbow.

"Sir?" Grady seemed to snap out of a trance. "Sorry, sir." He quickly cleared his throat and relayed the order in a loud voice. "Prepare to fire."

The galleon closed the gap quickly, pulling alongside the black frigate.

Two distant, deep and very distinct explosions resounded from far away.

"Smoke out to sea," the lookout shouted. "The dragons have taken down the two frigates fleeing to the west, sir."

Suddenly, the frigate by their port side opened its guns upon them.

Splinters erupted around the galleon crew. A dark cloud formed over the deck.

"Fire," Zakhar commanded.

Grady repeated the order.

The vessel rocked violently as the cannons spewed a barrage of iron into the side of the enemy ship.

The screams of men on the vessel resounded through the chaos.

"Reload and fire when ready," Zakhar instructed.

"The other frigate is turning about," the lookout shouted, pointing to the black vessel that had turned towards the sea.

"After seeing what those dragons just did to their friends," Grady said, smirking, "who could blame them. They'd have a better chance against our fleet."

Zakhar nodded, agreeing with the comment as another round of gunfire erupted from below deck.

A loud explosion erupted from beneath the port side frigate, breaking its mid-deck open with a great orange fireball.

The heat was immense.

Grady lifted his arm to shield his face.

Zakhar felt the deck tilt under his feet.

"Shit," the lookout called as the ship rocked back and forth, side to side, as it settled on the water.

More cannon fire ensued from behind the galleon. With too much smoke blocking his view, Zakhar turned to the lookout again.

"Our fleet has surrounded the black frigate. They're filling her hull with holes," the crewman testified.

"What of the other one?" Grady shouted. "The one that was on fire?"

"She still burns," the lookout answered. "But she is sinking slowly. I can't see any survivors."

Zakhar watched the frigate beside them, broken and shattered, disappear below the surface.

"Let it sink," he said coolly. "Resume course to Meadowmoor."

Twenty-Nine

"We number only two hundred and fifty able fighters," Brondt reported. "Not counting present company or those on the ships from Dendadia."

"I have three hundred and sixty men who can fight," Commander Zakhar offered. "But we are better sailors than swordsmen."

Alice, seated upon a log by the fire, turned a stick around in the snow by her feet as she considered their words. Mud had mixed into the white frost, creating a strange slush.

"How many wounded?" she asked Brondt.

"Not many," Brondt replied. "A few. Nothing too serious. They can all carry a sword."

With a deep sigh, she looked around the fire to those gathered about her. Her mother and sister sat by her side, Amicia and Ursula next to them. Thornton and his men sat across the hearth from her with the Agrodien warriors. Gruloch and one of the Kazrekh riders sat by Yuri. Commander Zakhar, Schoenbach, Karlena, and Akasati closed the circle to her left.

"We'll stay here until dawn," she told them, dropping the stick in favour of toying with the iron claws hanging about her neck. "Then, we march hard and fast to the north."

"What if more ships come from the north?" Zakhar asked.

"We have your fleet to deal with that," she answered.

"It would be nice if your dragons could lend a hand," he put in.

She gave him a small grin. "Consider it done."

"We should destroy all the ships we find," Gruloch offered. "Manned or unmanned, they pose a threat."

"Manned, yes," Alice agreed. "Unmanned, we should claim." She turned her attention to Zakhar. "If need be, can you sail and fight from one of those ships of yours with a smaller crew?"

"What are you thinking?" the fleet commander enquired.

"I'm thinking that we could increase our fleet size, if your men are able to man each vessel with limited numbers."

Thornton scratched his beard.

"You think they might have left some ships for us to take?" he chuckled.

"Perhaps," she replied. "I just think it strange that we saw only six vessels with the golden banner."

"More could be on their way," Emily suggested. "Or they could have all been destroyed when Blackshore was attacked."

"You destroyed all the ships at Blackshore, correct?" Alice directed to Gruloch.

"Correct," he answered. "We left nothing floating on the water by their docks. The ships we saw today were not from Blackshore."

"They would have come from Erimoor," Akasati deduced. "It's the only place with a docking yard large enough for ships of such size, apart from Wintermarsh."

Alice saw Schoenbach agree with a nod.

"We've sailed the *Adelandria* along the west coast several times," he told the girl. "Erimoor was once a great merchant port. It would be ideal to harbour a large fleet. It offers a sheltered bay of sorts."

"Then that's where we'll find our ships," Alice told them all. "Unless they have all sailed to the west or have been summoned elsewhere by Takmel."

Commander Zakhar rubbed his fingers together nervously. He looked across the fire and found Catherine peering at him. She glanced away to the fire. He supposed he still had more work to do in earning her trust. He moved his attention to Alice.

"We could sail ahead to see," he proposed. "We could even possibly commandeer some vessels if we are able."

"No," Alice shook her head. "We'll send a scout on a dragon when the time comes. It's easier to see such things high in the air and at a far distance than it is from the ground, or by sea. I'll make my judgement of the situation then."

The fleet commander continued rubbing his fingers together, accepting Alice's response. He quickly looked to Catherine again. She was staring absently into the flames. He placed his gaze on the fire as well.

"Don't worry, Commander Zakhar." Gruloch smiled. "We won't destroy any ships this time."

Alice moved her fingers away from the iron claws, letting them fall against the bearskin cloak with a soft jingle.

"We should eat," she said. "We should get some rest. We have a long journey tomorrow."

***

The loud sound of axe hitting chocks of timber reverberated over the open ground that gently sloped away to the river. It bounced off the tall stone walls that protected the eastern side of the city and back into the ears of the one-armed boy.

He leant the axe against the large stump sticking from the snow and picked up each of the two pieces of wood he had just cut. With a hefty toss, he threw the pieces of wood onto a pile he had been adding to since noon.

As the sun moved across the sky, sinking towards the west, the boy's father watched patiently from atop of the wall with a building sense of unease. The shadows cast by the magnificent structure stretched and grew, creeping slowly over the snow towards the pile of timber. Towards his boy.

Arthur placed another chock of timber on the stump. The axe was lifted and swung over the lad's head before being thrust downwards with tremendous force.

A single blow.

The chock split in two.

"He's getting good with that thing," Lor said to David, stepping up to his side to lean against the battlement. "I think we have more than enough wood for the pyres."

"He's not cutting wood for the pyres," David replied, his eyes fixed upon his son. "He's frustrated. He needs his wife. He misses her."

"And, so he cuts wood?"

David turned to face the other.

"When I lost both of my wives, I took to hunting," the large man explained. "I then took to blaming Alice."

"That was Takmel getting inside your head, my friend," Lor reminded him.

"I know." David frowned. "But, I still let it grow. I fed it with my hatred."

"You think that's what Arthur is doing?" the other enquired. "Feeding his hatred?"

"I think he sees Takmel's head in place of each of those pieces of timber," David answered.

"He blames Takmel for Alice being away?"

"Don't you?" David questioned. "She's your niece. I know I blame him. I blame him for everything that has happened to us since we brought him into our homes."

The sound of the axe splitting another piece of timber resonated up the wall.

"You think he was working against us then?"

"From the very moment his mother died," David said.

"He was just a boy," Lor put in.

"And look at what he could accomplish in such a short time," the big man replied. David let out a long breath and turned to climb down the ladder.

"Where are you going?" Lor asked, following a short distance behind.

"To get some more wood for my boy," he answered.

"I guess we could use it to burn those dead creatures," the other surmised.

***

General Saruun Versel stood by the bar in the tavern, scrutinising the two women seated by the fire and their guards standing nearby. The man with long, dark hair and four deep scars on his face drew her attention for the most part. The one who belonged to the Lilac Queen.

His hand never left the hilt of his sword, resting upon the round pommel that stuck out from beneath his cloak. His steely eyes moved cautiously over Versel's nine men, who sat casually throughout the room, silently watching their commander and the two queens.

The other man stood rigidly. He was a trained officer whose black uniform was adorned with polished brass buttons and a golden sash that fell across his right shoulder to his left hip. Versel surmised that this one, belonging to the Gold Queen, had seen little battle; perhaps no conflict at all.

It caused her to distrust the newcomers.

The room had been cleared. She had seen to that, ordering the innkeeper to empty the place out of patrons. They made warm meals for the two women and hot beverages served.

Now, with the innkeeper gone, and his staff instructed to leave also, Versel believed she could speak openly with the queens.

"Why are you here?" she asked finally.

"You dare speak to the Queen of Erimoor with such disrespect?" the rigid officer chided.

"I know full well who she is," Versel replied. She gestured to the Lilac Queen. "This one is also a queen. Knowing that doesn't tell me why they are both here. So, I'll ask again, and I expect an answer. Why are you here?"

"You should learn your rightful place, woman," the officer said, stepping forward and pulling his sword from its sheath.

Like a flash, Versel's men were on their feet and had their swords drawn.

The officer hesitated, stopping in his tracks. He moved his hand away from his blade and opened his fingers to show his bare palms.

"We were attacked," the scar-faced man informed them. "Blackshore was completely destroyed."

"By what army?" Versel asked.

"Dragons," the other answered.

Versel's men exchanged looks. A small amount of fear, mixed with disbelief, swam over their faces. They looked to their commander, who maintained a blank composure.

"We barely made it out," the Lilac Queen added, her eyes filling with tears as she recalled the escape into the hills.

"And Erimoor?" the general pressed. "Was it destroyed too?"

The officer looked at the Gold Queen. Her chin quivered before turning her head to face Versel.

"No," she replied softly with a shake of the head. "We fled before anyone attacked."

"Were the dragons on their way to Erimoor?" Norris asked as the men returned their swords to their sheaths, relaxing before returning to their seats.

"Who are you to question Her Majest—" the officer began.

"We don't know," the Gold Queen responded, interrupting her personal guard. "We didn't want to stay and find out."

Versel let out a sigh as she leant her elbow against the bar. She picked up a mug of ale and sculled it.

"What is now the bulk of our fleet, harbours there," she said. "Does it not?"

The Gold Queen hesitated, peering to the fire as if in search of the right words.

"Let me guess." Versel pointed to the Lilac Queen. "You arrived in Erimoor and told this one," moving her finger to the other woman, "that dragons destroyed your city. That scared this one so much that she ran away with you, hoping that the Maji would take you both in with open arms. Am I near to correct?"

Both women looked ashamedly to the floor.

"The fleet?" the commander asked, looking at both of the queens' men.

"Many vessels fled," the rigid officer answered. "All, or nearly most of the naval personnel, with them."

"How many ships?"

"Almost forty have gone," he replied.

"How many remain?" she asked.

"Nearly thirty."

"And no men to sail them?" Versel queried.

The officer shook his head.

General Saruun Versel turned, placed both hands on the bar and stared at the empty mug she had drained. She wished it would refill itself so that she could empty it again and again.

"In which direction did the fleet run?" she asked.

"Most fled west," the officer answered. "We sent a few ships south to see if anything remained in Blackshore and to scout the waters to the south."

"And you haven't heard from them?" Versel questioned.

"The orders were to sail north to Wintermarsh and report directly to me there."

She stared at her empty mug.

"West," she muttered softly, thinking out loud. She raised her voice a little. "Why west?"

"Sorry?" the Gold Queen asked.

"Why did the others sail west?" Versel turned to face them again. "What's to the west for them?"

"Home, mostly," the scarred man told her. "Most of the navy was made up from pirates and men looking forward to filling their purses."

"Sellswords," Willis put in. "Just like a great deal of those men in your garrison, General."

"Pirates," Versel corrected him.

"What's the difference?" Willis asked.

"Pirates sail ships," Norris answered. "Sellswords are a pack of scum."

"Sadly," the rigid officer began, "we would not have had a fleet without them. Fortunately, we can say that none of our men accompanying us are mercenaries. They are all well-trained and dutiful soldiers in the command of Her Majesty the Golden Quee—"

"Oh, shut it, pansy boy," Norris growled.

"Oy!" Grosset, one of Versel's lieutenants, suddenly called to the queens, placing his feet on the table. He had obviously downed a few too many mugs of ale. "Why couldn't you two just wave your hands, or something, and wipe those dragons out of the sky?"

The officer gave the man a reprimanding glare. Grosset ignored the look and kept his gaze on the two women.

"It," the Lilac Queen began. She paused for a moment and swallowed. "It doesn't work like that. Our power has been fading."

"Why's that?" Grosset requested.

"Our sisters are dead," the Gold Queen answered.

"Oh," Grosset said apologetically. "Sorry to hear that."

"She means the other queens, idiot," Norris told him.

"Our prime was taken and three more since," the Gold Queen continued. "With each one passing, a little more of what we are is taken with them."

"Must be why the Maji wanted those two little girls then," Grosset said, lifting his mug to his lips.

"What girls?" An expression of fear swept over the Lilac Queen's face.

"Two girls," Grosset told her. "Both twins. Can't talk. But, by golly, they can tear the meat from a man's bones pretty fast. And all that with their magic. Two of them. How many of you lot were there before all this? Seven, wasn't it? There's only two of them."

"You best watch yourself," the scarred man growled. His hand tightened around the hilt of his sword.

"Or what?" the other tested. "There's one of you and nine of us. That pretty boy next to you won't stand a chance, and he knows it. Look at him."

Versel turned and gave each of the men a stern look.

"I'm First Garrison Commander," she told the two men, "appointed by the Maji himself, and I outrank all of you. Stand down." She looked over at her own men. "Everyone."

Grosset held up his hand apologetically and resumed drinking.

The scarred man took a little longer time before relaxing his hand and submitting to the order.

The general looked to the empty mug again. She could really use another drink.

"You and your men will stay here tonight," she told them. "In the morning, half of your soldiers will accompany you and these ladies on to Wintermarsh. The rest will remain here with me in Ironfields."

"Half?" the Lilac Queen asked, sounding like a child who wasn't getting what she thought she was entitled to.

"You heard Captain Willis mention sell swords before," Versel said. "And after what you told me about the fleet running away, I need soldiers who will follow orders. And this one," she pointed to the rigid officer, "just told us that all the men with you are well-trained..." She looked at Norris.

"Well-trained, dutiful soldiers in the command of the Golden Queen, is what he said, General," the older soldier answered.

"Thank you," she said, turning back to the queens. "As First Garrison Commander of the Maji, I am commandeering half of your men to serve the defensive force under my direct authority. You may each keep your personal guards with you. However," she looked to the Gold Queen, "you may want to reconsider who you keep by your side." She gestured to the rigid officer in his pristine uniform. "This one looks to be more interested in his appearance than protecting you, my queen."

It was an insult. A challenge.

Versel's men placed their mugs on the tables, feet squarely on the floor. They all turned to see what the well-dressed officer's response would be.

Even the queens moved their eyes to him.

The scarred man stepped back a few paces.

The officer looked around at all the staring faces, colour draining from his own.

He was nervous.

Frightened.

Cornered and put on the spot.

"I..." he stuttered. "I won't fight a lady," he managed.

"I will," Versel told him.

Another insult.

The officer looked to his queen, to the scarred man, to the nine others seated about the room.

He laughed uneasily, tensely. He glanced at the door.

"Going to run?" Versel asked, stepping towards him slowly. "Like the fleet?"

There was anger behind his eyes, but she saw a greater amount of fear beneath it all.

His hand went to the hilt of his sword.

Hers did too.

A silent recognition passed between them.

She could see that he understood what would happen to him if he lifted his blade from its sheath.

With one more glance around the room, and a last lingering, apologetic look to his queen, he dashed out through the door and into the cold street.

Willis and Reilly jumped to their feet in order to pursue.

"Let him go," Versel said, relaxing as she turned about, returning to the bar. The mug was still empty. "He'll be dead by dawn if no one takes him in for the night."

The Gold Queen stared at the door, mouth agape.

"Sorry, my queen." The scarred man bowed slightly. "I offer my services to you, with my queen's permission."

"Of course," the Lilac Queen agreed, placing her arms around the woman seated beside her. "Braden can protect both of us."

Versel lifted herself onto the bar to reach over the other side. She found a corked flask sitting on a shelf just beneath the counter. She lifted it to the countertop and uncorked it, emitting a loud pop.

"He just ran away," the Gold Queen said, still gawking at the door.

"Because he's a coward," Versel offered, pouring something of a brown texture into her mug. "I'm betting he advised you to ride to Wintermarsh. Didn't he?"

The woman in gold looked at her, astonished, and nodded.

Versel drained her mug dry and poured again.

"Half of your men," she reminded the queens. "You and your men will stay here for the night, but in the morning, I will appropriate half of them into my forces."

Thirty

The traditions of Woodmyst were always to be upheld by all. Those who Richard and Becka raised expected it from any seeking permanent refuge in their community. No matter from whence you came, there were certain things that Woodmyst always did, and would always do.

One such thing included the setting of pyres. Regardless of the god each individual worshipped, every elder held the right to speak their words over the dead. It was a tradition set in place during the time of Chief Tomas Warde, who didn't believe in any of the gods, but didn't prevent others from doing so. It was only fair then, for all believers of all beliefs to have their say during a ceremonial pyre.

Another such thing included that all ceremonial pyres were to be set on the ground between the western wall and the edge of the Forest of Lunkhul. And such a thing needed to be performed once again at the edge of Woodmyst.

They mourned the men that perished upon the wall during the battle with the dark creatures as flames enveloped their bodies. Wives, mothers, sons and daughters wept bitter tears as they bade their loved ones farewell. Many from the city had gathered to show their respects and pay tribute to those who sacrificed their lives for the sake of all others.

Elders were asked to speak, to offer kind and meaningful words to help soothe aching hearts and quench the fiery anger that many experienced after the assault. The guards tolled the chimes in the towers by the gate, slowly, methodically, as if signalling the gods to open other, unseen gates to allow the departed through.

Finally, with the pomp said and done, Magistrate Stephen Latham stepped forward to address the crowd.

"Fellow citizens of Woodmyst," he began. "These are hard times. Heavy times. Fathers, husbands and sons taken from us before their time, ushered through the door to the safekeeping of Grolle.

"How many times have these grounds borne the ashes of the dead? How many times have we laid a torch to the pyres here? How many more times are yet to come?

"Though some of us lost husbands, sons and fathers here," he continued, "we must remember that word is still yet to reach us from the west, where other fathers, husbands and fathers have gone. Our future lies here, and they have gone to secure it. These brave men we honour today remained here to protect it.

"Let us not forget their sacrifice," Latham said to all of those gathered. "The living and the dead. For Woodmyst."

"For Woodmyst," the crowd chorused sombrely.

***

To the east, far across the pastureland outside the East Gate, beyond the hill and by the river, another pyre was lit.

It was a rough construction with wood piled untidily with the bodies of dark creatures thrown on top. Their arms and legs sprawled and jutted in all directions.

Alan and David held torches, lighting the fire beneath the dead beasts as Lor and Ruttger watched on, standing by the horse and cart that had carted the creatures and kindling to the place they now stood. Arthur wasn't too far from them. He bandaged his hand after blistering and splitting the skin on his palm from overusing the axe.

After a while, the fire took hold and lifted great flames into the air as it burned the bodies of the beasts.

The wood crackled.

The smoke grew thick and dark.

"Takmel could accomplish at least one fell deed at the expense of these creatures," Arthur said. "Those poor devils in the prison cells didn't stand a chance."

"I hate to say it," Ruttger replied, "but I'm glad there weren't much left of the old bookkeepers. I dare say we would have had the task of building another pyre for them as well."

"Pails, cloths and water," David said, dousing his torch in the snow before leaning against the cart. "That's what Andris said. The only way they could clean up that mess was with pails, cloths and water. There wouldn't have been enough of them left to put in the kitchen stove."

The older man beside him shuddered at the thought.

***

At the glade, they ignited a large fire pit in the centre of the lower ground. There, the northern men and older male younglings of the Agrodien, had set ablaze to the remains of the dark creatures that they had encountered.

In the days that followed, a bond had formed between the younglings and the four men. Each rising of the sun, after the men had left the warmth of their huts, was met with eager reptilian faces that wanted to go hunting and fishing.

The Agrodien mothers urged the men to take their children, male and female, on small quests. Glaun surmised it wasn't to teach the younglings anything that they didn't already know. After all, he had seen them rip the dark creatures to shreds with his own eyes.

He guessed it was to give the mothers a little time for self-reflection, possibly to mourn lost husbands or, in Galonia's case, place thoughts upon those who were with their Kayl'sro.

Glaun was enjoying his moments with the younglings, learning their ways of trapping and throwing a spear, and teaching them words of the common tongue. He found them to be much quicker at absorbing his lessons than he was at receiving their knowledge.

He was trying.

"We should try for a child," he told his wife Lilen over supper one night.

"The bug has bitten you, hasn't it?" she replied.

"Bug?" he looked about on the floor of their hut.

"I mean, that you are feeling this way because you are fond of the younglings," she told him.

He nodded.

"Yes," he admitted. "I so enjoy being around them. We should try for one."

"You think I've been holding out on you?" She smiled.

He gave her a puzzled look.

"What do you mean?"

"Every time we join," she said, leaning over the bowl of rabbit stew before her, "I hope and secretly pray that this will be the time. But, it never is. What if I am not able to?"

He leant back in his chair, looking as if something had drained him of all joy.

"I never considered..." he said, peering at the fire flickering inside the stove. He moved his gaze to her. She was still peering at him, sadness in her eyes, waiting for him to say something meaningful. "It doesn't matter. I have you, and that's all I need."

"I can try harder," she offered.

He smiled at her lovingly and shook his head.

"I'll pray more," she told him.

"You are an amazing woman," he said, reaching over the table to take her hand. "If it is meant to be, it will happen. Besides, what if it is something wrong with me that prevents us from having a youngling of our own?

"Forget the prayers," he continued. "Alice always says that there are no gods, anyway. Besides, I like joining together with you because I really like it. Let's not make it a chore."

She giggled and squeezed his hand.

***

"With the docks completed, and the city under repair," Monteacute said from behind the bar of *The Petty Beggar*, "shouldn't we consider sending a ship or two to reopen trade with Dendadia?"

Landon Wake, seated at a table by the hearth, Captain Davine Staiger upon his lap, lifted his mug of ale to his lips and drank it dry. He held it up for Monteacute to see.

"The problem with opening the trade routes is that the Dendadian fleet has their ships acting as a blockade for the time being," the sub-commander replied. Kateryn Crane brushed her red hair from her face as she took Wake's mug from his hand. She crossed the room and placed the vessel in front of the sheriff to have it refilled.

"Yeah." The other man screwed his face up. "I don't get that."

"No one gets in," Staiger explained. "And, no one gets out. It's that part that matters most."

"No one getting out?" Audrey Mountell asked. She was wiping the tables down to prepare for the coming night's business. "Like the Maji?"

"Exactly," the captain of the *Gypsy* returned.

"But he's not even anywhere near Newholt," Rose Heron offered.

"That we know of," Wake replied quickly. "They say he can turn to smoke and travel anywhere."

"Who says that?" Monteacute chuckled. "Vagabonds and travelling merchants who have spent too many years in the Core Lands."

"Maybe," Wake answered as Kateryn placed his freshly filled mug on the table before him. "But I have seen a girl upon a dragon. After seeing that, I'd just about believe anything anyone tells me."

***

Alice had led her army north, past the charred ruins of Blackshore and onward to Erimoor. There, they found twenty-one ships still tied to the docks or anchored a short distance offshore in a small bay. Other vessels floated freely away out to sea or have their hulks smashed against the rocky outcrops surrounding the harbour.

"There are people watching us, sir," one cavalryman said to Brondt.

Alice, standing on a boardwalk that hemmed the harbour a few paces ahead of the commander and his riders, peered along one dock to three ships swaying gently on the rising tide. The Agrodien warriors surrounded her, thick cloaks draped over them as a gentle snow-drift fell.

Erimoor was a well-sheltered township. The land, just to the north of the settlement, expanded far to the west, where it culminated at a point. Through the grey haze, Alice could see a tall beacon tower there, made of stone and currently unlit.

The ground curved around the water to the south, almost enclosing the bay, leaving a wide enough space between the headlands for ships to pass through. Large hills, sharp and craggy, surrounded Erimoor like a natural defensive wall, offering shelter from the harsh winds that swept down from the north. Whatever gusts made their way into the village were thwarted and dulled into nothing more than a gentle breeze.

Guard towers stood at intervals on hilltops surrounding the town-ship. The glint of iron still made Alice turn to them once in a while, uneasy and tense. She knew the towers were empty and what she saw was nothing more than the crude alarm chimes swinging on ropes attached to the towers' rafters.

"Send men to knock on each door and assure the people here that we intend no harm to them," Brondt told the cavalryman. "Find a magistrate or any elders willing to speak with us."

Alice moved her attention back to the beacon tower far away on the northern point.

"A few horses in the stable house," an infantryman puffed as he jogged to Brondt's side. The commander peered down at him from his steed.

"Are they fit to take riders?" he asked.

"They look like farm horses," the other answered. "And I didn't see any riding gear in there. Plenty of straw and grain, though. More than enough for our lot."

"Good man," Brondt said. "Find somewhere safe to shelter."

"Yes, sir." The infantryman saluted and moved away.

"We're not taking any horses," Alice said to the commander, her eyes fixed upon the lighthouse. "Not unless we really need to."

"Some of ours have suffered injuries," he informed her. "Minor cuts and bruises. Some have muscle fatigue from the move. Nothing too big. But still, replacements would be worth considering."

"We need to try and win these people over, Commander. We're not taking their workhorses from them," she replied. "I'll look at our horses and see what I can do."

He watched her for a moment, accepting her decision, but wondering why she remained focussed upon the sea. Zakhar's fleet had entered the harbour, dropping anchor away from the docks, but she directed her face to something beyond.

"What do you see?" he asked.

"A beacon tower," she answered. "It appears empty, but I'm uncertain."

He squinted, not able to see anything through the haze caused by the falling snow. Turning to a younger man sitting on a steed beside him, he gestured questioningly with a nod of his head. The other rider shook his head and shrugged. He couldn't see anything either.

"Is it lit?" Brondt asked.

"No," she replied, turning to face him. "If it was, you would be able to see it." She stepped down from the boardwalk and onto the ground, moving around the cavalrymen with the Agrodien in tow. "I need some men to pay a visit to the tower. See if it is empty. Try to convince anyone there that we are not here to harm them."

"And you?"

She stopped and met his gaze.

"I'll tend to your injured horses," she replied before continuing on her way.

Thirty-One

Arthur stroked the chestnut stallion, gently moving his bandaged hand over the steed's nose. His fingers were exposed enough to touch the horse's pelt. It stood motionless, its eyes half-closed, wanting more.

"You haven't taken him out for a while," Alan said quietly as he entered the stable house through the large open doors. It was dark, with only a few lit torches on the walls that cast deep shadows in the many corners of the large space.

The glistening of watchful eyes moved around in the blackness. Some snorted their protests at the uninvited individual.

"Too much snow," Arthur replied, watching the stallion's ears twitch as the other drew closer. "And my hand still hurts too much to hold the reins."

"Has the weeping stopped?"

Arthur shot a questioning look at his friend.

"Your hand," Alan clarified.

"Mostly," he replied, returning his attention to the steed. "It wasn't that bad. The bandage is Becka just being careful, I think."

Alan watched him for a moment, leaning against the door to the pen in which Arthur kept the stallion.

"You thought I meant you."

"What?" Arthur gave him a quick sideways glance.

"You thought I meant you when I asked about the weeping," Alan explained. "You've been crying."

"I haven't," the boy answered.

But Alan could see the streaks leading down Arthur's cheeks.

"It's all right," he said. "I think if I were away from her, and if I were her husband, I would cry endlessly."

Arthur felt a painful lump form in his throat.

"I just want her back home," he told the other. Tears welled in his eyes. "I don't like not knowing how she is or where she is. I want her to come home."

Alan put a comforting arm around Arthur's shoulders.

***

Christina, the Gold Queen, and Sarah, the Lilac Queen, resettled in Wintermarsh at the displeasure of their husband. He had placed them in rooms at the farthest end of the corridor from his own. His demeanour towards the last three women of the Seven had transformed. He had become quietly adverse towards them, avoiding them where he could.

Isabel's seat beside the marble throne had been taken away. Now, each of the twins had a place on either side of the Maji. He relocated the White Queen off the dais completely and positioned her on a small seat between two others against the wall to the right of the raised platform.

Subtlety wasn't one of Takmel's strongest traits. It was as if he was showing his willingness to toss old things aside in favour of the new.

She felt offended by the removal from her place. That he could so easily treat her so indifferently when her power waned. The concept that one person could discard another once they were no longer of any use, caused her to suffer some mild form of heartbreak. At the same time, her loathing for her husband had grown tremendously, making her grateful that she didn't need to sit so close to him when she was required to be in this cold, white room.

Her thoughts turned to the two little girls, the ones he now professed to love.

The ones he now called wives.

Soon, she believed, they too would outlive his interest, and he would cast them aside like her and the two women beside her.

The bruises on her face and the split lip he had given her were more than enough evidence to support her suppositions.

At least he was kind enough to give them seats to his right rather than inside the inglenook across the room from them. The flames burned high there, and she wouldn't have put it past him to have considered throwing the three of them into the hearth.

It was only that there was still a bond between them that saved them. Strength and power still linked them and couldn't be separated without the occurrence of death. Death to one of them would bring him pain and loss of power, and a draining of strength.

So, there they were.

A conundrum, kept alive and given accommodation only for the sake of his survival.

Five silent wives, three of which were powerless against him.

Useless, for the most part.

"We shouldn't have come," Christina, seated on her left, whispered beneath her breath.

"Shhh," Isabel hissed, keeping her eyes upon Takmel.

"Report," the Maji said loudly, beckoning a soldier by the chamber door.

The soldier started forward, his boot falls echoing throughout the room.

"Say nothing, do nothing," Isabel told the others softly, "unless I tell you to."

"My lord." The soldier bowed, dropping to one knee at the foot of the dais. "Ironfields defences are set in place. We have sent scouts to Erimoor and await their return."

"We can assume that Erimoor is lost to us," Takmel put in. "She is on her way here. There is no doubt in my mind that she intends to take what once was mine and use it to her advantage." He shot a vile glare to the Gold Queen. "If only someone had thought to burn everything to the ground before retreating."

"There are people there," Christina said, standing up. "Innocent people. I couldn't burn their houses."

"Shhh," Isabel urged the woman.

"Where could they go? It's cold and there are children," Christina continued. "Alice won't hurt them or use them against you. She can't. They are loyal to you, Takmel."

The Maji was rapidly growing impatient and irritated.

He flicked his wrist in her direction, causing her to slip backwards, her legs flying into the air, knocking her head hard against the marble wall.

The sickening sound reverberated around the room as the Gold Queen fell to the floor. A minor wound opened on the back of her head and oozing blood matted her hair together.

The twin girls exchanged a look of shock and horror.

Isabel quickly dropped to her knees beside the fallen woman and pressed her hand to the wound. Sarah raced from her chair and lowered herself beside the White Queen, giving the Maji a disapproving glance.

He returned her stare with a wry grin.

"It would appear my wife has a soft spot for the people of Erimoor," he sneered. "Seems that she isn't much of a tactician. She doesn't realise that the people of Erimoor could easily be swayed to offer support to Alice and her menagerie of men and strange creatures. Burning them all would have prevented that possibility. Burning all the ships would have been a tactical advantage instead of leaving them there for the picking. Getting on board, loading them up with supplies and sailing them around the point to bring them here would have been even better.

"Instead," he continued, "I have a bunch of extra men and horses. More mouths to feed." He gestured to Isabel with a jutting finger. "Instead of one stupid wife with no real value, I now have two more."

Upon hearing his words, Christina and Sarah sobbed. They bit deep and hurt terribly.

Isabel, however, felt one tear roll down her cheek. She held Takmel's gaze, offering her intense, bitter hatred towards him.

He must have seen it in her eyes, or felt it in his bones.

"I'm done here," he huffed, lifting himself from the throne and starting down the steps of the dais. "Come, girls."

The twins hesitated, exchanging confused glances before following their husband through the room. They shot quick, worried gazes at the three women on the floor by the side of the room as they moved away in haste.

"What are we going to do?" Sarah asked quietly as Takmel and the two girls disappeared from view.

Isabel looked down to the sad eyes of the Gold Queen before turning to see the same expression on the Lilac Queen's face.

"Don't concern yourself with that right now," she said. "I have an idea." The White Queen looked over to the guard still kneeling on the ground, perplexed by what he had witnessed. "Help me get her back to her chamber."

"Yes, my queen," the guard replied, lifting himself to his feet.

***

Alice whispered to the animals as she crept through the stable house. She gently touched their wounds and ran her palms over their flanks, commanding the tissue beneath the skin to reform and heal.

She had spent much of her day tending to the steeds. The sun had dipped towards the horizon and the temperature had fallen.

Her intention was to make sure that each creature was well-prepared for the journey ahead; a journey she wanted to begin at first light.

She healed abrasions, ranging from grazes to deep cuts. With a touch and a whisper, she cured bruises beneath the skin. Knotted muscles relaxed, and the horses were made whole again. As she worked her way deeper into the stable, she sensed someone watching from the loft that stretched along the length of the buildings, above the pens to her right. She ignored it, pretending not to hear the rustling of straw and clumsy bumping the individual made in following her deeper into the building.

One horse nickered deeply, softly, as she touched an open wound on its shoulder. It bent its head towards her as she whispered into its ear, "It's all right."

"What are you doing to them?" a young voice asked from above her.

"Helping," she answered, peering up to the dirty face of a young boy. He looked to be eight or nine years old at the most. "Why are you here?"

"I'm the stableboy," he answered. His clothes were raggedy, with rips in the seams of his patchy coat.

"Where are your parents?"

"Where are yours?" he questioned. There was a hint of defensiveness in his voice.

"My mother is in the manor with my sister," Alice told him in as much of a friendly voice as she could muster. "My father died many years ago."

"Why have you got swords on your back?" he asked, pointing to the hilts sticking out from beneath her cloak.

"For fighting with," she explained.

"Did your father teach you?" he pressed. "To fight?"

"No," she replied with a grin. "I taught myself. You still haven't answered my question. Where are your parents?"

"Dunno." He shrugged, moving to a ladder a few paces away. He started down, but suddenly froze in place when he neared the floor. His eyes were wide with fear as he gawked towards the door.

Alice didn't turn to see what was there. She had noticed the enormous shadow spill into the room before the stableboy had seen the Agrodien.

"Kayl'sro?" Yuri called softly. His voice sounded deep and more like a growl. He spoke to her in his own tongue. "Are you all right? I heard another voice in here."

"I'm fine," she answered, using his language. "A boy is in here. Nothing more."

Yuri emitted a satisfied grunt and returned to his post outside.

The boy watched on, astonished.

"That's my friend," Alice told him. "He looks after me."

"He's so big," the boy whispered as he lowered himself to the floor. "I don't think I've seen anything bigger except for horses and cows."

"Dragons are much bigger," she informed him as she stroked the steed gently.

"Dragons?" he murmured.

She replied with a nod. "We have many."

"How many?" he asked, sounding doubtful.

"Thirty."

"No," he gasped. "I don't believe you. How come I didn't see them? Where are they?"

"On a field just outside of town," she explained. "Where most of our men are located."

"Can I see?" he asked excitedly.

Alice turned and looked him squarely in the eyes.

"Only if you help me."

He nodded enthusiastically.

"You must answer all of my questions, understand?"

He continued to nod.

"All right." She placed a hand on his shoulder. "What's your name?"

"Warren."

"Just Warren?"

"I don't know my family name," he told her. "I don't know my parents. The Headman took me when I was little and they placed me in the care of the stable master."

"Where is the stable master?"

"Gone with the others," he replied. "They put on armour and rode north."

"And the Headman?"

"Gone with them," Warren explained. "He went with two ladies dressed in different colours. One in gold and the other in purple."

"Lilac," Alice corrected him. "How many went with them?"

"All the horses," the boy answered. He gestured around the stable house. " Except the old farm nags. This was all pretty well empty until you lot put your horses in here."

"And the men," she continued, "the ones who put their horses in here. They didn't see you?"

He shook his head.

"I was up there the whole time," he told her, pointing to the loft. "Hiding in the straw. Listening to them. They kept talking about the Maji and how they couldn't wait until Alice killed him so they could all go home. Other things like that." He looked at her in question. "This Alice lady must be powerful if she is going to kill the Maji. I've heard things about him and how he uses magic, and how powerful he is. She must be pretty powerful, too. Do you know her?"

She nodded. "I'm Alice."

He took a step back and sized her up. Slowly, his head shook back and forth.

"No," he said, a disbelieving smile spreading over his face. "You can't be. You're just a girl."

"I am," Alice affirmed. "And the Maji is just a boy. Not much older than me."

"And you're going to kill him?"

She looked to the boy for a seemingly long time.

"I don't know," Alice answered. "I'll try."

The boy looked at the door of the stable house, remembering the gigantic shadow that stood there only moments before, the monstrosity of his form, the giant sword strapped to his waist.

"Will you kill the people in this town, too?"

Alice shook her head. "No. The people will be unharmed if they don't pose any threat to us."

"Lots of old people here," Warren told her. "Some children like me. Some men and women. All the fighting men have gone. All the weapons are with them. There are only farmers and merchants left behind. I don't like them too much. They're all a bit nasty. Pushing me and kicking me when they want me to bridle their horses faster. Still, I don't think they should all get killed for that."

He seemed to plead for them.

"All right," she said. "I've told my people not to harm them. They'll be safe."

"Just don't go to the beacon tower," he suddenly urged her. His eyes widened as he gripped her sleeve in his hand.

She gave him a confused look. "What's that?"

"Don't go out to the beacon tower," he repeated. "There are things out there guarding it."

"Things?"

"Don't go out there," he insisted. "Stay here, in the town. Tell your people to stay here."

"What things?"

**

The road, although covered with snow, was well-worn and easy enough to follow. Mostly, it followed the water's edge, only diverting to move over or around steep rocky outcrops. Here and there, an empty, broken vessel, recently smashed upon the rocks, would creak and groan as the tide pushed and pulled at the hulk resting upon the shore.

It was almost tranquil.

The harbour appeared as if made of smooth glass, broken here and there by a sudden breeze that swept over the tall hills to their right or from around the point ahead of them, from the west. Thornton didn't like it when that happened. The head-on gusts were fleeting and rare, but when they came, they brought a terrible stink of salt and decay with them. The welcome northerly breeze would sweep it away, replacing it with the fresh aroma of a pine forest beyond the ridge.

He glanced over to the fleet sitting on the water closer to the town. Their sails were folded away. Their blue flags with the axe-bearing eagle waved every once in a while upon the gentle wind.

The number of vessels had grown from twelve to thirty-three as Zakhar and his men commandeered every able ship. It wasn't much of a takeover, as there was no one to oppose them.

Erimoor was far away behind them, shrouded in a white haze caused by falling snow. It too, was easy to conquer. No soldiers. No guards. Nothing worth taking out a dagger for, let alone his sword.

Only elderly, children and women ranging from the old to very young could be found, apart from some men who were ill-equipped to fight and quite willing to surrender. Thornton didn't regard them as cowards, like some of the other men that had come from the east. He considered them wise in judgement, knowing that they didn't possess the skills to overcome the army from Newholt and Woodmyst.

Alice had made it clear to all of them that only those who acted violently were to be taken by violence. After the episode with the straw men at the Griralith Pass, and knowing what was to come, none of the men wanted another battle.

Not yet.

Although he wasn't a genuine believer, he supposed this time that the gods were offering their favour.

His face contorted as the wind spun around from the west. A rancid, salty and sickly stench enveloped him. The steed he rode snorted in complaint.

"What makes that kind of stink?" Brook carped.

Thornton looked at the beacon tower. Made of dark stone, weather-worn and cylindrical, the structure stretched high into the air before them. Dark weed-covered its lower section, twisting about the base like webs, catching the snow along its tendrils. Dark windows dotted the side of the building, spiralling upwards at intervals from a large, rusted iron door on the ground, around the tower several times before reaching the top.

The captain pulled his horse to a halt. The steed lowered its head and gave it a mighty shake.

The stench was at its thickest here.

"I don't want to go in there," Jendryng muttered. "Smells like something got killed and is rotting away inside."

"We're not even inside, yet," Vawdrey said.

"I know," the younger man said. "That's what I mean. It's fucking bad."

"Language," Thornton reproved with a grunt.

"Well, it is," Jendryng continued. He gestured to the enormous iron door. "What's it going to be like in there? It's bad out here. Imagine what it's like in there."

"We have a job to do," Brook said, sliding from his horse. "You want to stay out here with the horses, be my guest."

"Yeah," the young man agreed. "I can do that."

"You stay with him, Vawdrey," Thornton commanded.

"What?" the other enquired, giving his commander a confused and questioning look. "I said nothing. Did I?"

"Five horses," the captain said in reply as he lowered himself to the ground. He handed the reins to Vawdrey, still atop of his steed. "Two-man job. So, you stay out here with Jendryng. I think the four of us can handle a smelly tower."

Cheyne handed his leads over to the younger soldier as Sparrow led his steed over to Vawdrey.

"Here you are," he said with a smile. Vawdrey took the reins with a shake of his head, offering the other a look of disdain. "We'll call down if we need you."

"Throw yourself off when you get to the top," the other snapped.

Brook pressed his hand to the cold door.

"There's no handle, and it's probably locked anyway," Jendryng offered. "We should just go back."

The door opened with a loud, metallic creak.

"Nope," Brook told him. "Not locked."

The potency of the foul odour increased.

Jendryng scrunched his face in disgust.

"Phfwar!" he blurted. "I really hope you lot have a great time in there."

Thornton shot him a reprimanding look as he pulled his scarf over his nose and followed Brook inside.

The stairs went up.

Made of hewn stone, they wound to the left, crooked and worn.

As they climbed, Brook noticed slender fissures cut into the stone wall to their right. They were just tall enough for an average man, barely wide enough for one of extremely thin stature to squeeze into.

"Where do you think those lead to?" he asked.

"To the centre of the tower," Thornton replied, trying to peer into one. Deep darkness and a face full of stink confronted him. "We should have brought torches."

He signalled the lieutenant to continue the climb.

They found more openings along the way. Cheyne was the first to notice something of a pattern with them.

"They have been positioned exactly between each of the windows," he blurted.

"What?" Sparrow questioned.

"Look." He pointed to a portal. "Window on the left here. We'll come across one of those holes on the right next. Then, another window on the left. You see for yourself."

Thornton saw. The pattern held true as they continued to climb. There were no other doors or passages, just the stairwell with small open windows that allowed light and air in on one side and thin gaps in the stone wall leading to darkness within on the other.

Eventually, after a lengthy climb, they reached the top.

The stair opened onto a level platform that spanned the top of the tower. Someone had constructed a shelter there with walls of stone and an old clay tiled roof. Several tiles had fallen and smashed upon the timber platform. The timber, both the flooring and the roofing frame, had rotted through in places.

Thornton could see that the structure was not just in urgent need of repair, but would need a total rebuild. The wood had turned dark from weathering. Great holes had formed in the floor. Each foot placement felt abnormal. The surface beneath him creaked and seemed to bow. It was dangerous, and he wanted to get back to the ground as quickly as he could.

Sparrow bent near one of the gaping holes in the floor. Directly beneath was the dark chasm of the tower's interior. The stench rose through the hole, wafting now and then into the soldier's face as if the structure was breathing.

But it wasn't the hole that had his attention.

"Look at this," he said to Thornton, brushing some snow away to trace over marks by the edge of the hole. "What do you think made these?"

The captain crouched and ran a finger along one of the marks.

They were scratches set deep into the timber and always in sets of four.

Dried, dark stains tarnished the edges of some of the score marks.

"Fingers made these," Thornton answered.

"Beacon's useless," Cheyne announced, crouching beside a rusted heap of iron. The shelter had housed the contraption well in its day, but the years had been unkind to it. Now, it is nothing more than junk.

Sparrow moved to the edge of the platform.

"Nice view of the bay," he said, peering back to Erimoor.

Even through the haze of falling snow, the quaint structures of houses and stores with their high, frost-covered rooftops appeared majestic. The large manor at the eastern edge of town, resting halfway up a hill, almost appeared regal. Its high walls and large buildings were hard to ignore, even with the falling snow somewhat obscuring the view. Just to see the township nestled by the surrounding, stony hills, decorated with white dust and the clear, mirror-like water of the bay, was well worth the climb.

A deep, orange glow from the setting sun gave the view an added element of beauty and caused the men to pause for a moment to soak it in.

All except Thornton.

"Sun's going down," he said, peering out to the ocean beyond the point. "Time to go."

He started towards the stairs as the sun dipped beneath the sea.

A deep groan filled the stairwell beneath them, rising upwards through the tower.

A loud clunk echoed along the stone walls.

"What was that?" Sparrow asked.

"The door," Brook answered.

Cheyne moved to the edge of the platform and peered over the side. Far below, he could see the other two men still seated on their steeds, holding onto the tethers of the other beasts. They were both gawking at the opening into the tower.

"Oy," he called down to them. "Stop playing games and open that door."

Vawdrey looked up at him and pointed to the opening.

"There's something in there," he shouted back.

Cheyne was about to consider the other's words as part of the jest, but Jendryng had his sword out at the ready.

There really was something inside.

Thirty-Two

The timber door suddenly burst open, bringing a gust of cold air into the cake store.

There were seven frightened young children huddled on the floor with three equally scared women pressed against the far wall. There were two shelves above them, lined with freshly baked cakes. They all looked at the intruder stepping into the room.

She peered at the colourful display. One had a dark chocolate coating with bright white cream jutting from its middle. Another was covered in white glazing with little pink flowers made of sweet, sugar-filled petals. Another had a message scribbled in runes made of icing.

The vision was delectable; something she didn't expect to see in a town under the control of the Maji.

"There," the stableboy said, pointing to an old woman under the shelves. "That's her."

Alice snapped back to reality and looked at the lady. She had a round face with large pink cheeks. A headscarf, adorned with colourful flora draped over her and tied under her chin.

"Warren," another woman gasped as she gave the boy a disdainful glare. She was very young and held onto three little infants tightly. Her eyes flashed back to Alice and the two swords strapped to her back.

"I'm not here to hurt any of you," Alice assured them, stepping on into the room. Warren followed closely, closing the door behind him. "I desperately need your help."

"Why would we help you?" the third woman questioned. Her voice shook with fear. "You want to kill us. Why else would you come?"

"We're not here to kill anyone in Erimoor," she said. "You have my word."

"The word of a little girl," the first woman muttered. "Who are you to make such promises?"

"She's their leader," Warren said with a smile. The old woman appeared to show interest in the statement, looking to the boy before scrutinising the girl carefully. "She has a dragon and can heal injured horses."

"You command them?" the old woman asked.

"Yes," Alice replied.

"Even them?" She pointed to the window, looking out to the street. Alice turned to see the Agrodien warriors gathering outside. The young children gulped in horror and cried.

"They're going to eat us," one child blurted.

"Shhh," the first woman hissed softly, pulling the child closer to her chest.

"They're my friends," Alice told them. "They answer to me."

"And your name?" the old woman asked, standing up. She was shorter than the girl and used a stick to balance herself.

"Alice," she answered.

"Alice," one infant hissed, as if it was a curse.

"Quiet, child," the second young lady chided.

"They all call me Amma Gertrude." The elderly lady smiled, suddenly changing her demeanour. "You look like a nice young girl, Alice. I bet all the young men in your army have tried their luck with you."

Alice felt her face redden in a mix of embarrassment and anger.

"I have a husband," she answered, offering a curious look to the other.

"So young!" The woman shook her head. "He must consider himself a lucky man."

"He most likely does," Alice said, stepping towards her. "But he and I are the same age. Look. I came because Warren told me you could help."

"Did he?" She shot the boy a sideways glance. The stableboy appeared uncomfortable until Amma Gertrude gave him a smile that was as sweet as her cakes appeared. "What can I help you with exactly, Alice?"

The girl looked at the two other women on the floor. They continued to clasp the children, still afraid of her.

"The beacon tower," Alice said.

Amma Gertrude seemed to tense. "You can't go out there," the old woman exclaimed. "It's cursed."

"Cursed?"

Amma Gertrude waved her hands dismissively. "Don't go out there," she repeated. "Stay here. Have some cake. I can make tea."

"I have people out there now," Alice informed the other.

The old woman gave her a disparaging look.

"Then they are lost to you," Amma Gertrude replied.

Alice peered through the window to where the Agrodien gathered. Their cloaks wrapped tightly around them as they stood sentry in the street.

"My friends and I will go out to them," the girl said. "We'll bring them back, curse or no curse."

"No, you won't," one of the young women said, standing up. "The tower is cursed. Any who enter never leave. It has always been this way. Every few years, the young boys forget the tales are true and they go out to overcome their fears. Always, every time without fail, at least one never comes back. We never go to the beacon tower. It is never lit. Something vile dwells in there."

Amma Gertrude leant upon her stick and took a deep breath.

"Ivette is right about most of what she says," the old woman said. "All except that it was always been this way. It wasn't.

"The tower was once our beacon. It guided ships into our harbour, keeping them from the rocks on the point. Our men kept it well. They used to say that you could see the light from all the way to Blackshore.

"When I was a little girl," she continued, "much younger than you are now, a woman came to Erimoor on a black ship filled with soldiers. She dressed in green clothes and looked beautiful.

"She tried to claim our town. Our men resisted and fought back. The battle didn't last long. Most of our men were killed, and those that weren't were imprisoned in the beacon tower.

"She cursed it then," Amma Gertrude said. "She told us that if any were to try to free those inside, they would join them and never escape. She said that if we didn't submit to her authority, she would curse the whole town. I will never forget her name. Yasmeen Svoboda. But she made us call her something else."

"The Sovereign," Alice said sourly.

The old lady nodded.

"She's dead," the girl said.

"The curse still holds," Amma Gertrude told her.

Alice looked through the window towards the sea. Towards the beacon tower. It was far away and shrouded in a white haze.

"It won't for much longer."

***

Thornton raced down the stairs with his sword drawn.

The revolting stench emitting from the slender holes to his left seemed to intensify.

Round and round the spiral staircase, he ran, his men on his heels. The portals to his right showed him that the snow was still falling, and the sky darkened.

"Should have brought torches," he grunted to himself as they neared the bottom.

The shadows had grown darker and darker as they descended the stone steps, but it wasn't quite dark enough to avoid seeing what waited for them by the door.

A man.

At least, Thornton believed so, until he had a moment to take in the spectacle.

Empty eye sockets stared up at him from an almost fleshless face. Dried pieces of rotted skin and hair clung sporadically to the decayed, discoloured dome sitting upon exposed vertebrae. Its neck creaked and cracked softly as it moved its head to peer at the other three men behind the captain.

Thornton studied the figure carefully. It wore raggedy clothing, ripped and rotting, hanging like strips of ribbon over its rib cage. In its right hand, gripped by bony fingers just held together by thin slivers of sinew, was a rusted dagger.

Cheyne pressed his face to the closest window.

"Get that door open!" he shouted urgently.

Jendryng and Vawdrey were already there, pushing with all of their might. Whereas Brook could open it with scarcely any effort only a short time before, they could not make it even creak under their combined strength.

"We're trying," the younger of the two called back.

"Get a rope on it and make the horses pull it off the hinges," Cheyne suggested.

Vawdrey stepped back to look up to the other.

"There's no bloody handle to tie a rope onto," he hollered. "There's no bloody anything."

Thornton kept his gaze fixed on the figure at the base of the stairs.

It simply stood there, moving its head slightly as if looking at each of the men.

Cheyne stepped back from the window and looked down to the bony spectacle.

"There's no way they can get that door open," he informed the rest.

"I heard," Thornton replied, frustrated.

Cheyne turned and climbed back up the stairwell a few steps. "Maybe we can go back to the top and climb down."

He felt something grab his leg as he spoke.

Dozens of arms reached suddenly from a dark fissure on the inside wall.

Some had greying flesh.

Some had barely any flesh at all.

Some limbs looked like those of adults.

Some were like those of children.

Grasping.

Snatching.

Gripping.

Clawing.

He screamed and swiped his blade down defensively.

Two of the limbs fell to the floor. The rest pulled him closer, closer, closer to the dark hole.

His stomach leapt to his throat as he watched the fallen limbs drag themselves back into the fissure, like insects fleeing away into the darkness.

More arms jutted from the slender passage, gripping his arm, his neck.

Pulling.

Pulling.

"Help me," he shouted.

Sparrow was first to intervene. He started hacking at the limbs closest to Cheyne's face. With each successful dismemberment came more, reaching hands and curling fingers jutting from the wall.

Brook and Sparrow attacked with ferocity, desperately trying to free their friend.

It was then that the lone figure near the door moved.

Each step appeared clumsy, awkward, as it moved across the floor to the first step. Its body swayed back and forth and its knees bent at strange angles.

"Shit," Thornton huffed.

He prepared himself to fight, seeing that the only way clear was either through the door that wouldn't open and was now blocked by the approaching ghoul, or to climb back up to the top, as Cheyne had suggested.

More severed limbs fell to the floor as Sparrow and Brook hacked into the attackers reaching from the wall.

It seemed to go in their favour.

Cheyne could move a little farther away from the dark hole with each strike that his friends made.

"Almost there, boys," he said, stabbing his own sword at the cluster of fingers stretching out to his ankles.

"Oh shit," Sparrow shouted, looking back up the stairs.

Numerous beings appeared from around the bend in the stairway above them.

Some walked, slumping with each step. Strips of flesh swayed from their bones. A few others crawled on their bellies, missing legs or sections below their ribs entirely, dragging their spines behind them.

Thornton pointed to Cheyne. "Get him out of there and help me down here."

The lone figure was climbing slowly towards him, the rusty dagger raised high above its head.

Most of the limbs from the things reaching through the dark hole were on the floor, crawling away back into the blackness. Only a few hands had hold of Cheyne. One was around his leg. One was on the collar of his tunic and three were burying their fingers into his torso in an attempt to get a better grasp.

He hacked anxiously at the one attached to his leg, but the angle was awkward.

"Hold still," Brook ordered, raising his sword to swipe at the hands holding Cheyne's body.

As he brought the sword down, another figure burst from the fissure.

Its skin about its face stretched and pulled into a tight smile. Long yellow teeth bit into Cheyne's arm, making him let go of his sword. The figure wrapped its arms around the soldier's waist and suddenly retreated into the hole, pulling Cheyne with it.

Brook's sword came down, slicing into his friend instead of his intended target. The blade landed deep into Cheyne's shoulder, almost taking the entire arm away from his body.

The soldier screamed in agony as the ghoul wrenched him into the slender passage.

Cheyne's head smashed and scraped violently against the wall. A fine spray of blood exploded over the stones.

A loud crunch ensued as the figure vanished into the blackness, tugging Cheyne behind.

The soldier's bones splintered and cracked as they carted away his body, forced to fit into a passageway not intended for someone his size.

"Fuck," Brook hollered.

Thornton swung his blade at the lone figure on the stairs beneath him and chopped into its skull.

A hollow crack and crunch resounded throughout the chamber.

Dust and particles burst from the being's head from the impact. It started thrusting its rusty dagger at the captain.

With a swift sidekick, Thornton sent the attacker rolling back down the stairs to the floor by the door.

"This way," he hollered to the others.

The band of creatures descending the stairs grew. More and more ghouls emerged from the dark fissures, some with weapons, others without.

Sparrow looked on, as if transfixed. More hands reached from the fissure beside him, where Cheyne had vanished. He thought one had taken him by the upper arm, and turned to see Brook glaring at him.

"You heard him," the lieutenant shouted. "Move."

The three men charged down the steps, away from the dead men approaching from above.

Slowly, the lone figure lifted itself from the floor, the dagger in its bony hand and jaw swinging listlessly from its left hinge.

It lunged towards Thornton with its knife above its head.

The captain chopped downward with all of his might, slicing through the attacker from the top of the skull and through its rib cage.

It fell to the floor, some of its bones falling away. It was not enough to keep it down.

Inelegantly, it pushed itself to its feet, keeping its eyeless sockets fixed on the older man.

Clunking, scraping and thudding noises echoed through the stairwell as more and more of the dead appeared from the fissures to join the forms already descending the stairs.

Sparrow clanged his sword against the iron door. There was no sign of a handle, release or locking mechanism on the inside either.

"Come on," he shouted, frustrated.

Thornton kicked the lone figure onto its back. Its dagger went sliding across the floor. The captain then stamped his boot down upon the skull of the fiend with a great crunch. He kicked the rest of the body apart, sending bones flying in all directions, separating his foe's pieces as best as he could.

Turning to the multitude of dead men on the stairs, he prepared to battle on.

"Fight until you can't," he said to his men.

Brook moved to his side, sword at the ready.

"Fight until you can't," he repeated.

Sparrow let out a long sigh and joined them.

"What else are we going to do with our time?" he asked in jest.

Thornton grinned. "That's the spirit."

Slowly, the figures approached, descending down, down, down.

The first of them reached the bottom step, placing its fleshless foot on the stone floor.

At that moment, the iron door beside them creaked and groaned.

The middle of the door buckled, as if something was pulling at it from outside.

The corners folded under tremendous force and the edges opened up to reveal what little light remained after the sun had sunk below the horizon.

Suddenly, the door was pulled from its hinges with a loud clang and flung into the sky.

Sparrow and Brook stood gawking at the spectacle with open mouths.

"Move, you idiots," Thornton growled, pushing the men towards the open door.

They charged outside, where they could see Alice with her hand outstretched towards the tower.

"Get behind me," she commanded them.

They didn't hesitate. As quickly as they could, they ran past the girl. There, they found Jendryng and Vawdrey still holding the horses and watching on in awe.

"There are dead men in there," Sparrow called to the girl. "They attacked us."

"I know," Alice answered, looking at the top of the beacon tower.

The men followed her gaze.

Sitting on top of the tower was Liana.

"Now girl," Alice said.

The dragon inhaled a deep breath, placed her snout against the opening to the stairwell, and filled the tower with flames.

Fire swept down the stairs, erupted from the tiny portals that wound around the outside of the structure before bursting through the doorway.

Thornton felt his stomach leap as a wall of fire sped towards the girl standing in its path.

Alice raised her hands again, pushing the flames back inside the tower, leaving the girl unharmed.

He could only imagine what was becoming of the ghouls inside. Turning to ash, he hoped.

The girl gave a shrill whistle, commanding the dragon away. Liana took to the air, starting back towards the township.

"Are you all right?" she asked, turning to the men behind her.

"We lost John Cheyne," Lieutenant Brook told her.

She frowned and nodded slowly.

"You should go back to the manor," she told them.

"And you?" Thornton asked.

She peered at the flames and smoke billowing from the beacon tower.

"I'll stay a little longer," she replied. "Just to make sure it is done."

Sparrow stepped to her side, staring at the tower in question.

"What was all of that?" he asked. "Who made this happen?"

Alice took a deep breath and let it out slowly.

"A remnant of the Mirikin."

Epilogue

Winter's curse had tightened her grip on Erimoor.

The gentle snow had continued to fall relentlessly, almost stubbornly, layering itself upon layers it had built throughout the day.

It heaped itself upon rooftops, gathering until it became too heavy before sliding to the street in massive clumps. It spattered against windowpanes and piled up in front of doorways, forcing people to remain inside, where warm fires were stoked and hot food was consumed.

It drifted gently upon the ground, slowly filling the hoofprints left by six steeds, ridden by five soldiers, as they returned along the road from the beacon tower to the township.

Alice caught Thornton peering back to her, giving her an uncertain look, silently questioning her if she wanted them to remain or not.

She waved her hand, signalling him to go as she sat upon the rocks across the path, not too far from the blazing tower.

He turned away, urging his steed into a trot, holding the reins of the riderless animal that followed close behind. Cheyne's horse.

Alice's thoughts turned to the fallen soldier as she looked at the great, monolithic structure before her.

He was in there.

A deep sorrow flooded over her as she gave thought to him.

This wasn't the send-off that he deserved.

His wasn't the pyre he had earned.

The flames lapped at the stonework, reaching through the many tiny portals around the shell of the tower, twisting and turning in the breeze.

The crackle of burning timber hidden within the structure reached her ears.

The warmth from the fire had been a welcome relief against the cold, but now it dwindled away slowly as the flames confined themselves mostly to what fuel they found deep inside the tower.

She heard a tremendous crash from above. Peering up, she could see thousands of embers rising, drifting higher and higher before being extinguished in the cold night air.

The platform on top of the tower had collapsed, she supposed. The noise of iron clunking as something large fell down the stairwell told her that the beacon had dropped.

She looked to Thornton and his men.

They had moved too far away to have heard the commotion. Oblivious to the sound, they continued along the road, fading into the haze of the falling snow, and the dark of the night.

Her gaze moved to the ships upon the glassy water as lanterns were lit on deck. Ripples in the water caused the reflecting light to dance rhythmically as the ships rose and fell gently upon the bay.

Tucking her knees up to her chest, she peered out to the ocean, where she could hear waves crashing upon rocks at the tip of the point. Beyond that, she noticed the faintest line of dark burgundy. The very last light of the day's sun.

Stars twinkled brightly in the sky. She arched her neck to see ribbons of dotted lights weaving their way across the expanse above.

She pulled her cloak tight around her frame as her thoughts turned to Arthur. She wondered about him every day but thought about him more so in moments when she was by herself.

On her own.

Alone.

Her eyes welled with tears.

She missed him.

She missed him so much.

She wondered if he missed her, too.

She smiled to herself, shaking her head slightly.

Of course, he misses you;; she thought.

The cold seeped through the many layers of clothing and slid its icy fingers over her skin. She shivered as she pulled the cloak about her, readjusting it over her shoulders.

The air had become increasingly colder and colder.

Glancing up, she noticed the flames had receded into the tower.

A thick drift of snow fluttered to the ground, carried by a sudden gust of onshore wind.

She shivered again, wishing she had the power to keep herself warm and do away with the cold sweeping into the bay area.

It was as if it were a curse.

Winter's curse.

If only there was some sword or shield to vanquish it.

If only she knew some incantation to drive it away.

She knew better.

Winter's curse was one enemy she had no power over.

Winter's curse was here to stay.

At least, for a time.

About the Author

Robert E Kreig was born in Newcastle, Australia and grew up in its outer suburbs.

He has always had a love for books, particularly well-told stories involving action, adventure and fear.

Some of Robert's favourite authors as a young reader included J. R. R. Tolkien, Stephen King, Orson Scott Card, Ray Bradbury and Frank Herbert. As he grew into adulthood, the list continued to lengthen, adding more influential writers such as George R. R. Martin, Matthew Reilly, Nathan M. Farrugia, Dan Brown, James Patterson, Michael Connelly and Lee Child just to name a few.

Inspired by movies like Star Wars, King Kong, Jaws, Jason and the Argonauts and other great adventure pieces, Robert listened to the voices in his head and entertained the strange visions dancing through his mind to assist him with writing his fantasy series The Woodmyst Chronicles.

Robert has penned ten books for the series which follow the lives of many characters, particularly focussing upon a family who must face many trials before the epic conclusion. Clashing swords, strange creatures, flying dragons and sorcery inhabit the world surrounding Woodmyst.

Robert has also written a standalone book, Long Valley.

Robert currently lives in Canberra, Australia where he hopes to one day become a full-time writer.

Other Books By This Author

THE WOODMYST CHRONICLES

From a faraway land...
...comes a new adventure.
The Woodmyst Chronicles is the story of a small community that faces the hardest of trials in a world filled with darkness, violence and magic.

Books In This Series...
THE WALLS OF WOODMYST
THE SONS OF WOODMYST
THE HEIR OF WOODMYST
THE WARLORDS OF WOODMYST
THE HUNTRESS OF WOODMYST
THE SHADOW OF WOODMYST
THE BRIDES OF WOODMYST
THE GODS OF WOODMYST
THE WEAPONS OF WOODMYST
A FAREWELL TO WOODMYST

LONG VALLEY

In the small community of Long Valley, nestled comfortably beneath snow-capped mountains, people quietly go about their business. Everybody knows everybody and there are no worries to give mind to.

But something has awakened.

A tragic accident near the valley's army base sparks a number of terrifying events, placing the local civilians in mortal danger.

A contagion is subsequently released into Long Valley, infecting pets, livestock, wildlife and people.

It's up to the local law enforcement and a small band of citizens to try to keep the town safe.

In the end, it becomes a struggle for survival as the people of Long Valley are overcome by the urge to feed.

www.robertekreig.com

www.whitekeepbooks.com

www.ingramcontent.com/pod-product-compliance
Lightning Source LLC
Chambersburg PA
CBHW020331120726
47904CB00002B/372